A Family Tree

James Ogilvie

Grosvenor House
Publishing Limited

The right of James Ogilvie to be identified as the author of this
work has been asserted in accordance with Section 78
of the Copyright, Designs and Patents Act 1988

The book cover is copyright to James Ogilvie

This book is published by
Grosvenor House Publishing Ltd
Link House
140 The Broadway, Tolworth, Surrey, KT6 7HT.
www.grosvenorhousepublishing.co.uk

This book is a work of fiction. Any resemblance to
people or events, past or present, is purely coincidental.

A CIP record for this book
is available from the British Library

ISBN 978-1-80381-291-5
eBook ISBN 978-1-80381-404-9

About the Author

A Chartered Forester and tree-lover, James Ogilvie has worked with trees, woods and forests all his life, including state forestry, private forestry and the charity sector. His other books include *Heritage Trees of Scotland* and *A Brief History of the Forestry Commission*.

Cover artwork by Kathryn Callaghan, Kathryn Callaghan Fine Art www.kathryncallaghan.co.uk

Dedication

Dedicated to Tree Lovers everywhere.

Contents

Introduction

Argyll glistened in the sunshine. An early morning rainstorm had moved on leaving the afternoon fresh with promise. A sleek company saloon sped towards Oban, rock music blasting from its speakers. It slowed momentarily before turning abruptly through some old gates marking the entrance of Ardcairn Estate. Drumming her fingers in time to the beat, Harriet glanced at her watch. As she concentrated on the narrow driveway she was occasionally distracted by a glimpse of sea loch flickering through the fringe of beech trees. In her rear-view mirror, carpets of fallen leaves danced like copper dervishes.

Harriet was the newest recruit to prestigious Estate Agents G K Saville and this was her first big break – the chance to seal the deal on Ardcairn estate. If she had been in less of a hurry, she might have spied a glimpse of otter beside a peaty pool or a shy roe deer bounding off into the undergrowth, but the beat anaesthetised her senses and she kept her foot hard on the accelerator. Passing an old cottage, she changed down a gear and decelerated abruptly onto the gravel that encircled the front lawn. She scrunched to a halt in front of some weathered steps leading to the Edwardian House and opened the car door. "Good timing," she thought to herself, glancing briefly at her watch. There were still a few minutes left to check the place over before her clients' appointment.

As she walked towards the house her attention was diverted by the surrounding scenery. A colleague of hers had once described the Ardcairn panorama as "nae bad" but in truth it was spectacular, though lately neglected. Below the front lawn, overgrown privet bushes and straggling lawns dropped in tiers towards the ruffled waters of Loch Etive. By the shore stood the remains of a once-impressive walled garden. Time had taken its toll. Two of its mock turrets had collapsed onto the ground and young trees were exploiting gaps in the masonry. Inside was a huge old straggling yew tree and to one side lay an oval pond choked by rushes, save for a small patch of blue water mirroring the gently moving clouds above. By the edge of the pond stood the sculpture of a heron: graceful, motionless, mimicked by the stance of a living heron in the inlet beyond. Far across the loch, below a line of crags fringing the horizon, shafts of sunlight played over late-season heather, browning bracken and yellowing tints of birch woodland. Harriet paused and inhaled a deep breath of fresh autumn air. She closed her eyes momentarily, savouring that unmistakable evocative tang of the Highlands: a blend of peat and wood smoke, salt and seaweed, bracken and dampness quite unlike anything else in the world. Startled by something, the distant heron gave a noisy 'cronk' and flew off. Harriet opened her eyes, wrenched herself from the view and turned her full attention towards Ardcairn House...

On three sides of the building stood the relics of a once-great collection of specimen trees: giant conifers nurtured from seed gathered from far-flung corners of the globe; specimens to rival the best of Scotland's arboreta. 'No doubt the legacy of former owners with a botanical interest,' she thought. But even to her untutored eye she could see that the arboretum was now a shadow of its former glory. Rhododendron bushes and birch scrub had spread unchecked, obscuring the original pathways and views from the house. Here and there, giant trees lay rotting on their side, neglected and uncared for, 'presumably storm victims from long-ago' thought Harriet. As her eyes took in the stately forms of two-hundred-year-old hemlock, fir and spruce she wondered whether the new owners would trouble to restore the arboretum. One tree in particular held her attention: a giant Douglas fir that towered above all the others, its foliage illuminated by the late afternoon sun. As she admired its grandeur something caught her eye. An old lady was making her way slowly but purposefully across the lawn towards the house.

"Will you be the new estate agent?" enquired the lady as she approached, her piercing grey eyes examining Harriet carefully, their intensity undimmed by advancing age.

Harriet had not expected to encounter anyone except her clients. 'Who was this woman?' she wondered, momentarily caught off guard. And then she recalled glimpsing the old cottage on her approach to the house. So this must be its tenant.

"Er, yes," replied Harriet, "I'm standing in for a colleague at the moment".

"I'm Ann McLeod," the old lady announced holding out her hand in greeting, "I was housekeeper for Miss Lacelaw. And Colonel Rutherford before her. My mother housekeepered Lord and Lady Robertson before that. Will you be wanting some tea?" she added disarmingly.

"No thank you," said Harriet, "I'm expecting my clients at any minute." Fishing around in her handbag she frowned as she pulled out a large bunch of assorted keys supplied by her colleague. She had absolutely no idea which one fitted the front door. But before she had time to work out which was which, Ann had swiftly inserted her own Yale key into the lock and pushed the door open. "I've been keeping the place aired since Miss Lacelaw departed," Ann announced breezily. "I'll bring you all some refreshment later in the drawing room. It's up the stairs on the left," she added over her shoulder as she disappeared off down a corridor.

Fighting the urge to remonstrate, Harriet decided that it would be best to leave Ann to her own devices and make a quick inspection of the house before the buyers arrived. She passed briskly from room to room, noting with approval that Ann had indeed been 'keeping the place aired' and more than that, keeping it dusted and polished as well. 'Devotion to duty' she thought, as she headed up the stairs. Presumably Miss Lacelaw had left her an annuity before she left. Certainly Ardcairn's infamous American heiress had been rumoured to be worth "top dollar" according to Harriet's colleagues.

Heading downstairs from the upper floor of the house, she entered the grand oak-panelled drawing room. Harriet had already seen several stately homes in her short time with G K Saville but whoever had designed this place had done a remarkable job, uniting house and grounds in a perfect blend of form and function. To the east - framed by a large picture window - stretched a majestic panorama of trees, sea loch and distant hills. Chief feature of the estate's arboretum was the lofty Douglas fir that Harriet had noted earlier, soaring above its neighbours: a protective leader guarding the estate. Gazing at the compelling view, Harriet became mesmerised once more...

Her trance was broken by the crunch of tyres on the gravel outside as a small car approached slowly but purposefully. Harriet reached hurriedly into her briefcase, grabbed the paperwork and checked her clients' names again: David and Eleanor Buchanan. Then she crossed the Persian carpet towards the windows at the front of the house and looked down. Had she remained staring towards the east instead of turning her back to the arboretum, Harriet would have seen the estate woodlands turning a deeper shade of gold and green as the sun started its slow descent towards Lorne peninsula and the islands beyond. Deep in the conifer grove the forest floor was darkening and by now only an occasional shaft of light penetrated the gloom. As the sun sank gradually towards the western isles its rays ascended the trunk of the giant fir, embracing its rough bark and briefly anointing the remains of some old carved initials.

Gazing down from her drawing room vantage point, Harriet saw a young, good-looking couple emerge from the car, sharing some private joke. Watching them join arms and smile at each other she felt an unexpected twinge of jealousy that this special corner of Scotland might soon be theirs. What she wouldn't give for a place like this! The woman walked a few paces away to a dilapidated semi-circular garden bench that stood on a nearby rise. Bending over it, she shaded her eyes from the setting sun and surveyed the scene, just as Harriet herself had done only a short time before. Seconds later her husband joined her. He stood behind her and folded his arms above her waist. Standing there, one behind the other, they remained motionless for a full minute gazing at the golden Argyll sunset, before turning towards the house - and business.

Harriet went downstairs to welcome David and Eleanor Buchanan to Ardcairn.

* * *

Ann shuffled her way along the passageway towards the library bearing a tray laden with cups, saucers, a teapot and some home-made shortbread. As she approached, she could hear the sounds of muffled voices coming from within. The estate agent's crisp accent contrasted with the deeper, softer tones of the man. But what arrested Ann's footsteps so abruptly was the sound of gentle, tinkling laughter coming from his wife. There was something strangely and unnervingly familiar about it.

"And if you just sign here… and here," said Harriet, pointing to the documents spread out on the occasional table, "we'll have our lawyers send over copies of the missives to you next week." She glanced surreptitiously at her watch and added, "I'm sure that you will both be very happy at Ardcairn. It's a wonderful place… Oh, this is Ann," she added, looking up as Ann entered the room, "the current housekeeper."

Setting down the tray on the sideboard, Ann was at first unable to observe the face that belonged to the lady signing the papers but she did notice the long hair that flowed down to her shoulders.

David stood up to introduce himself, thanking her for the thoughtful gesture of tea. 'A kindly face,' thought Ann, observing him closely. Then David added "And this is my wife Eleanor," and as she turned around, Ann froze. It was as though - in that instant - the clock had turned back twenty years, for the eyes that looked up at Ann and smiled, were none other than Sophie's.

Dropping some spoons in confusion Ann exclaimed, "I'm so sorry. I… It's just that you remind me of… it's… no matter," but as she bent down under the low table to feel for the scattered spoons she stared at Eleanor as if she had seen a ghost. There followed a short but embarrassing pause whilst everyone tried to think of something to say. In the end it was Harriet who turned to David and Eleanor Buchanan. Breaking the silence she asked, "Are you intending to head back south this evening?"

David replied swiftly, "No we're staying nearby tonight. We're planning to walk around the grounds tomorrow. We've a charter flight from Oban in the afternoon."

Harriet was just about to continue the small talk when her mobile phone rang. Making her excuses, she removed herself from the room to take the call in private.

Filling the gap in conversation Ann blushed, "Can I be of further service to you, Mr and Mrs Buchanan?"

"Thank you Ann, please call us David and Eleanor. You've already been most kind. That was a very welcome cup of tea after our long trip up here."

"You're more than welcome," replied Ann, rather flustered and unsure of exactly what she should say next. "It's just that, well, I wondered, if you haven't booked an evening meal... perhaps you would like me to prepare something for you here?"

David and Eleanor glanced at each other. Outside they could hear Harriet's voice saying, "I should be finished soon. I'll get back just as soon as I can."

"That's very kind Ann, but we wouldn't want to bother you," replied David, echoing his wife's thoughts.

"It's not a bother. It'll no' take me long to prepare something. Maybe you'd like to know a bit more about the place? I was housekeeper for Miss Lacelaw these last twenty-five years and for a while before that, in Colonel Rutherford's days."

Another telepathic moment passed between David and Eleanor. "Well, we would love to hear about it," ventured Eleanor. "It's just that we wouldn't want to put you to any trouble."

"It's no trouble at all Soph... Mrs... Eleanor. I would be happy to prepare something for you both."

David looked at his wife. "Well, why ever not? We'll check into our hotel first, but please don't make anything elaborate: we had a big lunch. What time would you like us to appear...?"

A minute later Harriet re-entered the drawing room and proceeded to fiddle restlessly with her watch. It was clear to the others that whilst she was distracted and keen to be heading off, she didn't want her clients to think she was rushing them. Sensing her unease, David said tactfully, "I think that we're finished with business now. Let's not keep you any longer, Harriet. Why don't you make tracks. We can arrange to lock up, if you show us what's what."

Harriet went through the motions of demurring, then shortly afterwards she and her expensive company saloon disappeared the long driveway.

* * *

Sometime later the new owners of Ardcairn were to be found examining leather bound volumes in the hushed surroundings of its library. In the corner, a grandfather clock measured out its slow metronomic beat. A log fire blazed in the hearth, its soft flicker augmenting the glow of a shadowy candelabrum. David and Eleanor were relaxed and content as they poured themselves coffee. But something had been troubling Ann ever since she had first set eyes on Eleanor Buchanan that afternoon. In her own psychic way she sensed that events in her life had been leading up to this moment and she felt a frisson of anticipation in the thought that two worlds were about to collide. She sat down in one of the Chesterfield armchairs, looked knowingly at Eleanor and said, "You were born on the night of the great storm, which would make you... twenty-two years old, am I right?"

Eleanor jumped. It was her turn to be startled. "Good Lord, how on earth did you know that?"

Ann avoided the question and continued to look closely into her eyes. "And your mother's name... Sophie, that's right isn't it?"

Eleanor's confusion deepened. Her hand shook as she put her cup down, spilling some coffee onto the faded ornamental rug. "Y, yes, but… how did you know that?"

Ann ignored her repeated question. "You look so much like your mother," she continued implacably. "How is Sophie?"

Eleanor frowned, her eyes clouding over. "My mother…" she started and then paused. She looked down at the carpet and swallowed. "Mum died not long ago. It was… complications. She had a… diabetic condition. How did you know her?"

Ann sighed softly. "I didn't know that. I'm so very sorry to hear it. I miss her very much." At this, Sophie looked up at her again, her flushed face expressing her confusion, while Ann continued, "She and Neil loved this place."

"Neil? Who's Neil?"

Ann hesitated, knowing that what she was about to tell this young woman would certainly turn her life upside down. And though her sixth sense told her not to hold back she hesitated once again.

"Who is Neil?" insisted Eleanor.

"Neil McLeod was your father," she replied, simply.

"What are you talking about?" Eleanor's mood changed abruptly and her usually melodic voice rose in anger and anxiety. "You're very much mistaken. My father's not called Neil."

Again, Ann paused. She looked at David who was clearly as taken aback as Eleanor. Then she re-examined Eleanor's face. Wild blue eyes flashed back. How much like Sophie she looked! In that moment Ann realised that she would be unable to keep the burden of that secret to herself. She had no choice but to tell the truth to this innocent beautiful young woman seated before her. She took a deep breath and said, "So: Sophie didn't tell you? Well, I'm not really surprised after all that happened. She wanted to make a clean break of it. Start her life over again back in Edinburgh." Ann put her cup down deliberately and gathered her thoughts, aware that the new proprietors of Ardcairn were staring intently at her in confusion and resentment. It should have been a contented end to a wonderful day, crowned by their becoming the new estate owners, but now their feelings had been thrown into turmoil by this clearly deranged but quietly confident woman. At that moment Eleanor experienced an intense feeling of déjà vu. She felt as if she were on the edge of a cliff, about to jump off into the unknown, not knowing where she might land. David's mind was also in confusion. Not knowing what to say and looking for something to displace his conflicting emotions he got up and put another log onto the fire.

As the flames leapt higher Ann continued, "Well maybe it's best not to talk about it after all."

But it was too late. The genie was out of the bottle and they all knew it.

Eleanor's tone was emphatic. "No. No. I'm sure that it's… important."

"Very well," declared Ann, smoothing her skirt over her knees. She stared at the fire for several seconds, cleared her throat and began...

"It was twenty-three years ago that Neil - your father - first met your mother here at Ardcairn. It was a wild night. Sophie - your mother - had been hiking in the area and had got into difficulties..."

Chapter 1

"Come on Sophie! We'll be late for the train." Charlotte and Fiona were champing at the bit, sensing the end of their four-day ordeal.

Although Sophie Montgomery had looked forward to her gold Duke of Edinburgh's Award expedition for several months, the reality was proving to be quite different from the anticipation. In the Common Room at St George's when the four girls had discussed details of their fifty-mile hike in the Great Glen area, the idea had seemed alluring, even exciting. But on the train journey north from Edinburgh the summer weather gradually worsened. Intermittent showers deteriorated into an incessant downpour that had lingered heavily, dogging their footsteps for most of the next three and a half days. And when it wasn't pouring, the Argyll midges had lived up to their troublesome reputation. But Sophie, Fiona and Charlotte had slogged stoically through the moors and the miles and were now into the final few hours of their expedition. Only five more miles to go now until their ultimate destination: the Taynuilt Tearoom, their appointment with Mr Edington - maths teacher and St George's 'D of E' assessor - and the train journey home. And after that? Well for Sophie, a successful expedition would complete her Gold award, bridging the gap between school and university. The cherished prize would be a visit to Holyrood Palace, a certificate presentation and perhaps even the chance to speak with the Duke himself.

But as can often happen on these expeditions, things had not gone altogether smoothly. Blistered feet and soggy clothes had contributed to frayed tempers and fractured relationships. Originally four of the St George's 6th formers had planned to take part in the expedition, but at the eleventh hour one had had to drop out. Sophie knew that the chances of three individuals remaining as a coherent team were low, but she had managed to hold things together, mainly by the force of her own personality. Stronger than Charlotte and Fiona, she had been annoyed at their general lack of effort and esprit and their continual moaning about the food, insects, dampness and lack of creature comforts. It fell to her to organise the tent, most of the cooking and just about every other damn thing besides. Now, having managed to guide the trio safely through tricky Argyll terrain with only the odd wrong turn along the way, all she wanted was some peace and quiet and to be alone by herself for a while.

"Are you coming or what?" repeated Charlotte, pursing her lips and tightening her backpack hip strap.

Sophie ignored her insistent demands and bent down to open the side pocket of her own rucksack. Yes, there it was: her prized travel watercolour set that she had carried, all for nothing so far. Here was the first proper dry spell of the expedition and she wasn't going to waste this precious opportunity. A light breeze was keeping the midges at bay and the view that stretched out before her was nothing if not stunning. It was time for a little restorative art therapy.

"Look guys," she said, reaching for her map and unfolding it. "We're almost back at civilisation now. D'you see that track there?" Her fingers traced a line on the paper. "You just follow that along the lochside until it joins the road there," she continued, pointing her finger at the thin yellow line on their map. "It's only a short walk from there to Taynuilt. Let's see… it's less than a mile. You two go on and I'll catch you up later."

Charlotte and Fiona knew that Sophie was a much faster walker than either of them. In fact it was she that usually had to urge them to catch her up. But although they sensed her need to be alone, they were not altogether comfortable about losing their acknowledged leader and they began to voice qualms about splitting up. Ignoring these misgivings, Sophie reached for her mobile phone, switched it on and examined the display. "Look, there's a good signal here," she said. "We can keep in touch. It's stopped raining I'm just going to do a quick sketch and then I'll catch you up in Taynuilt. I'll not be long."

The two girls still were still hesitant. "Go!" Sophie commanded them with finality in her voice that made them realise that arguing was pointless.

"Please yourself," retorted Fiona, unable to hide a hint of truculence. "We'll phone you from the Tearoom," and shortly afterwards she and Charlotte disappeared from view around a bend in the track, grumbling audibly.

If truth be told, Sophie hadn't been feeling too great that day, although she had done a good job at hiding it from the others. Of course, her teammates knew about her diabetes, but they also knew that it had never slowed her down before. So it was with a certain light-headedness that Sophie placed her phone on the rucksack, filled her plastic camping mug from a nearby burn, sat down on a rock and opened up her box of watercolours. With a brief sigh of contentment, she gazed in anticipation at the Loch Etive panorama.

In the distance a dark line of crags framed the moorland with its hidden folds and muted tweedy colours. In the foreground the ruffled blue waters of the loch contrasted with occasional white horses and a scattering of dark islands. Further down the loch towards Taynuilt, Sophie observed the monotone green of commercial plantations contrasting with the lighter green shades of native oak woodland, whilst in the distance she could just make out a group of taller fir trees thrusting up above their neighbours.

Settling down to her task, she was soon absorbed, immersed in trying to capture the spirit of the scene before her. Sophie's nimble hands worked their magic, her adept brush strokes conveying three-dimensional coherence to the empty sheet of paper. So lost in her creation did Sophie become that she failed to notice the brooding storm clouds amassing behind her.

Then two things then happened at once. A couple of large raindrops spattered on to her painting and her phone rang, its strident ringtone shattering the afternoon's tranquillity. "Blast!" exclaimed Sophie, momentarily startled out of her wits. She reached clumsily for her phone and accidentally knocked over the mug. "Blast!" she said again. Then flicking back her hair she put the phone to her ear, "Oh, hi Charlotte. You're there already? Gosh you guys were quick." She looked at her watch. 'Christ, it's late,' she thought to herself. "No, I'm fine, I'm about halfway there," she lied, holding her phone in one hand and frantically trying to pack up her paints with the other. Her brain was racing. "Can I speak with Mr Edington?" A short pause ensued. "Um, good, yes Sir. No, I'm making good progress. I think there's a later train to Edinburgh isn't there?" Then a pause. "There isn't? Oh. Yeah, I know we should have stuck together but…" Mr Edington was clearly not interested in her excuses, as the angry buzz from Sophie's receiver indicated. Her thoughts continued to whirl. "It's OK Sir, I have an aunt who lives in Oban" (another lie). "I'll phone her and arrange to stay there tonight. No, I'll be fine," she added. "Really. I'll phone my Mum and let her know. I'll call you at, what, about eight or nine?" She waited until the rant at the other end had finished. "Yes Sir, sorry Sir," she apologised, and hung up. Then she swore softly but thoroughly under her breath. It was, after all, vacation time. In only a few days she'd have left St George's. Next stop would be St Andrews University to study History of Art and then she could do what she damn well liked without kowtowing to petty and controlling schoolteachers.

Donning her wet-weather gear yet again, she set off down the track. If she was honest with herself, she was feeling pretty ropey now. The strengthening wind, the increasing rain, and knowing she was going to miss her train weren't exactly helping. By now her insulin supply was finished (she had stupidly forgotten to pack the extra needed) and the initial telltale signs of glucose deficit were getting stronger. "Sugar, na na na na, na na..." she sang out loud, "...oh, honey, honey" and she stopped for a minute beside a boulder to retrieve some sweets from her rucksack. Rummaging first in one pocket then another she felt a sense of panic starting to rise. "Shit!" she swore loudly, "I must have left them behind at lunchtime". At a makeshift lunch stop earlier that day the three girls had taken shelter from the rain in a corrugated iron shed that had 'seen better days'. But that was miles back. It was getting darker now and Sophie knew that all the other expedition sugar had been used up. Charlotte and Fiona had taken the tent between them so she couldn't make a camp. She had no other option but to press on. She knew that it couldn't be more than four or five miles back to civilisation. But the rain was becoming very heavy now and the landscape around her was gradually losing its sharpness. Familiar-looking objects were starting to become ill defined and hazy. The more energy Sophie used up walking towards help, the more fatigued she became. With every footstep she took, her condition deteriorated, and she realised that things were starting to get serious.

Losing her balance from time to time, she somehow continued to stumble her way through the curtain of rain towards civilisation – and precious sugar. But now something barred her way. A high padlocked gate completely blocked the track. From either side of the gate, tall deer fences stretched out into the far distance. Even in her befuddled state Sophie knew that she was in serious trouble. She was feeling hypothermic. She didn't have the strength to climb over the gate and if she didn't get help soon she would pass out. She took her phone out of her inside jacket pocket to make an emergency call. No signal? "Shit!" she exclaimed again, this time in desperation.

Leaning wearily against the fence she stared with unseeing eyes through the wire mesh at the track ahead and her exit route, so cruelly denied. They had no right to padlock a track like this. Her world started to swim in and out of focus. She vaguely thought that she could make out some green things up ahead. Were they figures? They seemed to look like figures: giant green druids in fact. Or were they trees? Anyway, they seemed friendly enough. And they were now appearing to beckon her with their giant green swaying arms, gesturing her onwards. She felt sure that they were there to help her. In a final effort of will she stumbled uphill, searching desperately for some sort of break in the fence line. The rain was stair-rodding down now. One of the druids in particular was beckoning her onwards. He seemed strangely reassuring to Sophie, suggestive of shelter, safety and salvation. She somehow chanced upon a gap in the fence, stumbled blindly towards the druid's protective green shroud – and then blacked out.

The last thing Sophie recognised before losing consciousness was the huge trunk of a mighty Douglas fir.

Chapter 2

Neil McLeod thought he'd kill two birds with one stone. Walk Robbie and take a look at that felling job on the American woman's estate. Well, it had seemed like a good idea at the time.

Even for a small Border collie Robbie had a lot of energy and demanded at least two long walks every day. Denied this, he would look reproachfully at his master with pleading eyes until Neil eventually caved in and uttered the magic word "Walkies!" Robbie was able to sense his master's moods so well that he knew when to bring a lead and drop it expectantly in Neil's lap. Today he was in luck. A pre-breakfast romp along the lochside; a run uphill to a forest thinning site that Neil was preparing and now evening walkies as well. Sometimes Neil had to leave Robbie in his extra long wheelbase Landrover if the site was potentially dangerous. He knew that would be the case tomorrow when he started on the next job, so today he was being especially kind to Robbie. Not that Robbie would understand that tomorrow of course.

And so it was mainly on impulse that August evening that Neil once again declared "Walkies!" and Robbie came running, his tail wagging furiously. Neil had some slight misgivings: he supposed that he should really have cleared his visit with the estate beforehand, for if the rumours (and there were many) were to be believed, Miss Lacelaw - the colourful American heiress who had bought Ardcairn three years before - wouldn't take kindly to an out of hours business visit. But Neil knew Duncan Fraser - the estate's manager - very well. He and

Duncan had been fellow pupils at Oban High School. Both had an interest in the countryside and whilst Neil had gone into forestry, Duncan had become what he called 'Miss Lacelaw's Factor', what others generally called 'Miss Lacelaw's factotum' and what Neil uncharitably referred to as 'The Lacelaw lackey'.

Neil had decided to go into forestry against the advice of his father, Jim. During a working life that had seen profound social changes, Jim McLeod had started his career with the Forestry Commission, helping to establish the great post-war spruce plantations throughout the west of Scotland. There wasn't a corner of Argyll that those planting gangs didn't know well, although theirs had been a tough life: up early, out in all weathers for piecework payment, hard graft. Neil's mother Eleanor had died of cancer several years ago, but his father showed no signs of ill health. Partly to save money and partly to keep his 'old man' company, Neil continued to live at home in the ex-Commission cedar shingle house at the edge of Taynuilt village, prosaically called 'Cedar Cottage'. Though recently retired, Jim - who had progressed from planting seedlings on the hillside to servicing forestry machines at the Forestry Commission workshop - enjoyed helping Neil maintain his growing collection of chainsaws and forestry vehicles. With no wife to care for now and with no hobbies to absorb his time, Jim was in the habit of spending long hours in his workshop, leaving Neil precious time in the evenings and weekends to catch up on the demands of paperwork and form filling.

Neil was gifted academically and had left school with a set of very good exam results. He could have gone to any University of his choice - his teachers had even suggested Oxbridge - but instead he enrolled on a Business Management course at the University of the Highlands & the Islands. Although he did well in his first-year exams, student life didn't really suit him and he was impatient to get on with his working life. Ignoring his father's advice to 'work in an office' Neil took the bold step of starting his own forestry contracting business at the youthful age of twenty-one. He was hard working - and it showed. His firm grew quickly and now comprised three full time employees, one apprentice, Jim's assistance, and a reputation amongst Argyll's forest-owning community for delivering results. Neil McLeod understood that long term success depended upon maintaining professionalism: knowing the sites to be worked, knowing the markets, knowing his men and knowing his machinery, not to mention developing a rapport with landowners and their agents. Neil's timing was felicitous. Many of the plantations established by his father's generation were now coming into maturity and there was literally a growing need for skilled contractors to harvest the timber and then replant the sites with the next crop of young trees.

Though some of his contemporaries went into fish farming and one or two - like Duncan Fraser - went into general estate work, they were the exception rather than the rule. Few contemplated the outdoor life seriously. They just weren't prepared to roll up their sleeves and work in remote places in all weathers and under difficult conditions. All that many of them wanted was the next weekly pay packet and a weekend of binge drinking. Neil knew who the local freelance forestry 'cowboys' were, and he also knew that they were only interested in making a quick buck and an even quicker exit. If they left sites in a mess, well, that was someone else's problem. Realising that they risked bringing the profession into disrepute Neil generally tried to avoid them. But despite his father's warning about the rigours of forestry work, Neil found himself suited to the life and with his father's help and a general lack of any serious competition he was able to grow 'McLeod Forestry' quickly. The only drawback was having to work most weekends. In fact, things were so busy that Neil sometimes wondered whether he actually owned the business or whether the business owned him.

It was this drive to succeed that found him preparing to visit the American's estate late that August evening. Robbie picked up his ears at the word "Walkies!" and rushed over, wagging his tail frantically. Neil tucked the little dog into his two-sizes-too-big biker jacket, slung his haversack into a saddlebag and kicked his trusty old Triumph motorbike into life. Robbie was used to riding pillion. He knew that it was a prelude to an outing and he enjoyed the breeze whistling about his ears as his head poked out of Neil's jacket. Neil knew of a little-used track that led around the back of Ardcairn estate close to the Norway spruce plantation that Miss Lacelaw had wanted to be harvested. Most of his contact over the work had been with Duncan but Miss Lacelaw had appeared on one occasion, bringing Suki, that ridiculous white overgrown poodle of hers. Neil frowned as he headed down the track, trying to remember what Duncan had called the animal. Oh yes, the "Powder-puff Pooch", that was it'. Neil chuckled as he recalled a particular incident at Ardcairn. Suki had become extremely curious – amorous, even – towards Robbie and clearly regarded him as some kind of canine sex symbol. Miss Lacelaw had been less than enamoured herself, definitely not amused in fact, and warned Neil from taking "that tiresome mongrel of yours" onto the estate again. Knowing her reputation as an imperious despot, Neil had shrugged the incident off, but it was with a sense akin to a schoolboy breaking the rules that he opened up the throttle of his motorbike as he sped down the estate drive that evening. He had informed neither the owner nor 'The Lackey' about his visit and furthermore Robbie was 'canina non grata'. Still, the dog could do with a walk, the felling site needed to be marked up and his team needed to have work lined up ahead of them.

In truth, Neil wasn't really bothered about taking on this job. He knew that Miss Lacelaw had alienated all the 'cheap and cheerful' forestry contractors in the area and that McLeod Forestry was probably her last resort. In fact the job had been half tackled already, abandoned when the previous cowboy contractor, having created an "unholy mess", had not been paid. Neil smiled. He knew who had created that mess. Argyll was a village and you couldn't blow your nose without someone knowing about it. Gossip was rife and in this business you were only as good as your last job. In fact, you had to be beyond reproach, since a tarnished reputation in the small world of Scottish forestry spelt eventual business suicide.

Turning off the drive, he snaked his Triumph up a muddy track towards the felling site, propped the bike against a tree and unzipped his jacket. Robbie jumped down enthusiastically, dislodging house keys, mobile phone and packet of mints. Neil gathered them up, stuffed them into his haversack and slung it over his shoulder while Robbie rushed round in small circles, his tail wagging frantically.

"Steady boy!" Neil commanded the dog, "No rushing off now," and he hung his helmet over the handlebars and strode off uphill in the direction of the 'unholy mess'. Soon he became immersed in his work, measuring piles of felled timber and marking trees to be thinned with a can of paint spray. So absorbed did he become that he failed to notice the dark billowing storm clouds piling up to the east. It wasn't until he emerged from an unthinned section of spruce that Neil realised the ambient gloom was actually due to the weather conditions and not the dim light under the forest canopy. Looking back towards the storm clouds he realised that he should be heading home as soon as possible if he was going to avoid a soaking. Hastily stowing his equipment back in the haversack, he looked around for Robbie's familiar features. The faithful collie never strayed far from his master - that was one of his good points - and always came when he called - that was another. But this evening was to be different. When Neil shouted Robbie's name there was absolutely no sign of the dog appearing. As the first fat drops of rain anointed his face, he became both annoyed and concerned. Though it wasn't far back to his bike, he'd get a soaking and he definitely didn't fancy carrying a wet dog. It was time to go home before the rain got worse. But where the hell *was* Robbie?

Five minutes later Neil was becoming visibly angry. Though he'd called and whistled, no vestige of a collie appeared. And then, just as Neil's anger was turning into concern, around a corner charged Robbie, his tail wagging furiously as he careered towards his master. But when Neil went to pick him up, the dog scampered off with its tail between its legs. "Robbie, come! Come here!" urged Neil. But instead of returning obediently to his master, the dog slunk off a short distance and looked back over his shoulder at him.

"ROBBIE!" shouted Neil in exasperation, the rain now pelting hard down onto his head and trickling down his collar. "I'm not playing games. Come HERE!" But again the dog trotted off in the wrong direction again and stopped still, looking back at Neil. This was so completely out of character that Neil felt compelled to follow. Robbie's tail now wagged hesitantly and he took off quickly along a track that wound its way through birch woodland towards the policy plantings around Ardcairn house.

"Not a good idea Robbie," warned Neil. Through sheets of rain he could observe lights from the house up ahead. The last thing he needed right now was a close encounter of an American kind. But the dog continued on regardless and his tail started to register off the wagometer scale as he threaded through the birch woodland and disappeared out of sight into a large rhododendron bush. Neil followed him to a small depression at the foot of one of estate's huge fir trees… and then stopped dead in his tracks. There, draped over the roots of the tree was the form of a girl: an arrestingly beautiful girl. Her rucksack still on her back, Sophie lay as still as a stone, her face pale and seraphic, her hand clutching a mobile phone.

"Sweet Jesus!" uttered Neil, bending down closer. His first thought was 'Is she alive?' Then his first aid training instinctively kicked in (how glad he was now to have put himself and his McLeod Forestry team through that course) and he swiftly examined her breathing (shallow), felt her pulse (irregular) and checked her lips (not blue but definitely beautiful, he couldn't help noticing). In truth, even in her bedraggled state she was clearly stunning. He stared, bewitched, at her limp wet figure, wondering what to do next.

Still gazing at her face, he instinctively brushed aside her hair and gently touched her cheek. Her face flickered into life. Her eyelids opened a little and her world started to come into focus once more. Neil could see a flicker of fear entering her eyes as they dimly registered the face of a strange man bending over her.

"Don't worry," he said, taking her hand, "I'm here to help you."

"H-help me?" She echoed his words, faintly squeezing his hand.

"Don't worry," he repeated, "you'll be OK." He turned towards the dog watching them so intently a few metres away, its head resting on its paws: "Good boy Robbie: Good boy".

Chapter 3

From her curled-up position beside the tree roots Sophie stirred feebly. In a slurred, barely audible voice she murmured, "Help me… diab…"

Neil struggled to understand. He couldn't see any obvious injury. "What's wrong? What do you need?" he asked gently. Perhaps she needed special treatment or medication or something.

But the beautiful girl lying in front of Neil could only mumble incoherently. As her whole body started to shake with cold the mobile phone fell from her outstretched hand. Picking it up Neil caught sight of the medi-bracelet on her wrist. "Insulin user ID" it read, "I have diabetes treated with insulin." Neil's knowledge of this ailment was rudimentary, but he did recall something about needing sugar. He slipped her mobile phone into her pocket and asked, "Are you diabetic? You need sugar?"

As she nodded pathetically Neil had a brainwave. He fumbled in his haversack, looking for the tube of mints. Thank God! His mind was racing as he split open the packet and placed three sweets into her mouth. He gave her a few moments for the effect to take place and then asked, "What's your name?"

"Phophie," she garbled, her mouth full of sweets and her brain still sluggish.

"OK Sophie, don't you worry. I'll get you to a dry place near here soon. Do you think you can walk just a wee bit more if I help you up?"

Feeling slightly revived by the infusion of energy she nodded her head slowly.

"Come on then, let's get you up and out of here. I'm Neil by the way," he said reassuringly, putting his haversack down and donning her rucksack. He stooped down, helping Sophie to her feet. "I'll take you to an old family friend who lives here in a lovely cottage, Rose Cottage it's called and she's called Ann and she's lived there forever and she's my Godmother and she'll help get you sorted and back on your feet…" Neil kept talking, trying all the while to comfort and reassure her as he placed her arm around his shoulder for support. With Robbie tagging along behind, they made their way slowly together towards easier ground and the lights of Ardcairn House.

But as they rounded the side of the building, Neil noticed with dismay that no lights were shining from Ann's distant cottage. "Damn!" he cursed, realising that she must be out, or even away. That was only going to complicate matters. Somewhat superfluously he said to Sophie, "Can you wait here for a minute while I see if Ann's about?" He set her down as gently as he could, propping her up next to a carved statue of a lion at the edge of the front lawn, before disappearing off into the darkness. Robbie kept darting to and fro, instinctively trying to shepherd his master and his new friend back together again.

Less than a minute later a canine commotion erupted from the direction of Ardcairn House. Let out for her pre-bedtime 'constitutional' and scenting an alluring whiff of Border collie, the spoilt Powder-puff Pooch rushed joyously out into the rain, barking furiously for her long-lost friend.

"Suki… Suki, come here Suki!" An unmistakable American drawl could be discerned coming from the direction of the house, and the silhouetted figure of Miss Lacelaw appeared at the front door. She switched on a powerful security light – and at that instant all hell broke loose.

The front flowerbeds became a battleground as Suki's doggie advances systematically destroyed the chrysanthemum beds. At the same time, her carefully groomed coat transformed from powder-puff pale to camouflage brown. Equally determined, Robbie tried to evade Suki's cavorting, generally adding to the floral carnage. Meanwhile Neil, who had failed to find anyone at home at Rose Cottage, was halfway across the lawn on his way back towards Sophie. Just at that moment the powerful security lights came on, temporarily blinding Neil, who froze like a rabbit caught in the glare of a car's headlights.

Miss Lacelaw let out a piercing scream which trailed off into a kind of yelp when she recognised Neil's face.

"What the hell do you think you're doing here?" she shrieked at him.

Looking towards the house, Neil shaded his eyes from the powerful glare of the halogen bulb and wondered what to say. But before he could speak, Miss Lacelaw's attention was diverted by the carnage in the flowerbed and she shouted in exasperation "Get off of my property or I'll call the police. And get your animal off of my property," adding, "I've warned you already." She started to go inside to phone the police when, off to one side, she spotted a bedraggled female figure beside the lion statue, desperately trying to get up onto her feet. Sophie picked herself up slowly, took two steps and then collapsed in a heap. Only at that point did Miss Lacelaw's hysteria subside a little. Later, after Neil had managed to blurt out a hasty explanation and stressed the seriousness of the situation, Miss Lacelaw ordered him to bring Sophie inside.

When he looked back at the bizarre events of that evening it seemed to Neil that the American woman's apparent concern for Sophie's welfare may have had more to do with her legal liability as a landowner than her compassion for a fellow human being in trouble, but at the time he dumbly carried out her orders without demur. He gently gathered up Sophie in his arms and carried her across the threshold of Ardcairn House. "Bring her into the library," barked Miss Lacelaw, and "Suki leave that alone," she commanded, pointing at Robbie. Wheeling around and marching inside she said sharply, "Not there!" as Neil, searching for the nearest comfortable to place Sophie, made for a sofa. After ordering him to leave Sophie on the floor and tie his dog up outside, Miss Lacelaw left the room in order to find some towels, muttering under her breath that it was quite insufferable that Ann was away. After she had disappeared, Neil and Sophie looked helplessly at one another. Even in her distress Sophie managed to raise a half smile and murmured, "I'm so sorry… Neil."

He grinned back and remarked, "Don't worry, she's always like this. You'll be fine." For a minute there was a bond of empathy, two souls united by a common adversary. Glancing at each other occasionally and feeling like naughty schoolchildren hauled up before the headmistress, the two of them connected in a brief moment, before the human maelstrom returned…

* * *

Some time later a semblance of order had been restored to Ardcairn. Tied up at the back of the house, Robbie was assuming an attitude of canine martyrdom. Sophie was sitting in the kitchen sipping a reviving mug of cocoa and feeling much, much better. Miss Lacelaw was still nursing her wrath towards Neil for being on her property "without permission" and particularly since he had brought Robbie after expressly being instructed not to do so, but at least she realised that he had quite possibly saved Sophie's life. Having finally been given a chance to explain himself, Neil was given a small disposable torch with which to find his way back to his motorbike and sent packing with a large flea in his ear. It was made abundantly clear that the services of McLeod Forestry would most definitely not be needed on the estate now or indeed at any time in the future.

Miss Lacelaw contemplated calling an ambulance for Sophie but then decided that she didn't want her own details appearing on any official record in connection with the incident. She imagined that after all that had happened, this young lady's family might decide to sue her for damages. So she compromised instead and despite Sophie's protestation that she was "perfectly alright," insisted that she be checked out by a doctor at the Oban hospital, calling a taxi to make sure that she did so. By the time the Etive Taxi appeared half an hour later, Sophie - punch drunk from repeated lectures about the dangers of hiking alone - was only too willing to vacate the premises.

As the taxi driver negotiated the twisting estate road in the driving rain, he surveyed his latest fare in the rear-view mirror and grinned. For an in-patient she was certainly putting on an Oscar performance, though she seemed to be interrupted frequently. She flicked back her still damp hair as she put the mobile phone to her ear. "Hi Mum - No, I'm fine… I've decided to stay on for another day… Yes of course I'll be back for my birthday tomorrow… Yes it went very well… Char and Fi went back this evening with Mr Edington. Actually, Mum, could you give him a call? He didn't seem too keen on my staying out here. I told him I had a relly in Oban just to keep him off my back but… look my battery's getting low. I'd better call you tomorrow. I'll let you know when I'm back in Edinburgh. Byee Mum. Love you."

It was only when the harsh fluorescent glare of the hospital lights drew near that Sophie realised how extraordinarily tired she was. Bringing his taxi to a stop outside General Admissions the driver turned around to face the girl whose tinkling voice had sounded so pleasant. "That'll be thirty pounds please lass." Sophie frowned. She hadn't imagined that she'd actually have to pay for the journey. She'd supposed that when Miss Lacelaw insisted on a taxi, she'd have put it on her account or something. This was not the best time for Sophie to learn that the very rich usually lacked the imagination to know what it meant to have much less. She was both annoyed and upset. She hadn't wanted to be taken to hospital in the first place and now she was having to pay for the experience. Too tired to argue however, she rummaged around in her wallet. "I'm s-so s-sorry" she said, I've only got twenty-five pounds. Could you possibly take me to a hole-in-the-wall? I can get some more cash out for you."

The taxi driver was not west Highland, intuitive and empathetic for nothing. He could see that she was upset and tired and even though she'd been evasive with her mother, his instincts told him that she had just been through an ordeal. "You've an honest face," he said, "It's a wild nicht and the nearest machine's back in toon. Dinna fash," he continued in his soft accent, handing her back twenty pounds. "That's ma birthday present tae ye. I'll just tak a fiver for me fuel." Rebutting her protestations he added, "Let's just say that Miss Lacelaw may have the odd wee pricey journey this month," and winked at her slyly. Tired though she was, Sophie managed the vestige of a laugh, which lingered in the taxi driver's ears long after he had vanished. She clambered unsteadily out of the Etive Taxi, shouldered her rucksack and turned around to wave her appreciation to her charitable chauffeur, but he had already spirited away into the wild Argyll night.

Unable to think rationally about any alternative course of action, Sophie shuffled on autopilot into the hospital reception area. As she gave her particulars to the receptionist, sparing most of the details except for her diabetes, she was long past caring where she stayed that night. All she wanted to do was to rest and then get home.

Before long, a young duty night nurse bustled down to assess her. Despite the lack of any audience except for Sophie herself, Morag clearly relished making an entrance. A feisty, buxom, no-nonsense redhead of Neil's age, she and Neil had been Oban High School contemporaries where they had had an on/off sort of friendship. After leaving school their friendship had drifted into a relationship or, more accurately, a physical relationship. Passionate and fiery, Morag was a demanding lover but also an incessant talker. As a good listener and happy to please, Neil had proved to be an ideal partner in the bedroom, or indeed any other place that offered sexual potential.

"They'll probably keep you in for observation tonight," Morag announced to Sophie. "Doctor Liston will see you later. What's that? When can you go? You've only just arrived!" she remarked dryly. "It'll depend on what doctor Liston has to say. If he signs you off then you can go home tomorrow. Edinburgh?" she continued, "Nice city… mind you, that Parliament now, what a carry on… my cousin knew the architect, and…" With this nurse chattering incessantly at her as she walked down the brightly lit corridor Sophie felt new waves of fatigue sweeping over her. She registered only certain words and phrases, struggling to concentrate as Morag continued her relentless monologue. By the time they reached the ward, Sophie was dropping with tiredness.

But several minutes later, as she lay in bed, sleep strangely eluded her. She found herself replaying the bizarre events of the evening in her head: her tension with Charlotte and Fiona (God, that seemed like days ago!) her watercolour (had she kept it?) her blackout (she could still feel Robbie's tongue licking her face) and then that Good Samaritan, ('what was his name?') She racked her brains trying to remember but failed. When Sophie did eventually drift off, the Samaritan's name was still on the tip of her tongue. An hour later, she was so soundly asleep that when Doctor Liston came to take her pulse, she hardly stirred.

But when she awoke the next morning, the first word on her lips was 'Neil'.

Chapter 4

Two days later on Ward 2 of Oban General Hospital, Morag was having a stressful day. It had started at six in the morning after a night of too little sleep. By mid morning, if it wasn't her pager ringing or the demands of patients it was frequent interruptions from phone calls. First there had been a member of the Ball Committee reminding her about an imminent deadline; then it had been a patient's relative asking if the patient's dog could be brought into the hospital "to cheer her up, like". Later it had been her mother wittering on about how Morag and her brother Greig had "woken me up last night with you gettin' in on his bloody bike at God only knows what time, clatterin' aboot like a scaffy waggon and leaving yer room like a Council tip…". For Morag, the only thing worse than being treated like a child was being treated like a child when on duty. Sometimes the other nurses covered for Morag, telling her mother that she was busy on the ward. At other times - like today for instance - when they fancied a laugh at her expense, they would simply hand the phone over, saying, "Important call for you, Morag" and then hover round, silently pulling faces, rolling their eyes and trying to annoy her. So when the ward phone rang for the umteenth time that morning and a colleague said, "Morag – another call for you," she bellowed in exasperation "Ward 2. Morag Govan."

"Oh hello" came the soft-spoken melodious voice at the other end, "it's Sophie Montgomery here."

* * *

Morag recognised her voice immediately. This was the annoying Missy who had discharged herself yesterday afternoon against the advice ("better stay in for another night, just to be on the safe side") of Doctor Liston. This was the cheeky Montgomery upstart who, yesterday morning, had blethered on about "this amazing good Samaritan who found me… blacked out… rainstorm… rescued me… if it hadn't been for him…" Morag, who was a much better talker than she was a listener, had only half concentrated on what Sophie had said at the time. "He was so strong and tall… and he had such a clever dog…" And at that moment, Morag had pricked up her ears, stopped what she was doing, and asked, "Did he say what his name was?"

Sophie replied innocently, "Yes, Robbie."

"No, you idio-" Morag bit her tongue "- I mean, what was your rescuer's name?"

"Oh, I see. Yes, it was Neil. I don't know his surname."

At the time of this conversation yesterday Morag had been about to give Ms Montbloodygomery a piece of her mind when her pager had gone off. Momentarily torn between attending the emergency and tearing a strip off Sophie her only thought was "Bloody cheek!" as she rushed down the corridor to answer the pager's demands. This cheeky besom had been referring not just to any Neil but to *her* Neil, her *boyfriend* Neil. As in they slept together even if they didn't live together. A sore point though, given that Morag Govan still lived at home, having to endure her younger sister's tantrums and her mother's tongue, being nagged and harassed whenever she spent a night out with her girlfriends in Oban and generally having her style cramped. Aged twenty, all Morag wanted was a place of her own like her brother, but on a nurse's salary and with Oban prices she couldn't even afford to rent. She had suggested several times to Neil that they get a place together. But by living at home with his father Neil was able to plough all his profits into his business instead of a mortgage. Both Morag's Mam and Neil's old man were still very full of life and the prospect of inheriting a house was years away. But the worst part of not having their own home was not having "a decent place to shag" as Morag put it. As one considerably experienced in the Kama Sutra, Morag resented not having what she called 'a decent fornicarium'. She and Neil had to wait until either house was empty (chancy) use her brother's place (unreliable) or make whoopee outdoors (unpredictable: after all, you could only take so much west-coast weather and midges in pursuit of a good time).

When they had first got it together Neil was up for anything, but over the last year he had been less enthusiastic about their al fresco shenanigans. They'd had a few near misses lately when they had nearly been discovered in flagrante. "Morag, I've got to think of my reputation," he told her after a particularly exciting but nerve-wracking occasion in the local woods. What if we were discovered eh? You know what a small place this is. My credibility would be in tatters." But Morag didn't care about his credibility. She'd had a number of previous boyfriends before him but she often boasted to her girlfriends that "Neil's the best shag ever." Whether that was true or whether she just wanted to make her friends jealous, even Morag couldn't tell. "When are we going to buy our own place then?" she would keep demanding, and "If you've got a problem going in the woods then let's buy our own wee But and Ben." And like a cracked record he would repeat his mantra about the need to build the business and about waiting 'til next year. But Morag was growing more impatient with every passing month.

After she had dealt with the pager emergency and eventually returned to her ward, Morag had fully intended to give Sophie a piece of her mind. But to her annoyance, her patient had simply disappeared into thin air. Discharged herself against doctors' orders. 'Good riddance' was Morag's main reaction at the time, and she had quickly put Ms Montgomery and the identity of her rescuer out of her mind.

But now here she was again, the interfering little besom.

* * *

"Hello? Are you still there?" came Sophie's voice down the receiver.

Putting the phone to her ear, Morag simultaneously took off her disposable gloves and her metaphorical gloves.

"Now you listen here," she snarled, "you keep your hands off my Neil."

"Your what?"

"Neil's ma property and you keep yer thieving maulers off him d'ye hear?"

"Look, I…"

"You heard me. You're not getting his number from me."

"I don't want his number. I want my ring."

"Your *what*?"

"My gold signet ring. I've lost it and I think it may be in the hospital."

"Oh." The wind taken out of her sails, Morag's tone became a touch less adversarial.

"You see," continued Sophie, "I noticed that it was missing halfway to Edinburgh but I called Scotrail and they haven't found it and it means a lot to me and I just wondered whether it had been handed in at the hospital? It's a gold signet ring," she repeated, somewhat unnecessarily.

A little mollified, Morag said, "Well nothing's been handed in that I know of. What does it look like?" Sophie spent the next minute describing its Oxford oval shape and Tree of Life motif, adding, "Can I possibly give you my number and maybe you could phone me if it turns up?"

Unable to think of a plausible reason why she shouldn't co-operate and relieved that no further reference had been made to Neil, Morag nestled the receiver against her ear. Holding a yellow hospital notepad with one hand and a pen with the other, she found herself writing 'Ring S Mongumery 0131 313 3210'. Then she put the slip of paper in the back pocket of her jeans. An hour later, preoccupied with the morning's responsibilities, she had completely forgotten about it. But later, on a cigarette break, it struck Morag that although Neil had spoken to her yesterday, he had never mentioned anything about rescuing a Ms Montgomery - or anybody else for that matter.

Then her phone sounded again. "Oh for feck's sake," she swore, "Not again." But this time it was a text from Neil. 'Babe – call me. Need something from you,' it read.

Neil was also having a stressful morning. Now that Miss Lacelaw had terminated the Ardcairn contract he was having to prepare another client's site in a hurry and he didn't like to be rushed. Driving to the new harvesting area along a muddy track, his Landrover had become stuck on a rogue stump and it took a while to detach it. When he finally reached the site, he realised with a groan that he had forgotten his haversack with the essential marking equipment.

"Bollocks!" he cursed. "Where the hell is it?"

In the back, Robbie wagged his tail and put on his most endearing 'why don't you take me for a walkies?' face. But Neil was in no mood for walkies. "Not now Robbie," he said grimly, suddenly remembering where he had left his equipment, "you and I are going to have to pay Ardcairn another visit."

En route to the estate he phoned Duncan Fraser to explain his mission. "Duncan, it's me. Listen, you remember that girl I told you about at Ardcairn?" There was a pause as some mild scolding commenced from Miss Lacelaw's Factor. "No shit Sherlock" continued Neil, "I know I should have asked permission… Very funny, no we weren't doing it, you cheeky sod… Yeah, you wish. Look mate, I left some equipment near the felling site… No, it's only a small bag. Just letting you know I'm on my way there just now to fetch it… Yes I'll be quick. I've far too much to do without getting a verbal from anyone, especially you-know-who." Neil listened, grinning as Duncan changed the subject. "What's that? The Ball? Are you gonna go then? Well I suppose we'll be going. Morag's on the committee, remember? OK mate, we'll make it a foursome. Listen, I'm getting out of signal. Speak to you later."

Ten minutes later he came across the motorbike tracks from his visit two days ago. Bringing the Landrover to a stop he turned to Robbie. "Not this time boy," he said, leaving the crestfallen collie looking pathetically through the rear window at Neil's disappearing figure.

As he approached the grove of Douglas fir, Neil could faintly hear Miss Lacelaw's voice in the distance calling to Suki. 'Poochy must have given her the slip,' he smiled to himself. 'Serves the harridan right.' A man on a covert mission, Neil pushed his way quietly through the arboretum, moving stealthily from the cover of one majestic fir to the next. Even in his subterfuge he found himself stopping for a few moments to admire their stateliness and his thoughts slipped back to the last time he had seen the trees, two days before. Eventually he spotted his haversack so hastily discarded when he had first caught sight of that extraordinary girl. But as he bent down to pick it up, an object flashed in the corner of his eye and a brief gleam reflected from something small on the ground nearby. A ring!

He picked it up and examined it carefully. As he did so a gentle breeze carried the cry "Suki! Suki! Come here Suki!" to his ears. The ring was a man's size. 'Bit large to be a girl's' he thought as he tried slipping it onto his little finger. Engraved on the flat oval surface was the image of a tree and the motto 'Garde bien'. 'Hmmm' he thought, 'Watch well'. 'Could it be Sophie's?' he wondered. 'Surely it wouldn't be Miss Lacelaw's.' It must have come off in his struggle to get Sophie up onto her feet. He should return it to her – but how? He didn't know where she lived. He didn't even know her surname. Miss Lacelaw might know, but there was no way he could ask her. She would want to know why *he* wanted to know. Given that he was hardly her favourite person, Neil was pretty certain that if he so much as mentioned it to her, Miss Lacelaw would demand the ring and then exclude him from any decision making one way or another. And she would also throw another conniption fit if she knew he had been on her property without permission yet again. No, he had to keep it quiet. There had to be another way to find out Sophie's details. Still admiring its motif, he pressed the ring absentmindedly to his lips before tucking it safely inside his zip pocket. And then in a flash of inspiration he guessed that Sophie was likely to have been taken to hospital, given the state she was in. 'Morag could find out her details' he thought.

Back at the Landrover Neil texted Morag. 'Babe – call me. Need something from you'

Seconds later a text came back 'A shag? ;-) you call me'

So he phoned her. But when Neil told Morag whose surname he needed, he was reluctantly cajoled into admitting that he had rescued this damsel in distress. Then Morag became less than forthcoming. "Why did ye no tell me about it?" she demanded. "They brought her in here but I didnae really see her much," she lied, "and anyway, she's awa' now. Took herself off." Why do ye want her number anyway? Why did ye no tell me about it yesterday?" she repeated. "Are you hiding something from me, Neil McLeod?"

Neil chose to reply to her first question. "No real reason," he replied evasively, adding, "I was busy. Anyway, she dropped… some cash and I wanted to give it her back," he lied. "C'm on babe, can't you get her address or something?"

But Morag, already annoyed, became increasingly belligerent. "Data protection. They won't release it to me. If she dropped some cash two days ago she wilna be expecting it back now. How much was it anyway?"

Neil became flustered. He was annoyed at Morag's questioning but glad that she wasn't there to see his face reddening. "Twenty quid." His web of deceit was growing steadily.

Morag cut in abruptly, "Look, forget it. Whoever this feckless tart is she can't be half as good a shag as me. Now do you want it or not?" she demanded. "Meet me at my place in half an hour."

Glancing at his watch, Neil realised that his day's work was in tatters anyway. He paused, gave Robbie a scratch behind his ear, then started the Landrover engine. As he headed down the road towards Oban he became immersed in thought.

But his thoughts were of Sophie, not Morag.

Chapter 5

As he drove towards Oban, Neil replayed in his head the extraordinary events from two days ago. 'What was Sophie doing on her own at Ardcairn? Where had she come from and, for that matter, where was she going?' There had been such a short time before Miss Lacelaw had burst upon the scene, taken command and banished Neil from her estate. During that time Sophie had hardly been conscious, never mind coherent. Neil realised that he didn't really know anything about her at all. 'And what about the ring? Was it even hers?' he wondered. 'How was she now? And *where* was she now? Clearly Morag was going to be about as much help as Miss Lacelaw,' he realised, as he approached the outskirts of town.

Robusta wood lay on the far side of Oban, close to the road that headed south towards Lochgilphead. For nearly two years now Neil had come to know its character, its moods and its secret places, just as he had come to know Morag's. At first it had proved to be an ideal setting for a secluded tryst and a spot of sex, al fresco. But lately it had become a much riskier rendezvous. A series of pathways had been created with grants from the Forestry Commission, opening the woods up to the public. So strong had been the local interest that folk had not only taken to the new routes but had also created a network of informal paths too. Over the summer months, walkers had beaten down the undergrowth and generally infiltrated Neil and Morag's favourite old haunts. On one recent occasion the two of them had almost been discovered in a compromising position. Whenever they heard distant voices their lazy afternoon sessions had, of necessity, become 'quickies' as Morag described them and although this risk of discovery added a certain spice to the proceedings, it also added unwanted stress, and at times proved to be a passion killer. These developments had led Neil to suggest to Morag that they find somewhere else for what they called "nookie". But Robusta wood had the great advantage of being only a short walk from Morag's home, and in a triumph of lust over experience she and Neil were too habituated - or perhaps too complacent - to look elsewhere.

As he drew near to her house Neil spotted Morag in the usual place close to the woodland entrance, sitting on a low wall, smoking a cigarette and looking bored. Seeing Neil's long wheelbase Landrover approaching, she flicked her cigarette butt away and jumped down, watching him park nearby. Then the two of them slipped quietly into the wood while Robbie watched dolefully from the back of the 4x4. He sensed that this place was good for walkies but for some reason his master never took him in there.

The couple made a furtive beeline for their favourite secluded place. Once there, Morag quickly removed her blouse and pulled Neil close to her. Already prepared for a spot of passion, Neil spread his old Barbour jacket on the forest floor and started unbuttoning his shirt. But as they became locked in a passionate embrace, they were vaguely aware of something rustling in the bushes nearby. A trembling of foliage heralded the sudden and dramatic entrance of a young brown and white King Charles spaniel that rocketed out of the bushes, careered straight towards them and immediately proceeded to lick their faces, its tail wagging furiously as it joined in the game. Morag giggled and patted its head.

"Maddie... *Maddie!*" shouted her owner from somewhere nearby.

"For God's sake don't encourage it," said Neil, but Maddie could smell eau de collie on Neil's old jacket and even if she couldn't see Robbie she too was intent on getting down and frisky. "Oh God," groaned Neil, setting off Morag even more.

"MADDIE!" This time the voice sounded uncomfortably close.

The spaniel looked up reluctantly in the direction of her owner's voice but still remained disobediently rooted to the spot, too distracted by the enticing smell of male collie. For a brief moment Morag and Neil looked at each other in mild panic. Then they hastily grabbed their clothes and started putting them on as fast as they could. Seconds later an irate woman in a tweed skirt and waxed cotton hat appeared at the edge of the clearing, red faced with effort.

"BAD GIRL!" she shrieked, though whether this admonishment was directed at Morag or Maddie wasn't entirely clear.

Reunited with her mistress at last, Maddie bounded back to her as if butter wouldn't melt in her little doggie mouth. It was clear to both Morag and Neil that they were the object of intense suspicion and doubtless seen as the entire reason why the dog had run off in the first place. Thin-lipped and disapproving, the tweedy tyrant glowered down at them for several seconds, put the dog on its lead, turned on her heel and marched off with a snort of disgust. With their unwelcome intrusion now over, Neil and Morag started to laugh hysterically. In mid-merriment, Neil noticed a scrap of something yellow on the ground. He bent down and picked up a piece of yellow paper as Morag turned away to adjust her bra. It hadn't been there before and must have fallen out of Morag's pocket. He picked it up and looked at it. Puzzled, he asked "Who's S Mongumery?"

"What?"

"S Mongumery. Friend of yours?" Neil enquired. "This says Ring S Mongummery 0131 313 3210. Looks like you've spelt the name wrongly anyway," he added.

Morag blushed slightly. "No-one you know," she lied, testily, and snatched the piece of paper back from Neil's hand.

"Alright, Miss Conspiracy," said Neil. "No need to be nippy. Why all the cloak and dagger then?"

"It's just a patient," she replied. "Anyway, it's none of your bloody business." And she screwed the paper into a ball and tossed it into the nearby bushes.

"Alright, alright," retorted Neil, confused at Morag's overreaction, "keep your knickers on."

At those words, Morag's scowl ceased and a smile started to form. "Actually, I can't," she grinned, making a show of pulling a pair of pink knickers from out of her trouser pocket. "I didn't have time to put them on." And when she improvised a mock striptease act, twirling the underwear round and round her head and draping it over the branch of a nearby tree, they both saw the funny side of it. Their spat over the piece of paper now forgotten, they both joked about her Damian Hirst artistic creation until Morag said, "I might have to leave this as a souvenir. I guess we'll have to find somewhere quieter in future."

Later on, after Neil had walked Morag back to her house, said hi to her younger sister, talked motorbikes with her elder brother Greig, accepted the cuppa offered by her mother, and started the drive home, he kept casting his mind back to the afternoon's drama. He frowned. His instincts told him that something wasn't quite right…

After a few restless hours of sleep he woke in the middle of the night realising what was wrong. "Of course!" he exclaimed out loud. It wasn't 'Ring S Mongumery', it was 'Ring. S Mongumery'. Sophie Montgomery's ring. That was it! He couldn't remember the phone number written on the paper but he knew it was an Edinburgh one, and now he knew Sophie's surname. Just to make certain he wouldn't forget, Neil switched on his bedside light, wrote 'Sophie Montgomery - Edinburgh' on his bedside pad, drew two x's underneath and drifted off again, this time to a sound sleep.

* * *

Next morning, before heading off to work, Neil made some phone calls. The first was to a friend in Edinburgh.

"Hi John, Neil here. How's things, mate? Still in bed?… Well of course *I've* been up for hours grafting." He paused, chuckling at the reply from the other end of the phone. "Listen, I was wondering if you could do me a wee favour… What's it worth? Well how about a pint sometime? OK, I'll tell you what it is. Have you got an Edinburgh phone directory there? Good. Can you look up Montgomery? Yeah, Montgomery. Are there many listed? Why? Well I'll tell you when I see you. Oh, c'm on mate." There was a long pause. John was clearly having difficulty either finding the directory or getting out of bed, or both. Neil drummed his fingers on the sideboard impatiently and then, "About thirty?!" he groaned. "OK who are they? Postcodes, phone numbers." For the next few minutes Neil scribbled away, grunting occasionally to show that he was capturing the information. Afterwards he said "Thanks mate, I owe you one. Look I'm coming down for the rugby in a fortnight. No, Morag's working, she can't make it. How about a drink before the game? Murrayfield Hotel, say one o'clock? OK, I'll see you there." He quipped, "Sleep well!" and then hung up.

His next fifteen calls were to random Montgomerys, four of which turned out to be answer phones. On the sixteenth attempt, a resonant alto female voice answered.

"Who is this?" she asked, when Neil had enquired if there was a Sophie at this address.

"I'm sorry to bother you. My name's Neil McLeod. I may have something that belongs to a Sophie Montgomery."

"Are you another of those exasperating boys who are always pestering her?" came the reply.

"No, I assure you that I really do have something that I think she's lost. It's a ring," he added quickly.

There was a short pause.

"What sort of ring?"

"A gold signet ring."

Then a longer pause. Time stood still for Neil at that moment and a strong feeling of déjà vu swept over him. When the lady then asked him for a description of the ring he said, "Look I'm sorry madam but unless I know that this *is* the right number for Sophie Montgomery how can I be sure you're not wasting my time?"

After yet another pause, the voice at the other end of the phone mellowed somewhat. "Good point. Well here's a suggestion. Why don't you show me the ring and I can show you a photograph which would identify it for certain and then we can all move forward."

Neil went on to say that he lived in Argyll but would be in Edinburgh a week on Sunday. "Hmmm," came the resonant voice again, "You have this address?"

As he took down the address Neil was thinking quickly. He was due to arrive in Edinburgh at lunchtime. The match started at two, which meant that it would finish just after three thirty. That would hardly give him time to see Mrs Montgomery and get back to Haymarket for his four thirty train home. But after this visit south he wouldn't be down in Edinburgh for ages. He realised that this was a chance he just had to take. "OK, I'll see you around three forty-five," he said, "My name's McLeod. Neil McLeod."

Chapter 6

The Murrayfield Hotel was a heaving mass of excited rugby fans. Welsh supporters wearing red outfits with dragon logos mingled with St Andrew's crosses, tartan and lions rampant. The hotel was doing a roaring trade selling drinks, snacks and bar lunches, the autumn sun was shining, and beer flowed in abundance. Team supporters were boisterous but not out of order and there was a pre match buzz of anticipation.

Standing beside the bar and true to his word, Neil had bought the first round of drinks. John grinned as he lifted his pint, smiled at Neil and toasted "Cheers!". "Slainte!" echoed Neil. With voices raised above the background hubbub the two of them bantered about Oban High School and old times, but their conversation was frequently interrupted by rugby supporters demanding lager and crisps from hard-pressed bar staff. Above the long wooden bar was a wide screen television showing the usual pre-match interviews, player assessments and vox pop interviews. Scarcely anyone in the packed lounge bar was paying any attention to it and in any case the loud TV commentary was drowned by even louder decibels from scores of raised voices. As the minutes passed, one round of drinks developed into another - at least for John - and after a while he shouted to Neil about having to take a leak, pushing his way through the throng of punters towards the gents.

Neil was in reflective mode that afternoon and had hardly touched his first pint. After John had disappeared, Neil absentmindedly drew out the signet ring from a pocket. Since finding it by the old fir tree at Ardcairn he had examined it many times and had memorised its intricate craftsmanship: the tree of life shape and the French motto 'Garde bien''. Worried he might drop it and not find it again in the crush of supporters, he put it back safely, then glanced up at the giant TV screen. Although the pre-match commentary was drowned by noise from the bar, it was augmented by subtitled messages. Distractedly Neil looked at the screen. Then in an instant his brain jumped to attention as a message flashed in capital letters on the screen: MURRAYFIELD SECURITY ALERT, KICKOFF POSTPONED UNTIL 3PM''.

"Shhhiiit!" cursed Neil though none of the rugby revellers even noticed him. With the last train back to Taynuilt at four thirty he would either have to sort out this ring business and miss the match or watch the match and miss the opportunity of seeing Sophie again. Neil knew that this was his last chance to do either for a long while: after today he wouldn't be back in Edinburgh for several weeks. "Shit!" he repeated, unsure of what to do. But by the time John returned from the gents, Neil had made up his mind. He gestured up to the TV. News of the delayed kickoff was spreading round the bar and the background noise level was becoming quieter now that the throng of supporters had turned their attention to the screen. "Sorry mate," said Neil "I'm going to have to abandon you."

"Are you aff your heid? What's up?"

"Something's cropped up; I'm going to have to bale."

"And miss the match? Have you gone completely off your trolley?"

"There's something I've got to do before I go home."

"What could possibly be more important than seeing the match?"

"Oh… nothing much," replied Neil vaguely.

John exploded. "For feck sake!" he exploded, "You haven't missed a Murrayfield match for years. You come all this way to see it and now you're telling me that you've got better things to do? Aye, right pal!"

But Neil would not be moved. "It's complicated," he said lamely.

"Complicated, my arse. It'll be some dodgy deal or a bloody bird I'll bet. Just wait 'til I tell Morag," he teased. But seeing Neil's lack of levity he changed his tone, adding conspiratorially, "Lighten up mate, your secret's safe with me. But you'd better let me into it sometime, *and* it'll cost you another pint to keep quiet."

Neil nodded. Competing for the barman's attention with the three-deep crowd, he eventually managed to secure his friend's liquid bribe. Setting it down beside John's two other empty glasses he slid his entrance ticket towards him. "Here, take it," he said, "See if you can flog it. You can buy the drinks next time." Then before John could remonstrate further, Neil articulated a half-apologetic, half-regretful, "See you then," and turned to go. He pushed his way through the hotel revellers and emerged onto Murrayfield Road. Taking out his Edinburgh street map he traced the short route to Ravelston with his little finger. Then he looked at his watch and drew a deep breath.

"Here I come, Sophie," he murmured.

* * *

Knowing his Edinburgh fairly well, Neil had expected the house to be a cut above the average, but he wasn't prepared for the imposing grandeur of The Grange, number five Ravelston Avenue, that confronted him some twenty minutes later. Through a set of ornate cast-iron gates he stared up at an impressive ivy-clad three-story house, which, unlike many of its neighbouring properties, had not been converted into flats. Preserved as the complete entity originally intended by its Georgian architect, it exuded an atmosphere of elegant but somewhat faded gentility. Neil whistled as his eyes took in the scene. The house conveyed an impression of wealth, but discreetly rather than deliberately. This was not a place where flashy cars would feel comfortable, Neil decided. In fact there were no cars to be seen at all. No, this place was more of a testimony to old money and old values, and Neil sensed a friendly atmosphere and a happy history. Pushing open a smaller gate beside the main entrance he walked slowly up the curving drive. Ahead of him, in the middle of a pool on the front lawn, trickled a small fountain. Though excited at the imminent prospect of seeing Sophie he couldn't help feeling a little self-conscious. He was, after all, a country lad not entirely at home amongst this city gentility and he felt rather dislocated amongst such established affluence. But before he had time to rationalise his feelings, a disembodied voice floated across the garden towards him "Ah, you're early. You must be Neil McLeod."

Neil looked around, failing to observe the owner of this voice.

"Could you possibly help me up?" the voice continued, "I'm not as agile as I used to be."

Still baffled, Neil searched in the direction of the sound and eventually traced its source to a spot somewhere behind a low hedge.

Next to a flowerbed, a full trug of weeds by her side, knelt an old lady. 'Probably in her late seventies' thought Neil. She wore a faded summer dress, a sun hat and a gardening apron bearing the modest slogan, 'World's Greatest Gardener'. The lady wiped her hands on her apron, looked Neil up and down and then proffered her hand. "How do you do. I'm Dorothy Montgomery. My arthritis hasn't been too good recently. Could you help me up?"

"Uh" he winced as she seized Neil's hand with a surprisingly strong grip. "I hope you found your way here without mishap?" she enquired. Now that she was standing upright, Dorothy was taller than Neil had expected. Even more disconcerting were her intense blue eyes. He gave an involuntary start. They were so similar to Sophie's and they seemed to bore into him, searching out his inner thoughts. Her face, though lined now, still echoed a beauty so striking and similar to Sophie's that he was quite taken aback, momentarily at a loss for a reply.

"I, er…" he said, conscious that so far he was not winning prizes for great conversation.

Still assessing him with her hypnotic eyes she said "Hmm," and paused, before continuing, "I thought we might have some tea? Would that suit you? I'm sorry to be so unprepared," she apologised, "It's just that I wasn't expecting you 'til later."

Not sure what to say, Neil simply said "Um" again, then realising that he must be coming across as a complete moron, added, "I got here sooner that expected." It was a lame reply but he thought it best to spare her the rather complicated reason as to why he had appeared so early.

"Well it's a good job you did," remarked Dorothy "all the roads around here have been very busy, what with all the rugby traffic. Do you follow it?" She regarded him once again with an unflinching gaze. Unable to hold it for long, Neil glanced away. "S-sorry?" he said.

"The rugby. I think Scotland might just win this time."

"Oh, y-yes." At last Neil was on familiar territory. But he still remained at a loss for words: how could this frail old thing be talking to him about rugby? His confusion only deepened when she went on, "Scotland is kicking much better now, but the Welsh team are very poor in the line-out don't you think?"

Neil still didn't know what to say. "I... you seem to know a lot about it," he said weakly.

"Oh Charles was very keen on his rugby. He was a Blue at Oxford. Then when we moved up here he used to drag me off to all the Murrayfield games. Wonderful times. Wonderful memories," she sighed. "He died two years ago you know," and she paused for a moment to wipe something from the corner of her eye. Then recomposing herself she continued, "Could you possibly take these things?" proffering the gardening tools to Neil. Realising that it was more of an instruction than a question, he gathered them up and trailed her towards the house. They made their way slowly to the front door and - not knowing quite what to do - Neil put down the tools in the porch. Following Dorothy inside he finally found his voice, explaining that he had planned to be at the match and mentioning the delayed kick off. "So I thought I'd come here early. After today I won't be back in Edinburgh for a while," he finished, starting to wonder where Sophie was.

"Good. Then we will watch the match on TV. I had set the recorder but now we can watch it live. But first you must have some tea. This way," she commanded Neil, leading him into the drawing room. Neil immediately recognised the pervasive scent of stargazer lilies. "Make yourself comfortable," said Dorothy, adding "No thank you, I can manage. Earl Grey alright?" and not waiting for a reply she vanished from sight. Reeling from this indomitable human whirlwind, Neil took a deep breath and looked around him, still wondering where Sophie might be.

Layers of family history adorned the room. Forty-year-old faded black-and-white photos of Dorothy and what must have been Charles sat side by side with newer colour photos, many of them taken in exotic locations. There were several images of beloved family dogs: mainly flat coat retrievers and Irish setters. In a display cabinet stood an engraved glass bowl bearing the legend "Presented to Sir Charles Montgomery Bt, JP, DL, for his valuable services as a Forestry Commissioner 1979 to 1989". On the grand piano were more images, several of Sophie and Sir Charles sitting together in the countryside, painting; others of Sophie with a rather stern looking woman. Her mother, Neil guessed. One picture in particular held Neil's attention: Sophie smiling shyly but proudly in the foreground, holding a painting of a sylvan scene, with the same woodland in the background. And there on the wall close to the piano was the painting itself. Even to his untutored eye he could see how vividly the brushstrokes had brought the landscape to life, imbuing the canvas with lightness and depth. And there on the wall beside it, was a portrait of Sophie herself, signed with the interlocking initials 'CM' in one corner. Neil was fascinated by the way in which her grandfather had captured the character of her beauty with a sparseness of brush strokes. He was still staring at it some minutes later when Dorothy swept into the room.

"Ah I can see you're admiring Charles' work." She set down a tray with an elegant silver teapot and Spode cups and saucers. "I'm not sure how hungry you are," she added, "so I've looked out some biscuits." Neil wrenched himself away from the painting and turned his attention to Dorothy, noting with approval a large pile of chocolate digestives on the tray. "That was the last painting he did before he died," she said, indicating the one that Neil had just been admiring. Charles loved Sophie very much. He passed on his love of painting to her you know," she added. Neil sensed the emotion in Dorothy's voice and partly to distract her from her distress while she wiped a stray tear from her eye, he took the ring from his pocket.

"Lady Montgomery, this is the ring I mentioned to you," he said proffering it to her and in an instant the wrinkles of sadness on her face transformed into lines of pleasure. "Ah!" she remarked, cradling it in her hand like an old friend. "Ah, yes. How kind of you." She examined the motif. "Garde bien. Well you certainly did that, dear boy," and Neil felt an unexpected surge of pleasure. Plucking up his courage he asked, "Um... Lady Montgomery, I wondered, is Sophie here by any chance?"

"Here? No, she's at University." Neil's heart sank as Dorothy went on, "Now I'd like to show *you* something." She had returned to her brisk and businesslike manner. "Here is it," she said, taking down an old album entitled 'Wedding 1945' from a shelf containing several volumes of photographs. She leafed through the pages. There amongst the black and white images were some photos depicting Sir Charles in army uniform proudly displaying the same ring. "That was the ring I gave to Charles when we got married. More than fifty years ago now," she added, her face wreathed in the memories of happy times. "He wanted a signet ring rather than a wedding ring. When he died, he left it to Sophie. It was a little large for her. She kept meaning to get it reduced to fit properly but she never did – silly girl. She will be pleased to have it again – it meant so much to her. But now you must tell me the full story," she insisted, pouring a cup of tea and handing it to Neil. "How did you find it – and me, for that matter?"

Bit by bit, Neil unfolded his account of how Robbie had discovered Sophie in a state of collapse within the fir grove, how unwell she had been and how he had taken her to a place of shelter and then, later, discovered her ring. He left out the details about Morag and the piece of paper. But to Neil's surprise, as he continued to relate this course of events to Dorothy, she became increasingly irritated, rather than pleased. Finally she interrupted, "Oh, that's so like Sophie, so typical. Putting herself at risk like that - and with her diabetes too. Just like Charles – he used to do some suicidally stupid things sometimes. I remember once, he…" She checked herself. "But how impolite of me, I'm so sorry. I am very grateful to you for retrieving the ring. I would like to reward you somehow" She went on briskly, "Let me see, would a hundred pounds be alright?" But Neil would hear none of it and the more she insisted, the more he resisted, until their battle of wills was interrupted by the timely ringing of a phone in the next room.

When Dorothy returned much later, the hint of a wry smile lined the creases of her blue eyes. "Well, that was my daughter in law Jane - Sophie's mother - on the phone. It seems that she is ignorant of what you have just told me. Perhaps I shouldn't be surprised. Sophie has chosen to be, how do they put it? *economical* with her mother as far as the truth is concerned. That puts me in a dilemma. If *I* give Sophie back her ring, the reason why she lost it will doubtless… emerge. I may say that that will not engender mother-daughter cordiality." Dorothy paused, thinking, her eyes narrow and her brow furrowed. "But now if *you* give her back the ring…" her voice trailed off, "well, that's an entirely different matter." She thought for a minute. Finally decided in her mind, she reached for a pen and paper and wrote down a number. "That's the number of Sophie's mobile telephone," she said, handing Neil the slip of paper. "She's just started at St Andrew's. History of Art. St Salvator's College." Her blue eyes once again held Neil's in a disconcerting gaze. "I know I can trust you to return it to her safely," she stated almost conspiratorially as she patted his knee. "She will be pleased."

"Now" she announced in a stentorian tone, "The Match!" Then, rather less formally, "Would you mind switching the TV on?"

And so it was during that eventful afternoon in Edinburgh that Neil found himself watching the rugby, not on a plastic seat on the Murrayfield terraces but sunk deep into a comfortable leather Chesterfield at The Grange, the television commentary punctuated by Dorothy's frequent cries of "Come on Scotland! Are you blind, referee? Fumbled again – what on earth are you doing?" and "Oh well done!" By the half time mark, Neil realised that he was going to miss his train home, but he was past caring. He was enjoying himself far too much. The match ebbed and flowed with neither team showing an overall advantage and although the end of the contest was a close-run thing, in the end the gods smiled down on Scotland. Neil and Dorothy whooped with joy at the home team's victory.

Resisting Dorothy's insistence that he stay for supper, and her continued attempts to reward him for finding the signet ring, Neil said his thanks, shook her warmly by the hand and promised to visit her again. It was with feelings of warmth and wellbeing that he stepped out into the post-match traffic. A plan that had half-formed in his mind was starting to solidify. But first, on a whim, he stopped by a jeweller's shop. Wanting to buy something special in which to present the ring to Sophie, he eventually settled - not for one of the many ornate silver boxes on display - but a unique wooden gift box. Though plain - almost nondescript in fact - it was very unusual, requiring a knack, obtained only through trial and error, to open it. Neil found the cryptic mechanism strangely satisfying. 'Perfect,' he thought, his excitement rising.

He directed his footsteps back towards Waverley station. There would surely be a train to St Andrews this evening. Nothing was going to stop him from seeing Sophie now.

Chapter 7

Like a giant electronic whirligig, the station timetable rattled through its self-important routine. Platform numbers and train station names flicked around in a frantic blur of black and white. Having asked at the information booth about the next train for St Andrews, Neil realised he had less than five minutes to board it. Armed with his ticket he waited anxiously for the flickering signboard to settle down into recognisable names and numbers. At last! Platform 15.

No time to call Sophie before boarding the train. He rushed onto the platform, grabbed an empty seat and switched on his mobile phone just as the guard blew the whistle. As the train clanked slowly out of the station Neil purposefully - almost reverentially - pressed the precious sequence of numbers that Dorothy had given him. Seconds later, just as the phone connected and a faint voice said "Hello?" the train - and the signal - were swallowed up by a tunnel connecting the short distance between Waverley and Haymarket stations. "Damn!" uttered Neil. He'd completely forgotten about that tunnel. A couple of minutes later, bringing Sophie's face to mind again, he pressed the redial button. This time the signal connected. Aha! Neil was mentally preparing his introduction, when... "The mobile phone you have called may be switched off. Please try later."

"Bugger!" Neil swore again. Some of his fellow passengers glanced disapprovingly in his direction. 'Well, I'm on the train now: might as well at least try to track her down in St Andrews,' he thought.

He waited until open countryside and this time punched in a different number. "Hi Dad. Yeah, great match. Fantastic result. Talk more about it when I get home. Yes, I'm on the train, but it's a different one. No, a different one. Long story. I won't be back until tomorrow now. Look, could you phone Craig to tell the team that I'll be late tomorrow and just to continue on that clearfell job? No everything's fine Dad. No worries," he said reassuringly. "I'm expecting to see a friend soon. What? No, no-one you know. Look I can't really talk here. I'll tell you all about it when I see you. Bye Dad."

The regular te-tum, te-tum; te-tum te-tum of the wheels broke into a random clatter as the train started rumbling over the Forth Bridge. Westwards in the gathering dusk, smoke plumes silhouetted the autumn sky, gas flares supplementing the sunset with their artificial orange streaks. Backlit by the setting sun, Grangemouth looked almost romantic to Neil: portentous perhaps. Although excited by his spontaneous mission he was also strangely nervous, afraid of Sophie's reaction. Would she be pleased to see him, or embarrassed? Would she want to forget his rescue instead of being reminded of it? 'Well, if she's anything like her grandmother she'll be fine,' he decided, willing the train to go a bit faster. But it obstinately continued its sedate self-important pace, rattling unhurriedly through the Fife countryside.

After a while Neil became lost in thought, brooding uneasily. Just as the sun sank below the horizon he tried Sophie's phone one more time, but it was still switched off. By now his misgivings were increasing. 'What if she's away on a study trip or something?' he reflected. Taking out the wooden gift box from his pocket he slid back the locking lever, unfastened the lid, removed the ring and started fiddling with it absent-mindedly. 'What corners of the world has this band of gold been to?' he wondered. 'What hands have shaken Charles Montgomery's hand? And come to that, Sophie's hand?' Turning to look out of the window at the lights passing by he became lost in thought, unaware of furtive glances and whispered conversation coming from two female students sitting across the carriage from him.

It was dark by the time the train eventually approached Leuchars. Neil had only been to this part of Scotland once before, as a young child, and his memories of the place were distant ones. He was disconcerted to see not the town that he had half remembered, but a small collection of assorted buildings instead. "Excuse me", he said to two female students as the guard announced the impending arrival of Leuchars, "Is this the right stop for the University?"

"Sure," said the taller of the two, a good-looking fair-haired American girl.

"Is it far to the town?" he asked her.

"To St Andrews? Well it is a long walk," she smiled at him "You'll have to take a bus – but you'll be lucky to get one at this time. Or a taxi."

"Thanks very much. Er, there's just one more thing?" As the train slowed down they all got up out of their seats and made their way to the carriage door. "Do you know how to get to St Salvator's College?"

The taller student smiled at him again. "St Sally's? That's my College," she said. "I was going to take a taxi there. We could split the cost if you want?" And so it was that, after making their introductions, Neil found himself sitting next to Annabelle - a warm, friendly and undoubtedly sexy American Classics student - who started telling him a bit about undergraduate life at St Andrews. As their taxi headed for town, Annabelle said that, yes, she knew of Sophie Montgomery. "She's in the year below me. Just started, but she seems to know loads of people already. She usually hangs out with a crowd of hooray Henrys here. How do you know her?"

Nil tried to imagine what a 'hooray Henry' was. "Oh we met briefly last month," he explained vaguely. I'm just passing through and thought I'd look her up.

"Just passing through?" joshed Annabelle. She turned to face him, "St Andrews isn't somewhere you 'just pass through'. This is the end of the line dude," and she swept back her hair, teasing Neil with her eyes. "Neil, do you mind if we stop at my faculty first? I've got to pick up my assignment. It's only a short walk to St Sally's from there - and anyway, you don't seem to have any luggage?" Her remark carried a hint of a flirtation, but this nuance was lost on Neil.

Ten minutes later Neil found himself in the centre of town waiting outside the Classics faculty whilst Annabelle busied herself inside. He tried Sophie's phone for a third time – still nothing. And then, in one of those bizarre and extraordinary coincidences that life can sometimes throw at you, he caught sight of her - at least he thought it was her - emerging from a nearby restaurant. For a few seconds the outline of her features remained silhouetted by the dazzling lights of the brightly lit doorway and then transformed itself into a vision of loveliness as she moved outside under the glow of a street light. His heart skipped a beat. Yes, it *was* her! She was wearing a green halter neck dress and high heels and her hair was up in a French plait. She looked gorgeous. My God, Sophie, at last!

As Neil started to cross the wide street he was abruptly checked by horn of a passing car. He hadn't even seen it, he realised with a shock. He called out her name, but the car driver was making his point by crawling past frustratingly slowly, making pointed gestures at Neil and gunning his engine, drowning all other sound. Neil was about to shout her name again when the restaurant door opened and another figure emerged from the brightness behind. A tall, dark, chiselled young man immaculately dressed in dinner jacket, silk scarf and cashmere coat, with a cigarette in his hand shouted "Sophie?" and sauntered over to where she was waiting, grabbed her by the arm and started to kiss her. Shocked into immobility, Neil - who was halfway across the street by now - froze to the spot, gawping in disbelief. Seconds later the young man drew away from her, threw his cigarette into the gutter and jumped into a Porsche convertible parked just outside the restaurant. He started the engine, revving it unnecessarily, as Sophie, briefly wiping her mouth, eased herself elegantly into the red leather passenger seat. Realising that his chance was about to slip away, Neil ran across the street and shouted "Wait!" to them. Paying no attention to him, the young man prepared to drive off just as Neil ran up to the car. "Sophie!" he gasped, flushed and panting.

She looked at him curiously. Then the penny dropped and a warm glow of recognition swept over her face. "Neil?" Her expression held a mixture of surprise, curiosity and pleasure.

"What the fuck Sophie?" The young man revved the powerful engine again and looked in his rear-view mirror, ready to pull out.

"This belongs to you," gushed Neil. He proffered the wooden box to Sophie.

"Thank you, but how…?" She was interrupted by the young man. "We're already late," he pronounced. "Gotta go. Can't wait," he added, gesturing at Neil.

"Henry, I…" Sophie started, but Henry was clearly in no mood to wait. He looked at his watch, then glanced at Neil's checked shirt and scruffy jeans and decided that this stranger was not worth waiting for. Disregarding Sophie's appeal to "hang on just a minute" he moved the steering wheel over, edging the revving Porsche out of its parking space and into the street. Neil was completely gobsmacked. He'd never seen such a display of arrogance and rudeness in all his life and for the second time that day found himself at a complete loss for words.

In all the confusion, Sophie struggled with a welter of emotions: anxiety about delaying Henry, amazement at seeing Neil again, curiosity about how he had found her and inquisitiveness about what he had given her. But before she could articulate the myriad of questions running through her mind, her playboy chauffeur had whisked them noisily up the road in an attention-demanding display of conspicuous wealth. Neil continued to stare in disbelief at the disappearing Porsche until it vanished around a bend. Still dazed, and shocked at the complete failure of his mission, he remained standing in the road, oblivious of some strange looks by a passing cyclist. His trauma was interrupted by Annabelle who by now had glided silently up to his side. She took his arm and steered him gently back to the pavement - and reality.

"I saw that display," she said disapprovingly. "Unbelievable. You get some crazy mofos here. Too much money and not enough manners." Then changing her tone she said brightly, "Come on, let's you and me go drown our sorrows. I've got nothing else to do tonight… except my essay!" she added, grimacing. Seizing him by the arm, she propelled him to a nearby pub and practically forced him inside. Still too bewildered to resist, he let her steer him across to the noisy bar, throwing a final glance over his shoulder at the empty street as the door swung shut behind him. If he had listened and looked carefully, he would have heard the noisy red Boxter return not long afterwards and seen Sophie jump out onto the pavement, clutching her grandfather's signet ring and calling Neil's name. But the bar was noisy and Annabelle was already ordering drinks.

They found a quiet space, tucked around a corner of the pub. By the time his second pint appeared, Neil was spilling out the full story to Annabelle, revealing how he had first encountered and rescued Sophie and how he had returned to the grove at Ardcairn and discovered her ring. Throughout his monologue Annabelle listened sympathetically. She searched his face closely, finding herself drawn to this romantic Highlander, half listening to the background strains of Dire Straits' 'Romeo and Juliet' while he talked on. She wrestled with conflicting emotions: on the one hand wanting to be motherly and protective, and on the other wanting to sleep with him and possess him. As time went on, the glow of three Bacardi and cokes fuelled her sexual desire and the possession emotion won hands down. She intertwined Neil's fingers with one of her hands and pushed back her hair with the other. Tucked into their corner, neither of them observed Sophie push open the pub door and look anxiously around the room. Neither did she see them, for after staring about her for a full minute, she left, still looking visibly distressed.

Half an hour later, when Neil had finally finished his tale, Annabelle smiled at him, gave him a lingering look and said, "Look, you've missed your train back to the west. I've got space in my room tonight if you fancy…?" her voice trailed off in a kind of question mark and her clear wide eyes looked directly into his, their meaning beyond question. From reliving the momentous events at Ardcairn a fortnight ago, Neil was wrenched back to the here and now and as the meaning behind her words struck home he twitched involuntarily, spilling some beer onto the table. "I…" he began, his voice tailing off in his confusion. Here was a very attractive American blonde making a pass at him – Neil McLeod. Conflicting thoughts rushed through his mind at the speed of light. 'Normally, well… she was definitely one hot babe, but… but.'

At any other time there would have been few second thoughts. But tonight Neil was racked with competing emotions: torn between the exciting prospect of a night with Annabelle and still tormented by the evening's sorry fiasco. If Neil had stopped to examine the whirlwind in his mind, he would have found one thought strangely conspicuous by its absence: any feelings of moral obligation to Morag. She, he suspected, was not always entirely faithful towards him, though he chose not to examine the clues too carefully. But should he extract some sort of comfort by sleeping with Annabelle tonight or should he somehow remain faithful to Sophie by refraining? 'What nonsense' he told himself. He and Sophie aren't an item anyway. How can he possibly be faithful to her?' And yet in an inexplicable way it seemed like that to him. After all, hadn't Sophie said, "wait a minute"? Hadn't she wanted to talk to Neil? It was her moneyed boyfriend who had impulsively propelled her away. Neil's mind went into overdrive. Here he was in a strange place. The pursuit of love had turned to dust but now he was being offered no-strings sex with an undoubtedly gorgeous girl. But sleeping with Annabelle would somehow... somehow what? Somehow be cheating on Sophie? Yes. He couldn't explain it but that's just how it felt to him. But then what was he to her? And in any case, she had her rich hooray Henry, whatever his name was... And then for the first time since the Porsche debacle the vestige of a smile came to Neil's face. That's what Sophie *had* called him: he *was* called Henry. That was rich in more than one sense of the word!

"What are you smiling at?" quizzed Annabelle, her eyebrows puckering briefly.

"Oh, I was just thinking how bizarre all of this is" replied Neil. "You and Sophie and everything. Listen, Annabelle, you're absolutely gorgeous and I absolutely would love to stay with you tonight but, well... you know. It's just that... I really ought to get back to Argyll. I should really have been back there tonight. There's people relying on me to turn up tomorrow..." his voice trailed off. He sounded feeble and he knew it.

Annabelle was a good a judge of character. She knew that he was in anguish and that what he probably needed to sort out his life out was space rather than sex. She didn't feel rejected. If anything, she kind of admired Neil for showing some resistance: most men were, after all pretty weak-willed. "Here," she said, prizing a circular beer mat apart and taking out a pen. "This is my number. Call me if – well – whenever."

Neil leant over the pub table and gave her a brief kiss on the cheek. "You are so sweet," he said again, and wrote his number on the other half of the cardboard circle. "And sexy" he added, handing it to her. "And if you ever find yourself in the Oban area, well, let's just say I owe you a big one Annabelle." They both laughed: the innuendo was not lost on either of them.

Outside the pub Neil and Annabelle kissed again, this time on the lips. Neil felt his passion rising and his resistance weakening but he was checked by the sight of an approaching taxi, its sign illuminated. He reluctantly prized himself free from Annabelle's embrace and flagged it down before he changed his mind.

As the taxi bore him back to the station once again, Annabelle turned back towards St Salvator's and hummed a line from Dire Straits' 'Romeo and Juliet': 'You and me babe, how about it…'

* * *

More than once during that long, draughty and sleepless night spent in the waiting room of Waverley station Neil replayed in his mind his happy encounter with Dorothy and his hapless encounter with Sophie. And more than once did he wish he had taken Annabelle up on her offer.

Chapter 8

During the next three months Neil threw himself into work, directing his contracting team by day and wrestling with paperwork during the Argyll evenings. But putting all his energies into building up his name and his professional reputation was starting to pay dividends. He took on another full-time worker, upgraded the Company's motley collection of chainsaws and purchased a second-hand forwarder machine with a higher output than the old one. Now his assistant Craig would be able to extract many more logs per day from the forest. With his client base secured Neil could be more selective about which jobs he took on and which ones he didn't, but even so he continued to work long days, whilst his father followed suit in the workshop. Neil's free weekend time was eroded by site inspections and even with no Edinburgh trips planned he found less time to see his friends in general and Morag in particular. Duncan – who had often dragged him off to the Taynuilt pub for a pie and a pint in the past – now had to use all of his persuasive powers to get his best friend to go with him. If truth be known, Neil was trying – mostly unsuccessfully – to forget about St Andrews and Sophie. But when Duncan did persuade Neil to join him for an occasional drink, the only thing that his friend ever seemed to talk about was Sophie. There had been times when Neil and Morag had rowed about accommodation and other times when he was feeling so low that he even thought about phoning Dorothy, but he never got further than the first few digits before abandoning the attempt. 'What's the use?' he would tell himself, 'Sophie's out of my league anyway and she and Henry are obviously an item.' And that view was reinforced by Annabelle, who phoned Neil a few days after that fateful St Andrews evening.

"Well they still seem together to me," she said. "Though I don't see them much, cos she's not reading my subject and anyway she's moved out of college. I think Henry's got a place out of town. I've sometimes seen the two of them in his tart trap," she added, with an unsubtle dig at the Porsche. Even though this wasn't what he really wanted to hear, Neil was grateful to Annabelle. She was the only person with whom he could have a meaningful conversation about Sophie and any scrap of news was almost better than no news at all.

By the time that December arrived, things were going so well for McLeod Forestry that Neil considered whether to surprise Morag by putting a deposit down on a small house. He had already discussed it a few times with his father. After Jim's wife Eleanor had died, being together in the same house had been an initial comfort to both Neil and Jim, and as time went on it had become the status quo. Although 'McLeod Forestry' had originally been Neil's idea and depended mainly upon his efforts, Jim's input to the business had been invaluable, keeping saws serviced and machines working. For someone in his sixties, Jim was unusually resourceful, but he wasn't the most domesticated of men. He had learned the basics of cooking for example, but basic was definitely the word. Fortunately for Neil and Jim, after Eleanor's death Neil's Godmother Ann had taken to coming over from her tied cottage on the Ardcairn estate to cook for them twice a week. Initially a pleasant change for father and son, after a while this had become a habit: an unspoken but welcome arrangement which they valued and appreciated. As cook for Miss Lacelaw, Ann was an excellent chef. For the years after Neil's mother's death, Ann's culinary visits had become something of a ritual for the three of them. Mindful that her cooking and her company always lifted Jim's spirits Neil called her his 'fairy godmother'.

Those evenings together at Cedar Cottage often echoed with the sound of laughter as tales were recounted of eccentric woodland owners and imperious estate owners. Neil had recently noticed the suspicion of a twinkle returning to his 'old man's' eyes, connected – he suspected – with the fact that Ann seemed to be visiting Cedar Cottage rather more often. "It's probably about time that I got my own place," Neil confided in Duncan one evening during a rare trip to the Taynuilt pub. "The neighbours must be getting fed up with all the machines and the squad coming and going. Anyway, the business is getting too big for Cedar Cottage." So when a nearby farmhouse with three acres and a barn came on the market, he considered putting down a deposit. But it needed fixing up and he didn't have time to do both that and manage the forestry business and he knew that Morag had neither the inclination nor the ability to repair and decorate the place herself. And besides, there was the major problem about where to base himself. He and the business needed space out of town but Morag needed to live close to Oban. She couldn't drive and her hospital hours generally didn't fit in with the local train and bus times. But houses in Oban were expensive and houses with space for Neil's business needs were prohibitively expensive.

Neil sighed. He was sure what he wanted from his business, but his romantic life? Now that was a conundrum for sure.

Chapter 9

For the last three months Morag had been in denial. The Oban Ball was approaching and although she had somehow found herself drafted onto the organising committee yet again, she wasn't naturally a committee person. To those people that were committee people, she could be very trying, but it wasn't always easy to get folk to help and Morag's autocratic style sometimes proved useful in dealing with recalcitrant creditors. But her main reason for agreeing to serve on the committee was a free ticket and free drink. This was Morag's third term of office on the Ball Committee and whether it was a case of pressure of work at the hospital or simply familiarity breeding contempt, this year she had been particularly lackadaisical about her duties. On a number of occasions other committee members had had to phone her at work to pester her to meet deadlines. Now aware of the Ball date fast approaching and aware that failure to meet these deadlines would be her fault, Morag was feeling stressed. She became increasingly defensive as the day of the Ball approached. Since Neil wasn't such great company nowadays, Morag took to going out more with her girlfriends: at least they knew how to have a good time. So much so that on two occasions recently she had woken up on a strange floor with a splitting headache and no recollection about how she had got there. Since the night that Sophie had appeared at Oban General, some indefinable wedge seemed to have driven itself between her life and Neil's, something elusive that Morag couldn't put her finger on. The day after Neil had gone to Edinburgh to see the rugby International, Morag had taken another call from that Montbloodygomery girl, mysteriously asking her to pass on her thanks to Neil. "He'll know what it's about," was all that Sophie had given out by way of explanation. 'For rescuing her,' Morag assumed wrongly, knowing nothing about Neil's impulsive and deeply disappointing trip to St Andrews. So, albeit with bad grace, Morag agreed at the time to deliver the message. But when Sophie also asked for Neil's address - something about wanting to send him a thank you card - Morag had put the phone down on her and in the end she decided not to tell Neil anything about Sophie's phone call at all...

* * *

A few days before Hogmanay, Oban's Volunteer Hall was a bustling hive of activity. There was a general air of excitement and anticipation with last minute preparations being made for the annual Winter Ball. In the dining hall, final adjustments were taking place to table settings, flower arrangements and name cards. In the adjoining ballroom, members of the ceilidh band were adjusting microphones and checking sound levels with a well-rehearsed routine of "one two, one two: testing, testing". At first the individual voices of duty staff were clearly discernible but as groups of ball-goers steadily drifted into the hall the volume of conversation rose until all voices became lost in a general hubbub of greetings – sincere and not so sincere. Though some folk had travelled from as far afield as Edinburgh and Glasgow, most of the revellers were local Argyllers. Old established families, professionals and enthusiasts mixed alongside students and a few less affluent Oban families. To some, the cost of tickets was of no small significance but like everyone else they enjoyed a well-organised Scottish dance. That love of reeling was the one thing that united everyone here, for most of those arriving at the Volunteer Hall were experienced dancers. Occasionally guests would arrive not knowing their Reel of the 51st from their Petronella. Their evenings were usually spent wishing in vain that they had done some preparation or wishing that there was a 'caller' to walk them through the steps, whilst they watched with envious eyes the gyrating kilts and swirling ball gowns of the ceilidh cognoscenti.

As the brief winter sunlight at this time of the year made for short working days outside, Neil had arrived in good time. Although he enjoyed a ceilidh as much as anyone, he had had a strange feeling about this one for some vague reason he couldn't put his finger on. He headed for the bar where Morag - wearing a plunging blood-red dress and displaying her remarkable cleavage - was clearly enjoying the lascivious attention of some early male arrivals. Whilst she smoked and chatted and made the most of her free drinks, Duncan and Lorna stood at some distance from the bar, people-watching and passing lewd comments and scurrilous jokes about the arriving guests. They could tell the newcomers, recognisable by their self-consciousness and immaculate highland dress, hired or perhaps even purchased at no small expense for the occasion. The old-established, often titled families were also distinctive. Completely at ease with a blend of formality and informality they were always 'hail-fellow-well-met' and seemed to know practically everyone else. 'Argyll certainly is a village' thought Neil wryly, observing the ritual exchange of kissings and compliments. Patriarchs of these old established families usually arrived in well-worn highland dress: Montrose and Prince Charles jackets that had seen a lot of ceilidhing but little dry cleaning; tatty kilts that had spent days on the hill stalking deer and evenings tripping the light fantastic. Sometimes these landowners also purchased tickets for a long-serving estate worker or two – but only if they knew their dances. Almost all of them did, though:

the culture of Scottish Dancing was alive and kicking on the west coast, with children exposed to ceilidhs from an early age and schools keeping a thriving tradition through classes and competitions. Duncan recognised several of the patriarchs and their spouses and he knew most of their names. The womenfolk were generally much better presented than their husbands although some of their dress styles had clearly been in fashion several years ago. Often they brought their smartly turned out offspring who quickly rushed off to the bar to join their friends for some drink-fuelled flirting and frivolity.

Neil nudged Duncan. He'd spotted the bishop of Argyll and the Isles together with various family members: accomplished dancers all of them. "He was good to me at my first Oban Ball," he said to Duncan. "Invited me into his set and made me feel at home," adding, "Wicked sense of humour!" Then Lorna announced, "Look there's Stephen and Gordon Grey." A striking family group appeared, the sons led by their father, all wearing identical kilts of a distinctive pattern. "Their father had the tartan made up for them all," remarked Duncan, "That cannae be bad!"

As well as older-established families, there was a sprinkling of wealthy merchant bankers and their well-heeled friends, some of whom chose to live in Argyll and weekly commute to London. They brought with them immaculately groomed partners or trophy wives half their age, most of whom looked as if they had stepped out of the pages of a fashion magazine, sporting unique and expensive designer dresses. As the evening advanced these femmes fatales drew increasing attention from the men, especially during the more vigorous dances. Duncan shoved Neil with his elbow just as a stunningly attractive girl made an entrance on the arm of a balding overweight man. "What the hell does she see in him?" he asked, his eyes practically popping out of his head. "Well Miss Pneumatic, what first attracted you to your millionaire husband?" Neil joked in a mock interviewer's voice, as the unlikely couple headed for the bar. As Duncan continued to stare unashamedly at the girl's backless dress, Lorna snapped her fingers playfully in front of his face like a conjuror bringing him out of a hypnotic trance. "Oi, Casanova, remember me? Your girlfriend?" and they all laughed. Clinking glasses with a collective 'Slainte!' the three of them made a toast to a successful evening. Neil turned round to clink Morag's glass but she was busy pouring drinks for a rather loutish young man and made a slight waving motion with her hand as if to say 'not now, I'm busy'.

As with every Ball, there were the 'characters': self-styled highland chieftains and wannabe romantics chasing their west highland dreams. One man – who wore an 18th century frock coat with a frilly jabot – was with a woman who looked as if she was auditioning for a film role as Flora MacDonald. But as the evening progressed, whether the dancers were rich or poor, young or old, long-established or newcomer; age and social class differences were firmly set aside. Through reeling, most of them connected with something larger than their own foibles and prejudices, united in a shared purpose driven by the power of music and dance. Social guards were dropped and feudal differences put to one side for an evening, for it was impossible to maintain an air of detachment when you knew that at any moment you could be holding hands and dancing with your rival, your landlord or your tenant.

Just as the moment approached for guests to take their seats for dinner Duncan turned to Lorna. "I dinna believe it!" he exclaimed, nodding towards the entrance. Sashaying through the doorway was none other than Miss Lacelaw swathed from head to toe in bright red plaid. "She looks like a tartan tablecloth," he remarked unkindly. "Does she no ken that it's the menfolk whit's supposed to wear the tartan?" Accompanying her was a shy American film producer wearing Andy Warhol style glasses and dressed - highly inappropriately - in a lounge suit, looking as if he wanted nothing more than for the earth to swallow him up. With some relief Duncan saw the two of them make their way to a distant table. Then, more from a sense of duty than desire, he made his way over with Lorna to acknowledge his employer's arrival and endure some awkward introductions. By now the last of the ball-goers were taking their places at the dinner table and as Duncan and Lorna made their way back to rejoin Neil they observed a scattering of unclaimed seats from late or absent guests.

Clutching two nearly full bottles of wine, Morag lurched a little unsteadily over from the bar to join her friends. Her official duties now over, she could really begin to enjoy the evening. She started by pouring a large glass of wine and promptly spilling it over the table. Although it was Chardonnay and not Claret, Neil, Duncan and Lorna failed to see the funny side of it, but Morag dissolved into paroxysms of laughter that continued as she also knocked her small handbag off the table. "Come on Morag," admonished Neil, "you'll be too bleuthered to dance if you're not careful."

"Don't tell me what to do Neil McLeod. I dinna need two mithers," she replied pouring an even larger glass. "One's bad enough" she added sulkily.

Cock-a-leekie soup arrived and the four of them soon forgot their differences and remembered their appetites. The banter began to flow and the group began to gel at last. Neil looked around approvingly at the packed dining hall, thinking that that he was going to enjoy the evening ahead after all. But just as he was about to take a mouthful of soup, he froze, the spoon halfway to his lips. His heart gave a lurch and his hand trembled slightly. Behind Morag he spied none other than Henry and the unmistakably gorgeous figure of Sophie Montgomery making their way into the dining hall. As striking as ever, with her long hair and elegant ball gown, she looked so different from that brief encounter in St Andrews. To Neil she seemed preoccupied, even agitated, and a thousand thoughts flew through his head. "Bloody hell!" he swore softly under his breath, staring in her direction, but she hadn't noticed him, intent as she was on reaching her place amongst a large table of fellow students. Not knowing what Sophie looked like, Duncan asked Neil what was wrong. "Um, nothing," he said dismissively. "The soup's a bit hot isn't it?" he remarked evasively.

"Ya daft eejit," remarked Duncan, looking in the direction at which Neil had been staring, "ye seen a ghaist or something?" Morag meanwhile was totally oblivious to what was going on. Laughing uproariously at one of her own jokes, she was tearing bits of bread roll and throwing them at a fellow nurse she had spotted at another table. But by now Duncan had noticed that Neil had stopped eating and that his good humour had mysteriously evaporated. "Come on big yin. What's wrong?" he asked.

"You're never going to believe this," admitted Neil quietly, "It's Sophie. She's here."

Duncan glanced quickly at Morag who was still dissolved in gales of laughter, then frowned. Not usually short for words, he was only able to utter one. "Sheeite!" he exclaimed, managing to extend the expletive into at least three syllables, "this could get complicated."

As the meal progressed, and Neil somehow managed to compose himself, he kept stealing glances towards the distant table where Sophie and Henry were seated, catching only occasional glimpses of the back of Sophie's head. Henry looked in Neil's direction a couple of times but there was no flicker of recognition on his face. When the time came for the first dance of the evening Neil's group hesitated; Morag from inertia, Neil from nervous anticipation and Duncan and Lorna from savouring their last chance to relax before the onslaught of intensive post prandial exercise. A gaggle of young locals took to the floor first, whirling their way through a Gay Gordon and then the space became crowded with dancers as the evening began in earnest. The second reel was a Dashing White Sergeant and - with Morag still suffering from drink-induced inertia - Neil joined Duncan and Lorna on the floor, searching for another three-some to join their set. The first long chord struck, and they were off in a blur of tartan, satin and silk. The dancers' stamp, stamp, stamp – clap, clap, clap punctuated the music as all six-somes divided in two, each group of three passing through the other group and on to join a new three-some. After a few repetitions of these steps, when Neil, Lorna and Duncan passed on to the next three-some, Neil found himself abruptly face to face with Sophie. The circle of dancers started to swirl clockwise but Sophie remained frozen to the spot. Not having seen Neil since St Andrews, she stared at him in shock and disbelief for a few seconds until the other dancers in Sophie's set shouted, "Come on!" at her. Jolted back to life she held out her hand to Neil and as she caught up with him and he touched her trembling outstretched hand, he felt a distinct electrical connection. Then they were back in the rhythm of the dance, their bodies yielding to the music and their movements flowing in unison, perfectly balanced, perfectly united. Though they were joined together for no more than a few brief moments, Neil sensed a powerful unspoken bond. During the last steps of the turn he gave her hand a gentle squeeze and she squeezed it back, those small actions conveying whole layers of meaning. Then, once again, they were forced apart by the music, whisked off in opposite directions by their respective dance partners to the next three-some and the next repetition of the dance. Neil gave a euphoric whoop. In that instant his reservations about the evening evaporated: forgetting Morag, he knew that with Sophie here, at last he would get to say those things to her that fate had cruelly denied him before.

Morag did eventually join the others on the floor for the next dance – a Schottish for couples. But her reeling was more connected to drinking than to dancing and Neil found her clinging onto him more for support than anything else. Every so often she spun out of control, to the annoyance of the other dancers who, whilst tolerating some occasional individualistic embellishment, frowned upon complete inebriation. Sophie was absent during that dance, having disappeared to the ladies, and as the music came to an end Neil made as if to sit down. But Morag had other ideas and when the next number was announced she said, "Come on you wuss, it's a Strip the Willow." And so it was that by an extraordinary twist of fate at that memorable Oban Winter Ball, just as the dance was about to begin, Morag and Neil found themselves in exactly the same set as Henry and Sophie.

For the first time that evening a palpable tension settled over the four dancers as Morag - drunk though she was - finally clocked Sophie, whilst Henry - somewhat uneasily - recognised

Neil's face. Even though he couldn't place where he had seen him before, he remembered that it had somehow been connected to an argument with Sophie. But there was no time for explanations or even introductions as the opening chord announced the start of the dance. Stealing several glances at Sophie out of the corner of his eye, Neil observed a kind of haunted quality about her. Something - or someone - seemed to be troubling her but he sensed that whatever - or whoever - it was, it wasn't him. Meanwhile, Morag was staring daggers-drawn at Neil. She was merely going through the motions of the dance, impatient for it to finish so that she could give him a piece of her mind for contriving this whole situation, as she believed. Henry, having tried and failed to remember exactly where he had seen Neil before and blissfully ignorant of the tense body language evident in the others, was - true to type - reverting to his usual boorish self. Like Morag, he too had had a lot to drink and was much more interested in leering at her cleavage than paying attention to Sophie. He yelled and clapped off beat and flung the female dancers around as if it was some kind of competition and when it was his and Sophie's turn to reel down the set between the two lines of dancers he threw her around with such force that Neil could see her wincing with pain. And then, at the height of their spinning, Neil spotted Sophie's ring flying off, wrenched from her finger by Henry, who was completely oblivious of what he had just done. As it rolled along the wooden floor towards a corner of the room Neil broke free from Morag's side and rushed over to pick it up. Sophie and Henry finished their turn. Sophie rubbed her finger and looked around in concern, trying to see where her ring might have ended up. "Here," said Neil, reaching her side. He slipped the ring tenderly onto her finger. "That's the second time," he grinned. Then, with his mouth close to her ear and speaking more softly so that only she could hear, he said, "Can we talk somewhere?" and flashed a knowing smile at her. As she grasped his hand Morag's jealousy reached erupting point. But the dance wouldn't wait and Neil had to rush back towards Morag to catch her up. She grabbed his hand with all the force she could muster and this time it was Neil's turn to wince in pain. As the dance was finishing, but before all the couples had left the floor she turned to Neil and berated him in a tirade of drink-fuelled expletives. "You two-timing bastard!" she swore, "You scheming shite. You invited that bloody bitch didn't ye? You expected me not to notice did ye?"

By now Morag's haranguing was attracting the attention of several people, including the Chairman of the Committee, Bill Turnbull. Though some distance away from this commotion he became visibly irritated as the disturbance progressed. Having waited for just the right moment in the evening to engage Lady Carrington-Smyth in a conspiratorial conversation of a somewhat sensitive nature, he now found himself awkwardly interrupted and, frowning, turned to observe the untimely source of the trouble. Morag's torrent of invective was becoming louder and louder and during this outburst Neil was unable to get a word in edgeways. Eventually during a brief respite he announced "Enough! It's over with us. We're finished Morag. You're nothing but trouble."

"And you can fuck off, Neil McLeod!" she shrieked at the top of her voice and slapped his cheek with all the force she could muster. There was a shocked silence in the Dining Room as a hundred people instantly stopped their conversations and turned their heads towards the source of this commotion. Forced to abandon his stimulating tête-à-tête with Lady Carrington-Smyth, Bill Turnbull realised that it was high time for him to exert his authority. People could be forgiven for not knowing how to dance properly but drunken arguments more befitting the Oban seafront on a Friday night were extremely poor form. "Excuse me," he apologised to Lady Carrington-Smyth, putting down his glass and frowning. He marched determinedly over to where the warring couple stood in a kind of Mexican standoff. By this time a trickle of blood was running down Neil's cheek where Morag's nails had torn the skin. "I'm afraid I must ask you both to leave," he demanded in a no-nonsense authoritative tone. But Morag was past caring. She swore loudly at him, the Ball and everything else she could think of and then headed for the door, aiming to make as dramatic and public an exit as she possibly could. But unfortunately for her, she tripped awkwardly on her dress, fell headlong into a table and upset a dozen glasses of wine, several dining plates and a collection of assorted cutlery, not to mention a rather elaborate flower arrangement. At the noise, the band abruptly ceased playing and by now all two hundred ball-goers were glued to this unfolding drama. Several gasps were audible as Morag's wine-streaked, food-stained figure could be seen hauling itself up clumsily from the midst of the carnage. But the reaction they witnessed was not the one they might have expected. Instead of tears or apologies, they watched spellbound as Morag clutched the spilt bunch of flowers and gazed drunkenly at the rows of gaping mouths surrounding her. Laughing hysterically, she drew herself up to her full height, pointed the bent flowers at her audience and shrieked, "Fuck off the lot of you." Then she lurched through the exit door and out into the night.

Sophie rushed over to Neil who was standing white faced and tight lipped. "You're cut," she said. "Here, let me wipe it" and taking a paper napkin, licked it and dabbed the blood from his cheek. "What happened?"

"We – well it doesn't matter," he said, "it's over now. She's gone," adding "and I've been asked to leave too. I had hoped I might dance with you but…"

"Neil, there's so much I want to say to you. I couldn't…I didn't know how to find you to say thank you. How did you find my ring? And how did you know to find me in St Andrews?"

"Dorothy," he said, a smile half forming on his face.

"What?"

"Dorothy - your grandmother."

"I don't understand."

"I could tell you all about it but I've been ordered to leave. When can I see you again Sophie?" He grinned. Just saying her name gave him a buzz.

A degree of order was returning to the dining room as serving staff bustled about, starting to clear up the mess. The rest of the gathering simply closed ranks and, for now anyway, appeared to ignore the whole unfortunate incident, pretending - in that stiff upper lip way that only the British can - that nothing particularly out of the ordinary had happened. However, Bill Turnbull would not be moved. Decorum had been breached and it was expedient, indeed necessary, 'pour discouragez les autres' to exert some authority and for justice to be seen to be done. He interrupted Neil and Sophie. "Young man I repeat, I must ask you to leave."

Henry, who was only now returning to the dining room after a lengthy visit to the gents, was the only person present amongst all two hundred ball-goers who was completely oblivious to the recent dramatic performance. He observed with annoyance that Sophie was wiping Neil's cheek in an over over-familiar fashion.

"Sophie?" he said, curtly.

"Not now, Henry."

He took a few steps over to her and grabbed her arm roughly. "This is not befitting," he drawled, his jaw clenched. Fiercely resisting his grip she pulled her arm away, whereupon he tried to grab her again. "Leave me alone," she spat through gritted teeth.

By now Bill Turnbull had had quite enough. Turning to what he figured was the common source of the problem he said to Neil. "I don't know what's going on but this has gone much too far. You will leave NOW."

Neil looked at Sophie and held out his hands in a gesture of helplessness. "I'm so sorry," he said, his expression a mixture of apology and amusement.

In that instant Sophie made a decision that would transform her life forever. She took his arm and announced, "I'm coming with you."

"The hell you are!" began Henry, at the same time as Neil said, "Look Sophie, I…"

"No, it's fine," she interrupted. "I've made up my mind. Henry, I'll see you back in St Andrews," and she gathered up her shawl and bag and prepared to leave. Henry, his mouth open like a fish gasping for air, found himself for once at a complete loss for words.

"I apologise for the earlier incident sir," said Neil to Bill Turnbull and added somewhat unnecessarily "I think my guest had had too much to drink."

Henry was still speechless.

When they reached the foyer, elated and giggling helplessly like school truants Neil and Sophie fell into each others' arms. Neil pulled her close and kissed her urgently, almost roughly. She returned his kiss passionately, her fervour fully matching his. Behind them through the closed door came the faint sounds of the band striking up again. For all the remaining guests apart from Henry it was as if the waters had simply closed over the events of the last ten minutes and washed them away like a bad dream. Several minutes later, Neil and Sophie were still oblivious to the sound of the music which swelled a little as the door half opened, letting a shaft of light penetrate the foyer. Neither of them noticed Duncan peering at them through the gap, his mouth opening as if to say something. And neither of them noticed the music becoming muffled again and semi-darkness returning to the foyer.

Later - much later - the two of them came up for air.

"What now?" murmured Sophie.

"Mmmm, well more of you for a start," murmured Neil, his hands still clasped around Sophie's body. Grinning like a loon he added, "How about a coffee in the meantime?"

Arm in arm they stepped out into the still, cold Oban night. It was only a short distance to the cheap local café that Neil remembered often stayed open late. All the other more presentable establishments had closed down for the night. As they took each others' hands and walked down the street towards the sea front, a pub-crawling posse of girls in their early twenties approached them from behind, whistled at Neil and made lewd remarks about his kilt. "What you got under there big boy?" and "You a true Scot then?" Sophie grinned at Neil. But as the girls drew alongside them their tone changed. "Hey, isn't that Morag Govan's boyfriend? Eh, whatsyername - Neil - you two-timing then?" Neil looked at Sophie, but she was still grinning. Turning to the girls Sophie exclaimed, "You can tell her that he's got a new girlfriend now," whereupon, like a pack of wild hyenas, they started taunting the two of them, mimicking her Edinburgh accent "Oh, we've got a new boyfriend now have we? Oh la di bloody da."

Neil managed to shake off their unwanted attention by guiding Sophie into the safety of the café. With most of the locals elsewhere in Oban's pubs and bars and with only a few tourists killing time there, the café was nearly deserted. Neil ordered coffee and guided Sophie to the quietest table he could find. An hour later, still hand in hand and deep in conversation, they remained the only customers. The proprietor - who could recognise a couple in love when he saw one - came over and announced apologetically that he was "sorry folks but it's time to shut up shop."

"There's something I want to show you," said Neil to Sophie and he guided her outside towards the multi-arched landmark of McCaig's Folly, its round colonnade illuminated on the hillside above them. Hand in hand they climbed the steps leading up the hill until they came to a convenient bench beside the arches of the grand folly. Below them twinkled the lights of Oban and in the still winter air they could hear a gentle humming coming from the Mull ferry docked overnight in the harbour. The moon was rising, bathing the sea in a shimmering path of light that stretched back from the harbour towards the open sea. Neil and Sophie sat on the back of the bench, their feet on the seat, absorbing the night-time scene and oblivious to the cool Highland air, until Neil muttered, "Uh oh, here comes trouble again." The strident voices of the feral girl-pack heralded their approach. Too late, they had been spotted.

"Oh I say, do look, if it isn't Lord Muck and his precious Lady Manure. Her ladyship's precious arse is simply too dainty for this seat," and so on. Neil knew that they'd get no peace with their gibbering gibes and jealous jeers. Leading Sophie back down to where he had parked his Landrover he said, "It'll be warmer in the car. Besides, there's something else I want to show you."

"It's long isn't it?" remarked Sophie, referring to Neil's vehicle. "Well I don't usually like to boast about it," he joked, enjoying the double entendre, "but seeing as it's you…" Sophie's tinkling laugh coincided with the striking of midnight and McCaig's folly plunging abruptly into darkness. Neil gestured to the equipment in the back of his car. "Sorry about the mess," he said, "At least Robbie isn't here. He'd be very pleased to see you but then again, three's a crowd," and Sophie smiled, remembering the collie's wet, reviving tongue at Ardcairn. "Jump in," announced Neil, "there's somewhere special I want to show you."

Inside the Volunteer Hall the remaining dancers were whisking each other around for the Last Waltz as Neil drove Sophie out of town along the empty highway. The fat waxing moon danced beside the car, waltzing its own passage along the Firth of Lorn. After a few miles Neil turned off the tarmac down a forestry road that became a track, then two vehicle ruts and then finally petered out altogether. But despite that he was sure of his overland route and after a few jolts and bumps across a patch of heather he brought the Landrover to a halt at his secret destination.

Neil had first stumbled upon this place when working on a forestry job nearby. He had been looking for a signal on his mobile phone but instead chanced upon a secluded rocky headland overlooking this quiet bay. No-one had ever mentioned this place to him and he felt sure that - apart from one or two local lobstermen - nobody else could know about it. Certainly he had never seen anyone else on the rare occasions when he had ventured there. Each time he visited, Neil felt the place emanate some indefinable quality, a cathartic tranquillity that left him refreshed and renewed. At times of stress or when he was unable to resolve a problem, he would make the effort to reach 'his' secret headland with its old, twisted sentinel pine tree. Looking out at the sea under the shade of that pine he could reflect, unwind and relax, letting nature's own ecotherapy salve his troubled mind. Invariably he came away clear-headed and feeling chilled. Now, as he switched off the engine, the image of Morag knocking over the table flashed briefly into his head. 'Funny that I never took her to this spot' he thought to himself briefly, as he turned off the engine. Through the windscreen stretched a scattering of islands surrounded by the silvery moonlit sea. "It's gorgeous," said Sophie, squeezing Neil's hand. They watched the moon gradually ride higher and higher in the western sky. And they talked… and talked.

Much later, when the moon had slid back down behind the horizon as if to allow the stars a turn to display their brilliance, Neil and Sophie eventually stopped talking and let their bodies do the communicating instead.

Several hours after they had arrived, but what seemed like only minutes later to the two lovers, a faint glow emerged in the east. Argyll slowly cast off her mantle of darkness and emerged refreshed and lovely in the pale winter sunlight. It seemed to both lovers that in that new dawn everything had changed. Their lives would never be the same again. The early morning cold suddenly struck Sophie and she shivered. "We'd better be getting back I suppose," said Neil. He hesitated. "Are you going to be alright? You know - about Henry I mean."

"Henry was a mistake," she said. "A huge mistake. He's not my type, but it's taken me 'til now to realise it. Anyway, forget him. I'm starving. What about something to eat?"

And so as the sun rose on the outskirts of Oban, Neil drew up at the only café that opened early, a greasy spoon establishment catering mainly for trawlermen and truck drivers. When the two of them entered wearing what was by now rather dishevelled Highland dress and a very crumpled ball gown, they attracted some strange looks and the odd innuendo from the patrons.

"Eh, you looking for Balmoral?" one quipped, and "You the new Highlander then?" and in a Gaelic accent too thick for Neil to follow, a quip about the two of them "looking as if they'd been hard at it all night" which had a few of the other diners chortling into their mugs of tea.

This last joke was lost on the two lovers, but they didn't care anyway. "Welcome to the Oban highlife!" Neil smiled at Sophie as they waited for their order. Full English Breakfast had never tasted so good.

Chapter 10

It didn't take Sophie long to move out of Henry's rented house in St Andrews. Moving in with him had been a great mistake in the first place she realised, a half-baked rebellious statement against her controlling mother and Edinburgh upbringing. But her freedom had come at a price. Falling for the first good-looking man she bumped into at university was, well, "frankly irresponsible" were the words her mother Jane would have used. But she realised that she'd learned her lesson. Meeting Neil had turned her world well and truly upside down. Hearing that Sophie had run off with 'a local' at the Oban Ball, Henry's circle of fair-weather friends revealed their true colours and turned their back on her. At first upset, Sophie realised that she was actually much better off without them and their expensive distractions. Unburdened of Henry, she could throw all her energies into studying towards her History of Art degree.

It was not easy trying to juggle her academic life and her love life but moving back into St Salvator's had its advantages: like getting to know her fellow undergraduates better. Annabelle in particular became a good friend. Over several shared cups of tea in Sophie's room Annabelle recounted the episode of Neil's impulsive visit to St Andrews as seen through her eyes. "He's totally besotted by you, you know," she revealed. "You're very lucky Sophie. If you ever get bored of him just let me know," she joked. But Sophie's problem was not boredom: it was distance. Although Neil drove to St Andrews as often as he could, that only amounted to two weekends a month, if he was lucky. Having no car, Sophie managed to get to Argyll once before the vacation, but it took her so long to get there and back by public transport that their time together was only fleeting. At the end of these visits Sophie and Neil hated the ritual goodbyes that signalled long days of separation. Spending most of their time apart but longing to be together was driving them both a little crazy. But no obvious solution to the problem of geography presented itself to either of the lovers.

One evening at Cedar Cottage, Duncan and Lorna had joined Jim, Ann and Neil for a meal. They were all enjoying a venison roast which - before ending up on their dinner plates - had spent a happy life as a roe buck bounding around Ardcairn estate. Miss Lacelaw was not aware of this fact. She did not allow any living thing to be shot on her property. But Duncan had no such qualms. He knew enough about deer to appreciate that the local population was multiplying out of control. The tell-tale signs of overgrazing - no regeneration of young trees and a lot of chewed foliage - were everywhere. Duncan knew that, left unchecked, the local population would eventually destroy the very habitats that lent much of the estate its conservation value and special scientific designation. Acutely aware of Miss Lacelaw's aversion to guns, not to mention his own future at Ardcairn, he had to plan his covert killing missions well away from the Big House, when Miss Lacelaw's back was turned - usually when she went over to The States.

Equipped with rifle, telescopic sights and silencer Duncan launched his discreet hunting operations with uncharacteristic efficiency, dispatching a beast or two as quickly as he could, then whisking them away into his deer larder at home, some distance away from the estate - and prying eyes. On several occasions Neil examined the butchered carcasses and asked his friend if he wasn't worried about being caught. If Duncan was bothered, he certainly didn't show it, for he reckoned he led a charmed life. Amused rather than anxious he knew that he was doing the right thing by the estate and if he did ever get caught – well, he would just have to take his chances. But as the 'hot goods' had to be got rid of somehow, and hating to waste good organic meat, Duncan found himself the local supplier of complimentary venison to virtually the entire Taynuilt neighbourhood. Everyone knew what was going on but - grateful for the free meat - nobody asked questions. And as a result, Duncan's generosity was often reciprocated: new fencing materials for his garden, an occasional salmon or the odd bottle of whisky left on his doorstep.

With the dinner plates cleared away, it was one of these bottles that Duncan produced with a flourish. Jim stood up to make a toast, "Here's to ye Duncan, provider of the feast." The others clinked their glasses together whilst Duncan grinned mischievously. "And Ann," continued Jim, "Ann, you're always a marvel," he remarked, raising his tumbler again. "Here's to the cook," and the chinking of crystal echoed Jim's heartfelt sentiments. Ann blushed. "Och it was nothing," she dissembled, secretly pleased that her culinary skills were so much appreciated. "But seeing as I've got your attention, I've some news for you all," she declared.

The others looked at her expectantly for it was very seldom that Ann made any announcements. Ann looked at Duncan and then at Lorna. "It could affect you two as well as me," she said, pausing.

"Well?" asked Duncan, after a few seconds had passed, "Don't keep us in suspenders."

Ann waited a moment longer whilst she regarded her friends and marshalled her thoughts. "Miss Lacelaw said to me that she's fed up with the men folk in Argyll, or the lack of men folk more like. She wants someone to help her share the burden of managing the place. That's what she told me anyway."

Neil nudged Duncan, "There's your chance, lackey. Sorry Lorna, you're about to become redundant now."

"Aye, right. She wants a rich plutocrat more like," replied Lorna. "Anyway, I hear that no man ever goes near the place. Or if they do they usually leave soon afterwards."

Ignoring this interruption Ann replied. "What I'm trying to say is that Miss Lacelaw is thinking of maybe selling Ardcairn. She told me herself yesterday."

This time there was a considerable pause as the potential implications of her words gradually sank in.

"She never told me," sniffed Duncan. "You'll be alright Ann, but I'd probably be out of a job."

"There's no guarantees for any of us," Ann replied. If the place was bought by a hotel chain they could bring their own staff, or anyone."

"Is it really the lack of a man that's making her sell up?" asked Jim.

"Who knows?" replied Ann, "It could be the terrible weather we've been having this spring. But she said she wants to move somewhere warmer and drier and she's going to be away for a month this Easter looking at places in France. She's asked me to take care of the house."

"I'll be out of a job," repeated Duncan gloomily, "and factoring jobs are no so easy to come by."

"Aye but you're a lackey not a factor so that doesn't count," mocked Neil rather heartlessly then, changing the subject, added, "Sophie's hoping to come up this Easter to do some painting."

The whisky was starting to take effect. "Painting my arse," joked Duncan crudely, "we all know what you two get up to. Etchings in the bedroom more like."

"Its not like that you hairy eejit. Lorna, you should give that one-track fiancée of yours a lobotomy."

"A lobotomy? Vasectomy more like."

"Aye aye? Is there something you're not telling us?" teased Neil.

"Dinna start," warned Duncan and then, turning to Lorna, "unless there is something you've not told *me*?" he asked, a note of anxiety creeping into his voice.

She laughed. "Oh you'll know soon enough when something happens, but there's nothing incubatin' the now."

Duncan clasped his hands together, raising his eyes heavenwards as if in silent prayer and exclaimed "Praise the Lord!" The others grinned. They all appreciated his off-beat sense of humour and guessed that this was Lorna and Duncan's way of telling them all that they were trying for a baby.

"The point is," continued Neil, "I'm not sure about Sophie staying at Cedar Cottage over the Easter holidays."

Jim started to remonstrate but Neil interrupted, "It's not you Dad – you know she really likes you, it's just that, well, this place is a bit small for the three of us. You know…" his voice trailed off.

At that, the hint of a smile crossed Ann's face, missed by everyone except Jim. "What is it Ann?" he asked.

"Well there is a possib… no maybe not."

"Come on, out with it," said Jim.

"Well, Miss Lacelaw will be away from the big House soon. She's going back to America for a while. You two might like to stay at Rose Cottage? But then I'd have to find somewhere else to live for two weeks…" her voice trailed off into a kind of question mark which was solely for Jim's benefit.

Appreciating the hint, Jim blushed. "Ye ken you're always welcome under this roof Ann. But are ye sure ye want to let my boy run wild at your place like a savage? Shouldn't we let's talk aboot it in the morning?"

Usually deliberate and measured, on this occasion Ann needed no time to come to a decision. "If that works for you, it'll be fine for me," she said. "Neil, please consider Rose Cottage yours and Sophie's for the Easter period. I'm sure you'll both take care of it."

Once she had resolved on a course of action, Ann was unwavering. Neil was genuinely pleased. "Ann, you're a real fairy

Godmother," he said, going over to her and giving her a hug. She pretended to be embarrassed by his show of affection but the others could see that she was secretly pleased.

"Well ye'll have the place to yourselves," remarked Duncan, "Me and Lorna are off to Corfu for a fortnight.

"I finally got him to think further than Glasgow for his holidays," said Lorna. "You wait, after some island life he won't want to come back."

"Well that depends on those Greek girls," he retorted "I hear they're quite partial to Scotsmen!" at which point Lorna threw a tangerine at him and then went across and sat down heavily on his lap.

"We'll see about that, Duncan Fraser," she said, as he groaned, and the others chuckled.

Neil turned to Ann again "If you're sure, Ann? That's really kind of you. And if there's anything I can do to help?" he asked. "I can split your logs, or something."

"Och, you don't need to do anything. Just enjoy the place. With spring late this year, it'll be looking just grand."

* * *

One evening shortly before Easter Neil found himself pacing up and down the platform at Taynuilt station, willing Sophie's train to arrive. Of course, it would be impossible to miss her: so few people usually got on or off there that it was never crowded. His pulse rate increased when the train drew to a noisy halt, but there was no sign of her. A couple of hikers alighted but Sophie was nowhere to be seen. Just as Neil started to panic that she'd missed the train, there she was, a vision of loveliness with an aura of grace and a bounce in her step. She'd been struggling to extract her rucksack from the compartment, the same rucksack that she had been wearing when Neil first set eyes on her in the fir grove at Ardcairn. Relieved and excited, Neil rushed down the platform towards her and threw himself into Sophie's outstretched arms. They kissed for a full minute and then Neil broke the spell. "I can't wait to show you round the estate – and Ann's cottage."

"Hmmm, maybe we could start with the bedroom?" she said suggestively, laughing her distinctive tinkling laugh. Neil smiled. He removed her rucksack, put it on his shoulders and took her hand in his.

"Hasta la vista baby," he declared as they walked towards the Landrover and two weeks of freedom.

Chapter 11

Those spring days at Ardcairn were amongst the happiest of Neil and Sophie' lives. Undisturbed by the outside world and with Argyll experiencing unusually clear and sunny skies, there was nothing and nobody to trouble their existence. During those precious days of freedom Sophie came to realise that her life in Henry's yuppie world had been just a mirage. Henry had only wanted to manipulate her, displaying her like some beauty trophy to show off to his friends. Sophie realised how naïve she had been, always finding it necessary to put on an act in his presence, playing the part of someone else, someone he wanted her to be rather that the real person she was. And even though there were moments of glamour and craziness, she realised deep down that it was just a chimera, a theatre of shallow characters and superficial friendships built on shifting sand rather than the solid foundation of the only thing that really mattered – love.

Life with Neil was so different. With him she felt grounded, truly herself; spontaneous, animated and passionate, counterbalancing his more purposeful and decisive nature without having to play to any agenda. With Neil she was almost always on the same wavelength. There was never any awkwardness, never having to think of what to say or how to react. Their conversations ebbed and flowed like the tides of Loch Etive and though pauses were infrequent, they were comfortable silences, never awkward. So often did they share each others' moods as they explored Ardcairn, walking beside the sea loch or exploring the oak woods and the hills, that they became completely attuned to each other. Some friends found their habit of knowing each others' thoughts - a habit that stemmed from those early days - almost spooky. 'Kindred spirits' was the phrase that they used to describe Neil and Sophie's connected relationship.

The morning after her first night at Rose Cottage, Sophie jumped out of bed, scampered over to the window and drew aside the curtains, letting the sunshine bathe the room in its fresh light. Bursting with the joy and energy that only an evening of passion followed by a night of sound sleep can bring, she wanted to embrace the whole waking world outside and sing to it at the top of her voice. Picking up a cushion from a chair she placed it on the windowsill and leaned over to gaze at the view. Though too early yet for Ardcairn's famous bluebells, there were carpets of daffodils greeting the morning light, lining a path that led towards the peaty dark Dubh burn. She could hear the gentle gushing of water cascading over stones and a faint breeze that carried with it the delicate scent of narcissi and undertones of bracken and damp soil. Sophie opened the casement window, breathed the distinctive Argyll air into her lungs and savoured the moment. A sleepy voice murmured from behind her, "Mmmm, you should see your booty, it's sooooo sexy."

Sophie turned round smiling, and faced Neil, her naked figure backlit by the sunrise.

"But your front's even better, boobylicious," Neil added, licking his lips suggestively.

Sophie playfully hurled the cushion at Neil's face. "Help ma Boab!" he shrieked as she bounded across the floor, leapt over the end of the bed and jumped on top of him with a yell, rocking Ann's bed alarmingly. Immediately below them, Robbie awoke from his doggie sleep in the kitchen. His dreams had been troubled due to the strange surroundings of Rose Cottage and the nocturnal noises coming from above. He got up out of his bed, yawned, stretched and purposefully picked up his lead from the floor. Then he pattered dutifully upstairs to see what all the commotion was about. But unfortunately for him, for the next half-hour his gentle pawing at the door fell on deaf ears as Ann's bed started to creak, gently at first, then more rhythmically and finally frenetically, before stopping abruptly.

The morning sun was much higher in the sky when the lovers eventually made their way downstairs for breakfast. "God, I'm starving," announced Neil, examining the fridge that Ann had thoughtfully stocked to the gunwales with home-made bread, bacon, eggs, cheese, mushrooms, tomatoes and all other manner of goodies. Used to helping his father with the cooking, Neil insisted on rustling up a large plate of bacon and eggs, with toast and a tall caffetiere of fresh coffee. Ann's home-made marmalade was much enjoyed by Sophie. "She's so kind," she said, munching through her second slice of toast. "We must think of some way to repay her."

By now Robbie was getting very restive. A thousand acres of doggie heaven lay just outside waiting to be discovered and yet all his master could do was slob around the house, eating. He trotted off purposefully to sniff the enticing air at the front door. Then finding his lead lying on the landing he dragged it clumsily downstairs again, every so often getting the end caught in a banister, until he finally plonked it at his master's feet. Neil smiled, "Yes Robbie, I know. You will get a walk" and at the magic 'W' word, Robbie cocked his ear expectantly, looking as irresistible as only he could. "In fact let's go now," suggested Neil. Leaving the dishes for later, all three of them tumbled out of Rose Cottage into the spring sunshine to explore the splendours of Ardcairn estate.

"According to Ann there's supposed to be some old settlements around here", said Neil as they started picking their way through the carpet of daffodils. "There's a stone circle somewhere, though no-one quite knows where it is. Ann says that it moves around in a mysterious way and that it's never in the same place twice."

They spent the morning quartering the estate, roaming through the overgrown remnants of an old apple orchard, and examining the nearby walled garden with its turrets and its old yew tree that Neil reckoned must be several hundred years old. They pushed through the rusty iron gates which had long ago ceased to be a barrier against roe deer and sat down against a corner of the high wall, basking in its reflected warmth. "This would have been a great place for nookie in its day," said Neil, watching Robbie rushing about trying to catch rabbits. "Mmm," agreed Sophie, letting her head rest on Neil's shoulder, adding "You're incorrigible, young man," and giving him a kiss. Later, they followed the path that led down to a crumbing lochside jetty below Ardcairn House. "We should borrow a boat. I know someone who could lend us one," said Neil, excitedly, "I've always wanted to explore the upper side of the loch."

"Well I can tell you it's wet. I've been there, on my Duke of Edinburgh expedition, remember?" teased Sophie and for a while they sat there on the jetty, their feet dangling over the water, lost in thought. Sophie then talked a little about her hiking experiences with Charlotte and Fiona. Neil listened, admiring the scenery. Close by, a heron stalked crabs on the shore, whilst the occasional mewing of a buzzard sounded from the clear sky above them. The lovers gradually became immersed in the peace that only a perfect spring day on the west coast of Scotland can bring. No midges, no clouds, just birdsong, the tang of seaweed and the gentle lapping of waves on the rocks. Neil looked at his watch. "Gosh it's three o'clock already!" he said. "You hungry?"

On their way back to Rose Cottage, they passed the big house. To one side of it was a new semi-circular garden bench that Miss Lacelaw had ordered from a local joiner. The lovers sat on it for a while, shading their eyes from the sun and looking up at the imposing Victorian edifice. Examining its turrets and crow-stepped gables Sophie remarked, "It seems such a shame, her living there all on her own. Surely a place like that was meant to be enjoyed by a family, by children? Not mothballed like a painting locked in a vault."

Neil nodded his agreement, "Well, if Miss Lacelaw's threatening to sell it, maybe a family will buy it?" he suggested.

The afternoon was well advanced when they ventured out of Rose Cottage again to do some more exploring. Though not as bright now, the Easter sun still gave out a convincing warmth signalling Spring, heralding regrowth and another cycle of birth and new beginnings. Robbie couldn't believe his luck today: more walkies and still no noisy forestry machines cutting down trees and spitting out logs. He rushed ahead, wagging his tail furiously and turned back every so often to see that his master and his friend were following. This time, as if by some mutual unspoken agreement, their footsteps led towards the arboretum at the back of the house. Neil talked a little about the different trees that he recognised, but there were some unfamiliar ones too. "I'm going to get my identification book from home and have a closer look. There's some really unusual species here and I bet nobody knows about them," he said animatedly. But the day was getting on and they couldn't linger for too long. Neil and Sophie both knew instinctively where they were going and why they were going and no words needed to be spoken. A moment of unfinished business had to be resolved. In silence they skirted around the back of the main arboretum and headed for the grove of giant fir trees.

Although the sun was dropping low in the sky now, its warmth could still be felt within the shelter of the grove as they pushed through the screen of rhododendrons. They emerged into the small dell where Sophie had collapsed all those months ago and where Robbie had found her and Neil had revived her. For a minute they were silent, each lost in their own thoughts. Then Sophie took Neil's hand and said, "Thank you." He felt her signet ring - he noticed it was still loose (she really *must* get it fixed he thought) and he gently eased it off her finger and examined it again. Garde bien – guard well. Well, I will do that,' he thought, 'til death us do part'. Taking her hand in his, he looked her straight in the eye and got down on one knee. Sophie gasped involuntarily.

"Will you marry me Sophie?"

As she looked down at Neil's solemn face her first thought - more prosaic than romantic - was about her diabetes and how it might affect their children. "Neil, I love you more than anything in the world. You know that, but we haven't talked about babies. What about my diabetes?"

"Sophie Montgomery, I love you for who you are and what you are. We'll cross that bridge when it comes. Now," he commanded with a smile on his face, "Are you going to make an honest man out of me or do I have to grovel?"

"Yes," she replied simply, holding out her hand for Neil to slip her ring onto her engagement finger.

They used to joke later on about Neil not having a ring to propose with, and having to borrow Sophie's, but for now it was enough for them to hold each other tightly beneath the old Douglas fir at Ardcairn and experience the happiest moment of their lives.

Chapter 12

To Sophie and Neil those Easter days passed with the speed and brilliance of a shooting star. Several times during that unseasonably warm fortnight they made their way to what they now regarded as 'their' grove. Sometimes they would spend a lazy afternoon making love under its green canopy, protected from phone signals, the outside world and all its interruptions. So secluded was their sanctuary that birds alighting in the branches above didn't notice the lovers below. Neil pointed out a Robin to Sophie and once a kestrel alighted on an upper bough, causing a commotion amongst the smaller birds. One lazy afternoon after an hour of unhurried passion, Sophie stretched out on Neil's coat and felt an object digging into her back. From one of the pockets she pulled out a strangely shaped tool a bit like a flicknife with a curve at the end. "What's that?" she asked.

"It's for gralloching the forestry competition," he joked, then explained that it was used quite commonly before the days of quick paint sprays to mark stands of trees - for thinning, for example. "Here," he said, twisting the mechanism and unlocking the blade. He went over to the Douglas fir whilst Sophie sat back on her haunches, hugging her knees and wondering what he was up to. After a minute he turned around, revealing a perfectly carved heart shape scraped into the bark.

"You're sure the tree will be alright?" asked Sophie anxiously.

Neil laughed. "No problem. I've seen many marked trees that never got round to being cut down. It doesn't harm them at all."

"Yes, but what about Miss Lacelaw?" Sophie asked uneasily, "She'll freak if she finds out."

"I bet she never comes near here," he replied, "This place is our secret and our secret's... well... *secret*," he reassured her. "In fact," he continued in a French accent, "ma masterpiece is not yet completed." Unlocking the tool again, he carved an 'S' beside the heart. "Alors," he said, "S for sexy Sophie. Picasso mange votre heart oot."

"Hmmm, c'est manifique mais it's still lacking a little je ne sais pas," responded Sophie. "Like artistic talent, for instance," she teased. "Here, let me have that thing."

Neil unlocked it again and, cupping his hand over hers, showed her how to angle the device correctly. In a few minutes Sophie had completed an elegant 'N' and added an arrow through the heart. "That's N for Naughty boy and S for Special tree."

Towards the end of the first week, having been out of touch with the world for several days, they both realised - though they would prefer not to admit it - that they were being a touch antisocial. They knew that they should really announce their engagement to the outside world, but they were enjoying their time at Ardcairn so much that they kept putting the moment off. Sophie wasn't sure what her mother's reaction to their news would be but she had a pretty good idea that Jane would be severely disapproving. It was easier to go into denial and wait for a while. Deep down they both knew that once they broke the news of their engagement to family and friends, things would change. Instead of their timeless, escapist, pre-honeymoon vacation, there would be a host of congratulatory but insincere phone calls from distant cousins putting up invitation markers for a future wedding. But there were more immediate and pressing reasons why they needed to make contact with the world beyond Ardcairn. Their food supplies were running low and Neil was keen to get his tree identification book from Cedar Cottage. For the last two days he had started to fret about how much - or more accurately, how little - progress his workforce was making. He had put Craig in charge of the gang for the first time and a couple of phone calls from him had not reassured Neil that all was going smoothly. He also had a mind to follow up an idea that had germinated ages ago but had only recently started to preoccupy him. Meanwhile, Sophie was itching to take advantage of the continuing good weather by spending the morning doing some uninterrupted painting outside. "Give my love to your dad, and Ann," she said, as Neil set off in the Landrover after breakfast.

When he returned several hours later it was minus the Landrover and Robbie and plus his trusty old Triumph motorbike. He roared up the Ardcairn drive and seeing Sophie walking down the driveway, popped a wheelie past Rose Cottage, much to her concern and secret admiration. "You know, you should be careful on that machine," she said but Neil mistook her concern for criticism.

"Me and my Triumph are always careful," he insisted, "You can judge for yourself soon. But for now?" he continued in his imitation French accent, "I ave my next trick. From nowhere, I magic for ze lady... ze dejuner," and with ostentatious flourishes he produced from his bike pannier some baguettes, cheese, houmos and taramasalata. "God bless the Taynuilt deli," he said. "Come on, I'm starving. Lots to talk about," he added, propping the bike up beside Ann's woodshed and leading Sophie towards the shade of a large beech tree not far from Rose Cottage.

"Where's Robbie?" asked Sophie.

"I've left him with Dad," he said. "Much as I love him, he's a pain in the arse in the mornings and anyway Dad likes to walk him sometimes. He and Ann seem very happy. That's Dad and Ann by the way, not Robbie and Ann," he joked. "If Robbie could talk, I bet his tongue would wag."

"As well as his tail," retorted Sophie. "Did you tell them about our engagement?"

"No. I wanted to wait until the right moment," he replied, sitting down on a garden bench and spreading a baguette "i.e. when you're around as well."

"Well how about throwing a party here for them next week? Duncan and Lorna will be back from Greece and I can phone Mum…" She hesitated. "I suppose you'll need to ask her permission…?" she added doubtfully, her voice trailing off in a kind of question mark.

Neil not so subtly changed the subject, "How's your painting getting on?"

Sophie showed him some rough sketches and the outline of a watercolour that she had begun from the semi-circular bench beside the house. "I was trying to capture the spirit of Ardcairn," she explained. "That bench isn't a bad place to paint from, but it's frustrating."

"What is?"

"Well, for one thing I think that gouache would be better than watercolour and for another the angle's not quite right. The perspective's too flat and that tree gets in the way," she explained, pointing to her sketches. "Look, do you see?"

"Hmm. It looks good to me," retorted Neil. "But did you try going higher up the hill?"

"Yes, I went up behind the house. The view's great but you lose the closeness of the garden and the picture becomes... well, it becomes Loch Etive rather than Ardcairn."

"What if you painted the view from the upstairs of the house?"

Sophie thought for a moment. "That might work," she said, but..."

Interrupting her, Neil instructed "Wait here a minute." and dashed off in the direction of Rose Cottage. Shortly afterwards he returned, dangling a key and grinning, "Your wish is my command, oh mistress mine..." Then changing to an oriental voice, he remarked, "Magic genie he haf special key to open secret treasure palace." And back to his usual voice again, "Ann's key to the house. Guess where we're going after lunch, Turner?"

"Yeah, as long as there's no Constable about," she joked, "Technically it's breaking and entering you know."

"We'll leave everything just as we find it. Miss Lacelaw won't even know we've been there. Ann won't even know we've been there. But can it wait for a bit?"

"Why"

"Because there's something I want to show you this afternoon. It's only a short ride on the bike," he added mysteriously and throughout their lunch under the tree he continued to keep her guessing.

"Is it safe?" asked Sophie later, regarding the Triumph anxiously.

"Safe as houses, silly."

"I've only been on a bike a couple of times before. I hope you don't drive like a maniac."

"Not when I've a passenger," he joked. Sophie's face remained apprehensive. "Don't worry, he said reassuringly, "ask Robbie, he'll tell you."

Sophie grinned uncertainly, remembering how Neil had told her about taking the collie for short rides on the bike and trying to imagine the improbable scene. "Now that *would* be a painting," she remarked.

"What?"

"You and Robbie on your motorbike. Anyway, when are you going to tell me what all this subterfuge is about?"

He jumped up. "Right now. Come on. Bring your sketch pad."

Handing Sophie his spare helmet, he made her put on her hiking boots and waterproof jacket. "I've got a spare set of kit. But it's at Dad's and anyway, we're not going too far," adding "Morag won't be using it anymore."

With Sophie's jaw constrained by the full-face helmet, her voice sounded crazily slurred. "Hath Morag twied to get in touch with you athter – you know – athter the Ball?" Sophie asked as she waited for Neil to get on the bike.

Neil laughed. "Nope, thee's thunk without twace." Then in a more insistent voice, "Forget her, she's ancient history," and he strapped on his own helmet and kicked the bike into life. "Hop on angel. It's show time."

Although much too fearful at first to derive any pleasure from the ride, Sophie became a little less anxious as they reached the end of the Ardcairn drive. She started to loosen her tight grip on Neil's waist and remembered what he had told her about relaxing and leaning into the corners. Contrary to her expectations Neil was actually a very safe rider who drove defensively on the open road. After the first mile or two, feeling much more secure, Sophie started to relax and enjoy the whole experience, delighting in the rush of the world gliding past. They turned off onto a minor road and then, after less than a mile, headed up a dirt track. In a short while a gate barred their way. "Watch the exhaust pipe – it's hot," said Neil steadying the bike with his legs as Sophie hopped off. Before them was a gentle rise. "You can leave it open," he said, gesturing at the gate and revving the engine "Come on!"

She unlatched the gate and climbed back on the bike. Ahead, nestling in a fold of the hill stood an old farmhouse with a nearby wooden barn and some outbuildings, sheltered from the northeast winds by a screen of mixed woodland. Though intact, the house had a neglected feel and the outbuildings and barn were in various states of disrepair and definitely in need of some TLC.

"Lonan Farm," announced Neil, "What do you think?"

"Ith's – well ith's great but whath's ith for?" Sophie's jaw was still constrained by the helmet.

"Us."

"You mean…?"

Neil took off his helmet and interrupted "Yep, it's for sale. Actually, it's been up for sale for a while," he said, helping Sophie undo her helmet strap. "I did a wee planting contract for the owner a year ago. He knows Dad. He told me he wanted to give up farming and move back east to his roots. He's already sold most of the farmland but he wanted to sell the house and inby fields for the right price. I couldn't afford it at the time but… well, my bank manager says its OK now, so what do you think? It needs quite a lot of work doing to it."

"Oh Neil, it's wonderful," she enthused, the reason for this mysterious visit now apparent. "And the view!" By this time, they were standing in what used to be the front garden but was now a sea of weeds surrounded by a dry-stone wall. Behind them a bay window jutted out from the house, while in front, a break in the low protecting hillside gave a distant view down towards Loch Etive.

They spent the next few hours exploring Lonan farmhouse and the barn and discussing the possibilities. Sophie's creative juices were flowing and her eye for design and feel for colours were already leaping ahead. "It's amazing," she said, getting out her painting book. "Lots of potential…" and she fired off sketch after rapid sketch. "I could make this a studio," she said poking her head into one of the outhouses. I could really paint here, and with these four bedrooms we could run a B&B. Maybe I could even sell some paintings."

"You run a B&B? Remember I've got a full-time business to run and machinery to keep here and you've got a Degree to think of."

"I'll do a distance Degree. I mean what else is the Open University for?" she added. "And there's loads of space." She enthused "I'm sure we can do both, Oh Neil, it's lovely. It's so right for us!" and she hugged him energetically.

* * *

That evening was cooler than it had been for a while and after dinner the two lovers spent a long time in the dining room of Rose Cottage discussing Lonan Farm and their future together. Sophie was torn between immediately wanting to roll up her sleeves and get stuck into fixing the place up, and finishing her studies at St Andrews. So much in her life was changing and so quickly that her mind was a whirl. Although talking plans over with Neil was exciting, she needed time to think and reflect. Painting was the one thing that always restored her equilibrium and enabled her to work her way through big decisions. So they agreed that the next day she would continue with her painting while Neil would catch up with his team's progress. And they settled on a date for their engagement party at Cedar Cottage in three days' time.

* * *

The next morning's plan was to sneak into Ardcairn House so that Sophie could start her painting. Neil knew from what Ann had told him a while ago that there was no burglar alarm but even so they both felt apprehensive and excited as Neil turned the key in the front door lock. This was definitely unlawful. But as they moved stealthily from room to room their nervousness gradually subsided. Climbing up the creaking staircase they entered the grand oak panelled drawing room and shuffled their way over the Persian carpet to the large window at the rear of the house. "Look Soph," whispered Neil, "it's our tree," pointing to the fir grove beyond the arboretum. For a while they gazed in silence at the tree's majestic form, each lost in their own thoughts, remembering that stormy night all those months ago and recalling more recent stormy afternoons of their own making.

"I'm feeling horny," whispered Neil.

"Why are you whispering?" asked Sophie, her voice sounding unnaturally loud in the panelled space.

"How about it?" he asked, but Sophie was already pulling him down onto the carpet.

Ardcairn hadn't seen anything like it since the wild bachelor days of Colonel Rutherford.

Afterwards they sat on the floor gazing out of the front window towards the line of hills beyond the loch. "Duncan's certainly been busy," whispered Neil to Sophie. "Look at those hedges," and "That grass in the walled garden must take some cutting." They admired the neatly clipped privet hedge and the smooth, even lawns dropping down towards Loch Etive. An oval pond with its heron statue reflected back the light blue of the afternoon sky. It was a view "to die for" as Sophie would remark years later. But for now it was enough to lie, naked, enjoying the warmth of the sun though the window and treasuring the moment. After a while, Sophie sensed the rhythmic rising and falling of Neil's chest. He had dozed off. She went quietly over to where she had left her artist's case, then crept back to the window. Setting up her easel she looked out beyond the loch to the distant craggy hills and birch woods, the bracken and the heather, and sighed. Hesitantly at first, and then with increasingly confident strokes she began the outline of her painting. For once the brushes seemed to take on a life of their own, capturing the spirit of Ardcairn with effortless perfection. After a while Neil twitched and woke up, smelling a whiff of turpentine. He rolled over and observed Sophie's naked body silhouetted in the light of the window, absorbed in her work. Resisting the temptation to give her a hug and sensing her need to be alone, he slowly crept away. For the next few hours Sophie remained immersed in her creation until her concentration was broken by the crunching of Neil's steps on the gravel below.

He waved up at her and put one hand in the crook of the other arm, rocking that arm backwards and forwards suggestively. Sophie smiled down and flashed her breasts back at him over the top of the easel. Then Neil gestured to his watch. Time to wind up.

Sophie packed up her oils and made her way downstairs. She could finish the painting later.

Chapter 13

After several days of spring sunshine, the Highland weather finally took a turn for the worse. A light drizzle blew in off the Atlantic and descended on Argyll. By mid morning it had become a more serious attempt at rain. Sophie realised that with her engagement announcement due to be made at that evening's party it was high time that they broke the news to Jane. After a late breakfast and prevaricating for half an hour they finally resolved to make the call. Sophie switched on her phone. "I'll speak to Mum first and then hand over to you," she said to Neil. I'm sure it'll be OK." But it didn't take a genius to sense the doubt in her voice. As Neil watched her flick back her hair and nestle the receiver against her ear, he could feel his pulse rate increasing, anticipating the importance of the moment to come.

"Hi Mum, I…"

"No, I'm still in Argy…"

"No Mum, I…"

"But we do. Yes, I know Mum." And so on.

For the next few minutes Neil fiddled with his own mobile phone, aware of the occasional "no" and "yes" and "no, Mum" coming from Sophie. She seemed to be getting more and more tense as the one-sided conversation progressed. Only after several minutes was she able to get to the point. "Mum I've some important news. I'm engaged!" she blurted out breathlessly.

There was a long pause while Neil listened to the loud insect-like buzzing coming from Sophie's phone. Although he tried - and failed - to work out what was being said, he could tell it wasn't good. Jane was obviously in monologue mode and Sophie's frown lines increased with every minute that passed. After some time, looking distraught, Sophie crept upstairs, still listening to her mother's ranting. Overhead, Neil could hear the occasional muffled comment from his fiancée. Just as he was just reflecting glumly that the rain outside was a perfect accompaniment to the mood of the morning, his own mobile phone rang. 'Morag' came up on the screen.

'To answer or not to answer,' he thought. Upstairs he could hear Sophie saying, "But I can finish my degree through the OU, Mum." Hers was clearly going to be a long call. He pressed the green button on his mobile phone and put it to his ear.

"Well it's about time you bastard," came Morag's acerbic tone.

"If you're just out to give me a verbal then I'm going to hang up," replied Neil.

"You're history, Neil McLeod."

"Tell me something I don't know."

"Yeah, and what's more my new boyfriend is a much better shag than you ever were."

Upstairs he could hear Sophie pleading "But Mum, I love him. I don't care about any bloody inheritance…"

Neil continued, "Well that's good because you're never going to get any from me again."

"Oh, finally discovered you're gay have you?" came Morag's spiteful reply.

Neil sighed wearily. Morag could be like a dog with a bone sometimes and he knew only too well that her agenda was to insult him and try to hurt him. But he was long past caring. He knew deep down that the seeds of destruction had been sown at the start of their relationship, and their breakup was a question of when rather than whether. The Oban Ball was the straw that broke the camel's back and Neil realised that since then he hadn't missed her one iota. Indeed, he had hardly even thought about her at all. From above his head came Sophie's voice again, "I have. I have thought this through Mum."

Neil continued, "No. In fact I was going to wait 'til later to announce it but you might as well be the first to know."

"Know what?" said Morag a little too sharply. Neil sensed an undercurrent of curiosity and a hint of unease creeping into her voice as she repeated "What are you talking about?"

"I'm engaged."

For about the first time in her life Morag Govan was at a complete loss for words.

Neil waited, letting his words sink in. He wasn't going to make the next move. As the seconds ticked by he realised that all was now quiet upstairs. Sophie had stopped speaking. Then his phone disconnected.

A minute later, had he been able to teleport himself to Morag's bedroom he would have seen her staring through blurred eyes at a photo of Neil, her eyes streaming with tears. As it was, he simply switched off his phone and went upstairs. Sophie was sitting on the bed, cradling her phone in both hands and crying quietly. Neil slipped into the bedroom, sat down beside her and put his arm around her. After several minutes he broke the silence. "So that went well then."

Sophie shuddered - a half sob, half tinkling laugh - and wiped her eyes on her sleeve.

"Yes, well, it could have been better, I suppose."

Neil decided that now was not the time to probe further and that maybe it wasn't the greatest moment to tell Sophie about Morag's call either. Instead he took her hand and said "Do you want to call off the party Soph?" Sophie thought for a while and then shrugged slightly. "No, it's okay. But it may just have to be a party party rather than an engagement party." Neil sat holding her hand for a few minutes more until his attention was diverted by something outside. Through the bedroom window a shaft of light penetrated a gap in the gloomy cloud canopy, spotlighting a small corner of the loch below. "Come on" he said, "let's go down to the loch and skim stones. That'll make you feel better."

Sophie sniffed loudly and gave a rather too contrived chuckle. "You maybe. Skimming's a blokey thing. I'll watch – that's more a girly thing."

So, arm in arm, they meandered down to the side of Loch Etive. Its drizzling stillness was broken only by the slack tide sucking at the seaweed and the crooning of distant eider ducks. After an hour of talking and sauntering and stone skimming,

Sophie's confidence was beginning to be restored. They made their way slowly back towards Rose Cottage. In the kitchen Sophie glanced down at her phone on the kitchen table. She wanted to turn the bloody thing off and forget all about it but she couldn't help noticing that it had registered a missed call.

"Dee called," she shouted to Neil who by this time was in the in the bathroom, "I wonder what she wants?"

"Who's Dee?"

"Dorothy"

"Oh. Why don't you call her?" he said, pulling the handle.

Sophie waited until the sound of flushing had subsided and then pressed the call button. As Neil emerged, he noticed again that slight side toss of her head and half flick back of her hair which she always made before putting the phone to her ear. God, she was so lovely!

"Hello Dee." There was a pause whilst Dorothy said something, then "You know already? Mum phoned you?" A lengthier period ensued in which Dorothy talked and Sophie listened. "OK," she said and handed the phone to Neil. "She wants to speak with you," she whispered.

"Lady Montgomery?" said Neil and then he laughed. "Of course. How are you Dorothy?"

"I gather you want to make an honest girl out of Sophie," chuckled Dorothy's voice at the other end of the phone.

"I… well… um, yes" he replied, disconcerted. Dorothy's disarming knack of catching him off guard had thrown him yet again. 'How *does* she do it?' Neil found himself thinking.

"Well I just want to say how delighted I am for you both," Dorothy went on, "You'll know that Sophie's mother is not exactly enamoured of the idea, but I… well lets just say that I will do my best to talk her round. I'll have a chat with her once she's calmed down a bit. I hope that once she's met you, she'll be prepared to review her… decision. Now, when can you both come to see me…?"

* * *

That Saturday evening the atmosphere at Cedar Cottage was positively festive. All afternoon Ann had been quietly getting on with preparing food and whilst Jim innocently imagined that it was to be a normal party, Ann - in her own psychic way - had half guessed the reason for the occasion. When Neil turned up, whistling and carrying a case of champagne Ann's suspicions were confirmed and she resumed her preparations with renewed vigour, keen to make this an evening to remember. Seeing all the array of appetisers and dishes she had prepared, Neil was impressed. "Ann, you're a marvel," he said. "Thank you so much for lending us Rose Cottage. It's been wonderful. Are you sure we can stay there 'til Monday?"

"Of course," she replied with a twinkle in her eye.

That evening was one they would never forget. The wine and the conversation flowed in equal measure and Ann's cooking was universally acclaimed. Jim quietly got on with making everybody welcome, whilst Ann heaped dish after dish of delicious snacks onto everyone's plates. Looking tanned and relaxed, Duncan and Lorna regaled the others with their experiences of Greek food, Greek dancing, and plate smashing. Duncan was all for demonstrating the latter and had to be forcibly restrained by Lorna. Throughout the evening Neil and Sophie were inseparable. It was obvious to all the other partygoers that they were deeply in love. They had decided to wait until ten o'clock to make their announcement but shortly after nine Sophie felt her phone ring on vibrate. Half inclined to ignore it, she looked at the screen. Dorothy! She indicated to Neil. "Let's find somewhere private," she said, and they crept upstairs to the bathroom. Sounds of hilarity drifted up from below.

"Hello Dee."

Neil watched Sophie's face intently, reading it for any sign of a reaction. Her growing smile was a dead give-away though, and after the call had finished Sophie said, "Apparently Mum's had a bit of a change of heart. Dee told her about the ring and everything and now she wants to meet you. She says that although she's not very happy about what's happened, she can't very well stop us anyway!"

Neil gave her a brief hug and the two lovers slipped back downstairs hoping that their absence hadn't been noticed. With a plate on his head Duncan was demonstrating his version of a Greek belly dance and everyone else was in stitches, absorbed in his perfect mime act and having missed Neil and Sophie's absence. But Duncan had not.

"Ah, the lovers return," announced Duncan, "We canna let you out of our sight for a moment but that you're sloping off upstairs for a spot of rumpy pumpy."

"Actually, ladies and gentlemen, we have an important announcement to make," said Neil grandly, clinking his glass with a fork. Ann gave a small gasp and put her hand to her mouth. Jim paused in mid drink. Neil dragged Sophie to the front of the room, beaming broadly.

"Sophie and I are engaged to be married!"

The plate fell off Duncan's head, smashing to smithereens on the kitchen floor and the room erupted in a general round of applause.

The party went on until the wee small hours. As if by telepathy, several uninvited guests from the neighbourhood turned up to share in the celebrations. 'News certainly travels fast in Argyll' thought Sophie. Neil decided that he had drunk too much to risk driving back to Rose Cottage on the main road and was going to return via the private track that led through the woods, but Sophie persuaded him to order a taxi instead. When the Etive Taxi finally did turn up at Cedar Cottage, no-one was more pleased than the driver himself to recognise the rosy-cheeked vision of loveliness who had climbed into the back seat of his car all those months before. "Well if it isnae the fair maid of Ardcairn," he chuckled. "You're looking much better than when I last saw ye, lass."

Sophie laughed and replied "Thanks. And thanks again for letting me off the fare."

"Yous know each other then, do you?" questioned Neil, taken by surprise.

"This gentleman let me off paying for a taxi ride," she said, "It was my birthday present," she added, with a sly wink.

"Please, call me Malcolm," said the taxi driver.

Still none the wiser Neil rejoined, "Well then, it's another free ride for us tonight, my good man."

"And why might that be, my bonny lad?"

"This young lady and I have just got engaged." This time it was Neil's turn to laugh.

But when the driver deposited them at the cottage and Neil fished in his pockets for the fare, he only managed to find a high denomination note. The taxi driver had no change and Neil, in expansive mood, told him to keep the change.

"I guess the last laugh's on me then," said Malcolm. "But if ye gi's a call about your wedding transport I'll gi' ye a good deal, mind," and he winked at them and drove off into the night.

Chapter 14

The lovers' last day at Ardcairn was also memorable, though not exactly in the way that Sophie and Neil had intended. Resolving to finish her painting, Sophie gathered together her canvas, easel and case of oil paints, took the key to the big house and disappeared up the drive. Neil left her to it and remained in Rose Cottage to catch up on some paperwork. But finding it difficult to concentrate on his accounts he went outside and started splitting a pile of unseasoned logs for Ann. Towards the end of the morning he thought he'd surprise Sophie with a flask of coffee and some biscuits. Making his way up to the big house he could see her features framed in the picture window, focussing on her work. When she spotted Neil, she waved down at him and he grinned and waved back. As he entered, he noticed that Sophie had left the key in the front door lock so he locked the door behind him, pocketed the key and bounded up the stairs to join her.

By now Sophie's painting was reaching its final stages. Even as a self-confessed art ignoramus, Neil couldn't help being impressed by the way in which Sophie had captured and subtly transformed the view onto the canvas. It was as if the quintessence of Ardcairn had been gathered, distilled and crystallised into two dimensions. Although Sophie pretended to be diffident about her work, Neil could tell that she was secretly pleased. He sat on the arm of a sofa, sipped his coffee in silence and watched her add a hint of yellow paint to the sea loch.

"There," she said, adding some final dabs, "that's about finished now."

"It's amazing. I never would have thought that Loch Etive would be yellow, but it definitely works. A few more paintings like that and you'll be halfway to your gallery."

"Mmm. Except that this one isn't for sale. This is our keepsake for the best two weeks of my life. And, I know what my next painting's going to be."

"What's that then?" he asked.

"It's a secret," she teased.

"Oh, come on, don't be like that."

"Well if I tell you, you must promise not to laugh."

He promised and so she told him about this idea she had conceived since the first time Neil had appeared on his motorbike. In the painting, Neil would be on his bike with Robbie looking ahead out of his open jacket and they'd be zipping up the drive towards Ardcairn House. Sophie was so enthusiastic and animated as she described her concept that despite his promise Neil couldn't help himself and laughed uproariously. Amused rather than annoyed, Sophie leant across and pretended to strangle him, whereupon he grabbed her arms and gave her a full-on kiss and quite soon they were both on the floor together. Maybe it was the warm afternoon, the Persian carpet, the frisson of being somewhere they shouldn't or a realisation that the sands of their time together in Ardcairn were running out, but whatever their reasons were for getting physical the two lovers didn't stop to examine them. From gentle caresses their passion escalated by degrees towards a full-on sexual frenzy. But at the height of their lovemaking, someone – afterwards they could never agree which one of them it was it was – managed to knock over a vase. Admittedly it wasn't best Ming china but it might as well have been for all they knew. Jolted sideways, the vase wobbled precariously on its stand for a couple of seconds and then crashed onto the floor, breaking into a myriad of small pieces. Aghast, Neil and Sophie simultaneously shouted "Christ!" stared at each other in disbelief and then burst into nervous laughter. This hilarity was more an outlet for their shock at the seriousness of the accident than a show of disregard for its consequences. Afterwards, somewhat chastened, they started to pick up bits of china and place them back on the table. But as they were halfway through fishing for hidden pieces of vase another unwelcome surprise was about to shatter the peace of their world. Neil's sharp ears registered the sound of a vehicle approaching along the gravel drive. Covering his nakedness, he rushed over to the window and looked out. Then he swore again "Jesus! It's her. She's back!" Seconds later a car drew up on the gravel. Drifting up from below came the sounds of a door opening and the unmistakable voice of Miss Lacelaw, imperiously commanding the taxi driver to "Be careful with those cases. They're Louis Vuitton," and summarily dismissing him with a "You know where to send the bill. I trust it will not be as expensive as the last one." Then in a less direct tone she said, "In, Suki. Come on in. Good girl, no running off now."

For the next few seconds the upstairs drawing room was a frantic whirlwind of activity. Thanking his stars that he had had the presence of mind to lock the front door behind him, Neil hastily pulled on some clothes while Sophie desperately dismantled her easel and quickly chucked paints, brushes and thermos into her carrying case. Meanwhile Neil finished picking up odd bits of broken vase as Sophie attempted to dress as quickly as she could. In a real panic now, they could hear the front door being opened and Miss Lacelaw entering the porch. Trapped like prisoners, Sophie and Neil knew that they were only seconds away from being discovered. That bloody dog would sniff them out for certain and raise the alarm. A host of thoughts flashed through their minds. They would probably end up with a police record, and even more worryingly, Ann would probably lose her job. But just as they thought all hope was lost, in a blessed twist of fate the lovers were granted a reprieve from the most unlikely of sources. In a sweet, divine intervention, Suki became their hero of the moment as the dog's naughtiness for once played unpredictably but gratifyingly into their hands.

Fed up after the confines of her long car journey, Suki had scented a familiar whiff of collie and human beings amongst the outside odours of Ardcairn. Her curiosity instantly aroused, Suki slipped her lead and made a quick getaway over the lawn. Miss Lacelaw's shrill voice could be heard echoing from the porch below.

"Suki. SUKI! Naughty dog. Come here now!"

"Let's go!" Neil urged Sophie, but she needed no second bidding. She grabbed the painting and bolted from the drawing room. As they rushed along the passage towards the rear of the house Neil remembered that there was an outside fire escape somewhere and he dragged Sophie to where he guessed it might exit the premises. In their second stroke of luck, just as Miss Lacelaw was catching the wayward Suki by her collar, Neil chanced upon the right room at his first try. He eased the stiff casement window open and stepped onto the metal platform. "Hurry!" he cried, helping Sophie over the windowsill and onto the attached ladder. It was one of those fire escapes that are common in the US and even as they started to climb down it, Neil's thoughts flitted to various film scenes.

"This is just like a gangster movie, eh?" he grinned.

"Jesus Neil, shut up. This isn't funny," was all Sophie could muster in reply through gritted teeth.

But like those ladders where criminals made their getaways from the cops, this one didn't drop continuously to the ground and Neil had to release the last part to let Sophie onto terra firma before he climbed up again, retracted the bottom section and jumped down.

In the front garden Suki realised by now that she was well and truly captured, but her keen hearing had picked up sounds of activity coming from the other side of the house. At once forgetting the enticing scent of collie pee lingering in the shrubbery, she turned her attention to the unfamiliar noises with renewed curiosity. Rather than having to be reluctantly dragged towards the house and captivity, Suki was now positively straining on her lead *towards* the house and barking excitedly, much to Miss Lacelaw's surprise. But this mini drama on the front lawn was entirely lost on Neil and Sophie who by now were running as fast as they could towards the bushes fringing the back garden. Reaching the security of the shrubbery they pushed their way furtively through the greenery, systematically skirting around to the front of the house again and making for the cover of the yew tree in the walled garden.

Breathing heavily Sophie gasped "I thought she wasn't supposed to be coming back 'til tomorrow."

"She wasn't," Neil panted. "She must have decided to come back early, God knows why."

"What are we going to do about the vase?"

"I don't know. I'll have to phone Ann as soon as possible," he added.

Even as they flitted through the trees towards Rose Cottage Miss Lacelaw was making her usual inspection of the house to see that all was in order. Fortunately, she didn't notice that the fire escape casement was no longer locked. But as she entered the drawing room, she became all too aware of the broken vase and a strange lingering smell, although her nose wasn't able to identify it as turpentine. Her extreme annoyance at finding the broken vase was not helped by Suki who, rushing around the room and wagging her tail excitedly, promptly peed all over the carpet. Her doggie nose had detected high notes of human passion above the lower notes of coffee and oil paint and she naturally wanted to leave her own calling card in return.

Out of breath and still on an adrenaline rush, the two lovers eventually reached the safety of Rose Cottage. Neil immediately dashed into the kitchen, picked up Ann's phone and dialled Cedar Cottage. Luckily, he caught Ann just as she was about to go out to the shops and while he blurted out the full story she listened to his hasty explanations and abject apologies with patient understanding. Meanwhile, Miss Lacelaw, picking up her phone to call Rose Cottage in order to find out the cause of the breakage, was irritated to find Ann's phone constantly engaged.

She hadn't seen Ann's car when she drove past Rose Cottage. What was going on? Impatient to the point of infuriation, Miss Lacelaw took matters into her own hands, deciding to march down to Rose Cottage herself and demand an immediate explanation.

"…so I'm really sorry Ann. Look if there's a bill for the damage of course I'll pay," repeated Neil in abject contrition for the third time. But as he embarked upon yet another apology for entering and breaking at Ardcairn he was suddenly aware of the line going dead. Had Ann hung up on him? She couldn't have; that would simply not have been in her nature. And yet when he tried phoning her back there was no reply. What he couldn't possibly know was that in the middle of his holding forth about how the vase had "accidentally broken", Ann had experienced one of her rare but intense premonitions and this one had told her to get herself to Ardcairn as soon as possible.

At the same time that the determined figure of Miss Lacelaw was marching her purposeful way down the drive towards Rose Cottage, Ann's grey VW Polo was shooting up the road towards Ardcairn. Ann didn't like driving fast at any time, but on this occasion she put her foot hard down to the floor and roared up the drive at high speed. Looking down from a thermal above the estate, a sharp-eyed buzzard might have had trouble guessing who would have won the race to Rose Cottage that afternoon: Ann or Miss Lacelaw. During the five minutes that it took to walk between the house and the cottage Ann performed the fastest drive home from Taynuilt that she had ever made or ever wanted to make again. Out of a corner of the kitchen window Neil and Sophie caught a flash of grey car streaking up behind the cottage and coming to a rapid standstill.

It seemed like only a second later when a knock at the door heralded the arrival of Miss Lacelaw. Luckily, she didn't spot the two lovers. Neil and Sophie froze, panicked, looked at the door and than at each other, and in that instant Ann emerged from around the cottage and said insouciantly, "Ah, Miss Lacelaw. I was just on my way out to get some more hoover bags for those china fragments when I heard you knocking. There's been a wee breakage I'm afraid. Were you no intending to come back tomorrow?"

The wind completely taken out of her sails, Miss Lacelaw replied curtly, "My friend left early so I decided to cut the trip short." Sophie and Neil then overheard her add, "What happened with the vase Ann?" her accusatory tone a jarring contrast to Ann's conciliatory overtures.

Ann had never been known to tell a lie and as Neil listened to her dulcet soothing tones setting out a credible and entirely rational explanation for what had been "an unfortunate and regrettable accident" his heart went out to her. He knew that she was compromising her own moral code in covering for him and he was overwhelmed with gratitude. But his euphoria swiftly turned to fear as he heard Ann asking, "Would you like to come in for a wee cup of tea Miss Lacelaw?" Now she really was playing with fire. She must have known that he and Sophie were inside. What could she be thinking about? Their cover would be blown immediately. He eyeballed Sophie in alarm and silently gestured 'upstairs'. But in the end there was no need to make a move. Miss Lacelaw was heard to reply curtly, "No thank you Ann, I have a lot of unpacking to do this afternoon. Please come up to the house this evening and finish the vacuuming," and she turned on her heel and marched resolutely back towards the house.

"Whew!" breathed Neil as her footsteps retreated up the drive, "that was much too close for comfort".

As she watched Miss Lacelaw depart, Ann brushed some unseen specks of dirt from her coat, then pushed open the door to Rose Cottage. She surveyed the two sheepish lovers looking for all the world like a couple of naughty schoolchildren. "Well, that's a muckle pickle you two nearly got me into."

So contrite was Neil during the ensuing minutes that Ann eventually found the amusing side of things. "I'm surprised you had the energy for chopping wood," she said in a rare show of scurrilous humour, after being shown the mountain of firewood that Neil had created. "Now I think it best if you two make yourselves scarce," she said. "Dinna worry about Miss Lacelaw. I'll see to all that," brushing aside all of Neil's repeated abject apologies and frequent suggestions that he pay for the breakage.

They packed up quickly, loading what they could onto Neil's motorbike which - luckily - he had parked behind the cottage. Just before they got onto the bike Neil said to Ann through his visor, "How didh you know that sthe wouldn't come in when you athked her?"

Ann chuckled, "I didn't but I'd a feeling that she'd say no. You see I've asked her inside several times before, but she's always declined. I think she's too uncomfortable with the idea. It's like she wants to keep a distance between us. Anyway, now she'll never suspect that my place was, em, occupied."

Neil swallowed. His estimation of Ann soared even higher. "You're a geniuth, thairy godmother!" he declared with genuine admiration and gave her a big hug before climbing on the bike.

"Och, awa wi' ye both. Ye'll be the death of me," she remarked as Sophie clambered on behind Neil. Ann was secretly pleased by Neil's remark, but she would remain worried about what happened for a long time afterwards.

* * *

Before Sophie returned to St Andrews the following day, she had one final request. Despite Neil's protests she made him pose with Robbie on the bike, just as she had described before and took several sketches and photos of them from different angles. Robbie seemed to enjoy it: he thought it was an elaborate prelude to going for walkies. But Neil was not a good sitter and when he complained about having to hold a certain pose for even a short while she dismissed his whinging. "Calm down Sam Brown. This is going to be my next masterpiece. I'm going to make you famous," she announced airily.

"I don't want to be famous," he retorted sulkily.

Robbie would have wagged his tail if he weren't squashed up in his master's jacket. He didn't mind what happened so long as he got his walkie.

Chapter 15

One rain-soaked Friday evening several weeks later, Sophie could be seen brooding at a desk in the faculty library at St Andrews. Her History of Art books lay open in front of her and her essay on *Russian Modernism: Theory and Practice 1908 - 1916* was half finished. Sophie's mind was not on her work. Instead, she was staring into space and fiddling absent-mindedly with her hair, reliving her Ardcairn experiences, thinking about her painting of Neil and wondering when she should tell him.

At the same time Neil was hunched over his paperwork at Cedar Cottage, wrestling with a complicated tax return. He knew that the deadline for its completion was looming and that he should really fill it in soon if he was going to avoid a fine. But to do so with accuracy meant banishing all thoughts of Sophie and their Easter holiday and every so often the photograph he kept of her on his desk kept smiling up at him and distracting him. Flashbacks of their time together kept breaking into his train of thought and upsetting his concentration. He sighed, turned to the form again and groaned. One of the questions needed an answer to which only Jim had the details. "Bugger it!" he exclaimed in frustration. Jim had gone out with Ann. Again. They were at the Oban cinema that evening and the last time they disappeared to Oban they didn't get back until midnight. In fact it was getting late already, Neil realised with a start as he looked at his watch: just before eleven. 'That's the second time they've been out together this week' he recalled with a frown. Then his frown changed to a smile. His father becoming a worry to him? That made a change! Neil wanted to phone

Sophie and tell her that the sealed bids for Lonan Farm were going to be opened tomorrow but he realised that he had left it too late that evening. So he sent her a text instead. 'Hi Soph. Call me pm 2moz. Miss u soooo much :-(N xxx'.

Sophie glanced at the library clock – eleven pm. It would be too late to phone Neil by the time she got back to St Salvator's. She idly thought about taking the early train to Oban the next day and surprising him, but she remembered he had said he was going to be busy on Saturday. What's more she should really attend the lecture tomorrow morning on *The Age of Klimt, Olbrich, and Mucha*. She sighed, turned back to her essay, looked at it for a few seconds and then abandoned it altogether. Her recent ice cream addiction was nagging at her, her painting was calling to her and she felt in the mood do some more exploratory work on it. When she reached the college, Neil's text awaited her. She smiled and texted him back, knowing that by now he would probably have switched off his phone. 'Willdo. Robbie, pl tell master mistress misses mister. S xxx'. Lately, with blood glucose levels yo-yoing like crazy, her diabetes had been giving her concerns, but ignoring her latest glycogen reading she made a large hot chocolate, grabbed a tub of ice cream and settled down to the start of her big artistic project. Absorbing herself in painting usually cleared her mind but tonight was different. Sophie just couldn't settle, troubled by the thoughts that kept crowding into her mind.

* * *

Neil was deep in discussion with Craig the following afternoon when his phone went off. Luckily it was set to vibrate because with all the background chainsaw noise at the harvesting site he wouldn't otherwise have been able to hear it. His gang was rushing to complete this job today - their bonus depended upon it - and they were felling trees and extracting timber hell for leather.

"One second," said Neil, taking his phone out and glancing at the screen: Sophie. "Got to take this call. I'll be with you in a minute Craig." He made his way down the track a short distance until the background buzzing of saws diminished by several decibels. His discussion about piecework rates abruptly curtailed, Craig snorted and climbed back into the cab of his forwarder. Boss or no boss, he was under a tight deadline and he wanted to finish the job today.

Before Sophie spoke, Neil blurted out "Soph, I've got some wonderful news. It's Lonan Farm. My offer was accepted this morning and the date of entry has been set for the end of June. Isn't that fantastic! When can you come up and see it?"

"Darling!" Neil thought that the voice at the other end sounded strained but decided that it could have been the noise of the chainsaws nearby. "Neil, that's great but I've got something important to tell you. I'm…." but just then her voice was drowned by the sound of the forwarder engine roaring into life. Neil picked up just the odd word here and there; "…news…" and "…only just discovered…"

"Yes, it's great isn't it," continued Neil, putting one finger in his non-phone ear and starting to walk down the track away from the cacophony of chainsaws, "When can you come up? It's not too long 'til the end of term."

Sophie said something inaudible again and, unable to hear her properly, Neil made general approving noises. It was several seconds before he eventually managed to find a quieter spot around a corner.

"But aren't you upset?" came Sophie's voice. At the same time Neil observed the loaded forwarder starting to make its way towards him along the forest road.

"Upset? Why should I be upset?" he shouted above the din of the approaching forwarder, "You love Lonan Farm."

"You're not listening to me," she said. "I said, I'm *pregnant*," but at that moment her voice was muffled by the din of the giant red machine thundering past with its load of logs. Craig grinned down from the cab and gave a mock salute to his boss while Neil nodded back at him. "Sorry darling, I can't hear you," he shouted as the forwarder disappeared down the forest road.

"I'M PREGNANT!" she bellowed.

This time there was no doubt. Sophie's message had been successfully transmitted, received and understood. Neil stopped dead in his tracks and uttered one pithy expletive.

"Sweet Jesus!"

Chapter 16

Still in shock, Neil made his way back to Taynuilt on mental autopilot. Instinctively he headed for home but at the last minute something made him drive past the village turn-off and continue down the main road towards the coast. He needed time and space to think away from the demands of work and the distractions of Cedar Cottage and there was only one place where he could be guaranteed to find peace, quiet and no phone signal: his secret headland. After a few miles he turned off down the forestry road and then bounced along the rough track that soon petered out. Jolting over some rough heather for a few hundred metres Neil drew the vehicle to a halt under the lone pine tree. His mind now disengaged from manoeuvring the Landrover, he switched off the engine and gazed through the windscreen at the nearby headland and brooding islands beyond. In Neil's mind one thought cast out all others: 'Sophie's pregnant'.

After a pause he clambered out of the vehicle, walked the short distance towards the cliff edge and stared down at the surging sea. The tide was coming in and his thoughts regathered themselves... 'Sophie's pregnant'. Instead of the usual white horses prancing about in the waters below, these were grey mare waves corralled by a troubled sea. He sat on the turf and gazed down at the rocks buffeted by the turmoil of surf and spray below. Each pounding breaker seemed to sough out her name: Sophie... Sophie... Sophie...

Neil thought back over their brief and very interrupted phone call at the harvesting site, trying to analyse the feelings behind

Sophie's words. It had not been easy, what with the constant noise and Craig's demands. Sitting on her bed in her college room, Sophie had known that the news would break like a bombshell in Neil's world and she imagined that he would probably need time to think it over and work things out in his mind. She was right. Sitting at his favourite spot at his secret headland, Neil's head was a frantic whirl of emotions and feelings. When Sophie had broken the news to him his first reaction had been one of shock of course, but had it been the shock of anxiety or of pleasure? Even he couldn't tell. Sophie had been very matter of fact about her condition and even mentioned the option of an abortion. Thinking about that now, he sensed that her suggestion might have been more for his benefit than hers, a 'get out of fatherhood free' card perhaps, or even a 'get out of their relationship free' card. He tried to envisage the reality of an abortion from her point of view but failed completely. So many questions churned around in his head, each one clamouring for an answer. How could he possibly begin to imagine what it must be like to face the decision whether or not to terminate a potential human life? If they did have a baby what would that do to their lives and lifestyles, his work, and her studies? What did he really want and what was his duty? What would Jim say, or for that matter, Dorothy? And could he and Sophie possibly continue to live apart now – or together for that matter? Maybe she thought that he thought that she had become pregnant to ensnare him. "Oh, for God's sake!" he shouted aloud to the breaking waves. Now he was just being irrational. Why on earth would she want to trap him? He knew that that went against every fibre of Sophie's being. She was always one for letting people be themselves, keen to understand them for who they are: not out to change them. He knew that her love for him was nothing if not unconditional and she would no more want to stop him from being himself than… he searched for an analogy in his mind… than she would want to stop the waves breaking onto the rocks below.

As he listened to those same waves crashing rhythmically beneath him, Neil's karma gradually gave itself up to the rhythm of the sea and little by little he felt his pulse rate starting to drop and a degree of calm return to his troubled mind. Gradually he could step back from the immediacy of the news and begin to think rationally about its implications. He concluded that if he did call time on their relationship she would probably go ahead and have the baby anyway. Did he feel a responsibility? Of course he did. How did that change his feelings for Sophie? He couldn't possibly know.

But by the time the tide had retreated from the rocks, the answers to all these questions were irrelevant. Neil had made up his mind: he and Sophie were already engaged: now they would get married. He wanted to stay with her and become the proper father of her child. When he had arrived at his cove, Neil's forehead had been wrinkled with concern. Two hours later, when he left his rocky perch by the cliff edge and walked slowly back to his vehicle, the frown lines had vanished.

Neil wanted to break the news to his father first. Thinking it over by the sea's edge he resolved to tell him just as soon as he returned to Taynuilt. But fate dictated that events should take a different turn that afternoon. As he neared the end of the track back to the public road his mobile phone signal kicked in and an assortment of tones indicated three missed calls and an incoming text. The last person he expected to have been contacting him was Morag Govan but that was the name displayed on the screen. 'Ironic,' he thought. He had meant to block her from his caller list but had somehow forgotten.

Neil wondered why she had waited all this time to pester him. It had been many weeks since either of them had been in touch - not since Neil had announced his engagement in fact - and he was in two minds about whether to read her text or not. It would probably be an abusive FOND 'Fuck Off aNd Die' message: 'I've got a new boyfriend and he's better than you in the sack', or some such vitriol. He could do without her insults right now he concluded, putting the phone back on the seat again. But seconds later, when the message tone rang again indicating a second text from Morag his curiosity was aroused. He stopped the car and read the most recent message: 'Yr dad awake asking 4U'. 'What on earth was that about?' he thought. But when he read the first text his puzzlement changed to alarm. "Yr dad in hspitl - accidnt."

Neil immediately wrenched the gear stick over, let the clutch out in a spray of gravel, gathered speed along the track and hurried towards Oban General as fast as the Landrover could go. Twenty minutes later he roared into the hospital car park, screeched to a halt and jumped out, not bothering to lock the vehicle. Shortly afterwards, having been directed to Ward 2 by Reception, Neil bounded up the hospital stairs two at a time just as Nurse Govan happened to be making her way down the same steps carrying a tray of assorted pills. He only just managed to avoid colliding with her.

"You can slow doon. He's no deid," Morag remarked dryly.

"S-sorry," he replied, steadying himself on the banister rail and glancing briefly in her direction. "What's happened?" he asked.

"Your faither was taken here about an hour ago. Seemingly he was in his workshop and had an accident. He blacked oot and fell doon. They're no sure what the problem is. They want to do some tests," she explained hurriedly. "I'll show you whereabouts he is," she added, turning around and heading upstairs again. They pushed through some double doors at the top of the stairs and walked down the corridor through Ward 2. Pointing to one of the side doors she said, "He's in there." Then she paused. I've got tae go now. On my rounds," she explained. Then her tone changed abruptly from civil to accusatory. "You're a difficult man to get hold of, Neil McLeod. You know they're clamping down on the use of mobiles in this place. They say it affects the monitors, but I think that's effing bullshit," she spat out the words viciously in his face.

Neil sensed that her savagery was really meant for him. He held her gaze with a steady expression and said, "Thanks for getting in touch." He paused, "Look Morag, I…" and she eyeballed him back, waiting for him to continue. He kept expecting the right words to emerge from his mouth, but they obstinately refused to come, "… just… thanks," he repeated lamely, pushing open the door and walking in to the room.

Behind a protective curtain lay Jim, unconscious, a bandage round his head. Two doctors were standing beside his bed, whilst Ann sat on a chair nearby, her face etched with worry lines. But her expression softened a little when Neil walked in, and for a second she looked almost relieved.

"Thank heavens you're here," she said, "I tried to contact you but your phone…"

"What happened?" he interrupted.

A doctor who had been leaning over Jim straightened up, turned to Neil and asked, "Are you a relation?"

"I'm his son."

"Your father had an accident earlier today. We're unsure of the details but it seems there are... complications."

"What sort of complications?"

"Your father was knocked out. We don't know exactly how. He managed to regain consciousness in the ambulance. He's been able to talk, but not coherently. He's clearly had a severe knock to the head and we think that..." the Doctor chose his words carefully, "...we aren't entirely sure whether something may have happened to his brain. We'll need to take a scan. It's possible he may need an operation. He's under sedation just now. We're taking the precaution of airlifting him to Edinburgh." As an afterthought he added, "Glasgow would be the usual place but they're very busy just now I'm afraid. But don't worry, the doctors at Edinburgh are amongst the best in Scotland – he'll be in very good hands."

"Edinburgh?" Neil was struggling to take it all in.

"We don't have the necessary facilities here. I'm sorry, this must be a shock for you. We think that... there are reasons to believe that your father's condition may be more... serious than first diagnosed. I am sure that this is in his best interests."

"But, but..." Unable to think straight, Neil was bewildered by this barrage of revelations. "When...? Will he be all right? Can I come with him?"

"We won't know the prognosis until tomorrow. We're co-ordinating with another patient here who's also awaiting airlift to Edinburgh Infirmary. We'll let you know what the hospital decides to do and we will of course also need to take details of…" He was interrupted in mid sentence by a nurse, who pushed open the door and announced briskly, "That's the chopper now Dr Anderson".

Neil and Ann looked on helplessly as two orderlies rolled Jim from his hospital bed onto a lightweight air ambulance trolley. They could see fresh blood oozing through the bandage around his head. One orderly pushed the trolley whilst the other held a drip. Dull-witted with shock and unsure of exactly what to do, Ann and Jim dumbly followed the entourage of white lab coats down the corridor that lead towards the external doors. Outside they could hear the dull rumble of rotor blades from the waiting helicopter, pulsating ominously like an executioner's drum roll. As the hospital doors swung open the drumbeat became a cacophony. Ann blocked her ears. Neil shuddered. For a long time afterwards, he could not hear the sound of a helicopter without feeling a sense of overwhelming dread.

Stopped dead in their tracks by a barrier and a large notice warning members of the public not to venture further, Neil and Ann stood helplessly, watching the well-rehearsed procedure unfold before them. 'This can't be happening,' thought Neil, 'It's a bad dream, that's all'. He couldn't be expected to recognise the classic signs of denial that immediately followed a trauma: the out-of-mind experience that refuses to take in the reality of here-and-now. The other air ambulance patient could be seen stretched out on his trolley, already secured inside the aircraft, with just enough space alongside for Jim. A few seconds later and the helicopter doors were closed. Its engine swelled from loud to deafening, its rotors flattened the grass around the concrete landing pad and the monstrous mechanical bird slowly lifted Jim up, around and away. Ann and Neil watched for the few seconds that it took for the chopper to disappear from view. Then all that remained was a loud silence and Jim's conspicuous absence.

Ann and Neil remained standing by the safety barrier, hesitating, unsure of what to do until at last a nurse appeared. "Could you please come this way?" she asked gently, "I'm afraid we need you to fill in a few forms." Neil took a sidelong glance at Ann. She was wiping tears from her eyes.

Two cups of tea and several completed forms later, Neil and Ann sat in the Landrover in the hospital car park, talking. Ann unfolded the full story of how she had discovered Jim with a big gash on his head, lying in a pool of blood on the workshop floor. She couldn't understand what had happened, but he had been unconscious and looked extremely pale. She had dialled 999 and the ambulance had arrived very quickly: luckily the crew had been on a routine assignment close by, and they bandaged him up immediately. Although he had lost a lot of blood, he regained consciousness on the way to the hospital, even pretending for a while that nothing untoward had happened. Then his mind had started to wander, and he became increasingly incoherent. Ann explained, "I hadn't intended to visit Jim this morning but something made me go over early today," and as she recounted the exact sequence of events, Neil realised that her timely discovery and prompt action had in all probability saved Jim's life. He marvelled at her coolness and her capability in the face of an emergency. For a while they sat in silence, each lost in their own thoughts, each trying to make sense of the situation. Neil wondered whether Ann's visit to see Jim had been prompted by another of her psychic premonitions, but he decided that now was not the time to ask her. Some time later, maybe.

He was first to speak. "I don't know what would have happened to Jim without you raising the alarm," he said at last, starting the car engine.

She brushed Neil's statement aside. "Anyone would have done the same thing," she said and trembled a little, the shock of it all starting to kick in properly.

Neil headed the Landrover in the direction of Ardcairn. As the turn off for the estate approached, Neil flicked the indicator switch distractedly, negotiating the driveway with unease. The last thing he needed right now was some kind of abrasive encounter with Miss Lacelaw. With his mind momentarily unshackled from morbid thoughts about his father he suddenly recalled the phone call from Sophie that morning: 'Gosh, was it only this morning?' he wondered in disbelief. Rose Cottage was now drawing closer and Neil slowed down, wondering whether this was a good time to break his - or rather Sophie's - momentous news to Ann. He stopped in front of the cottage and hesitated. Just as her hand reached for the vehicle door handle, he sensed his chance, blurting out "There's something I have to tell you, Ann. It's… it's not about Jim."

She waited patiently, seeing him wrestle with his thought, trying to marshal the right words to explain what had happened. "Aye Neil?" she replied.

"I… I don't really know how to put this," he said uncertainly.

Ann waited patiently. Again, Neil hesitated, unsure, his head still full of worries about his father. "It's about Sophie," he said and in the awkward pause that followed he cast about for the best way to put it.

Not for nothing did her close friends called her 'Fey Ann'. A strong feeling of intuition swept over her and she sensed what he was trying to articulate. "It's alright, Neil I think I might know," she said, not waiting for him to finish. "She's expecting isn't she?"

Neil would have been astonished if he was not already emotionally drained. "How…h-how..." he began, and his voice trailed off weakly.

"I just know." Then she looked up at him intently and in a fervent tone of voice said, "Neil – promise me ye'll pray for Jim."

He nodded dumbly.

She clambered down from the Landrover and was about to shut the car door. In an effort to cheer them both up she added, "And don't worry about Sophie. She'll be fine."

Neil turned the vehicle around and smiled weakly at Ann through the open window, his eyes moist with the emotional overload of the day's events.

"You'll make a great faither," she half shouted at him.

Neil sniffed, gave a weak smile, and signalled goodbye. "Thanks," was all he could muster by way of reply.

As he drove off, he could see Ann waving back in his rear view mirror but what he couldn't see were the worry lines returning to her face. As he reached the main road three thoughts competed for his attention. 'I hope Dad's going to be OK', 'I'm going to be a Dad myself' and 'Phone Sophie.' The first two matters were out of his hands and in the lap of the gods. At least he could do something about the third.

But before he did there was something he knew he must do…

Chapter 17

Like all local bikers Neil knew the twists and turns of Argyll's roads intimately. Normally he would have revelled in the exhilaration of banking his Triumph through their bends and throttling it up their gradients, but this evening was different: this evening he was deeply distracted. Taking the back route from Taynuilt in order to avoid the town and the tourists, he re-joined the Lochgilphead road, expecting to find the usual convoys of caravans and foreign number plates, but things were strangely quiet that day. Travelling on mental autopilot and with few other road users to contend with, Neil was able to think about matters besides the road ahead. But rather than admiring the stunning scenery unfolding around him that evening his thoughts centred around his fiancée and his father, and every so often something from the day's turbulent events would enter, play, and replay in his brain. Leaving the main road behind, he turned down a quiet lane that meandered towards Seil Island and the Bridge over the Atlantic. Although there were no tourist signposts pointing out his place of pilgrimage, Neil remembered the five-bar gate that marked the start of the moorland track. He propped up the bike beside it, chained his helmet around the front wheel, hopped over a style and marched off up the track towards his destination.

All the locals knew about the Argyll Wishing Tree but few of them ever visited it. It took determination to walk the several miles there and back, and people were generally too incurious or too lazy to make the effort. Neil himself had only been there twice before, once when his mother Eleanor had contracted cancer and then a year later, after she had died. For those who did make the effort however, the experience was always memorable, usually extraordinary and sometimes overwhelming.

After ascending for a couple of miles, Neil watched a fishing boat curling lazily out into the Minch leaving a wake of golden ripples in the otherwise mirror-calm sea. As he crested a small rise he caught sight of his goal up ahead - an unremarkable, stunted and rather forlorn-looking tree. From a distance it looked just like any other out-of-the-way hawthorn and although hikers might have wondered why someone had bothered to put a stock fence around it, those ignorant of its legend would probably just have walked past, not giving it a second glance. But remembering the wonder of his first encounter with the Wishing Tree, Neil quickened his pace. Yes, here it was, still the same old half-fallen hawthorn, almost leafless despite the season and blasted by the wind into a natural sculptural form. As he approached it, Neil observed for the third time in his life what it was that made this tree unique: numerous coins embellishing its branches, pressed into its bark and piled into the forks of its limbs. Generations of superstitious locals and travellers had left countless offerings in this way, making obeisance and asking wishes, acknowledging the tree's mythological powers. As he gazed at all the coins festooning the tree, Neil pondered the motives behind these offerings: something material in some cases perhaps, recovery from affliction or illness undoubtedly, and then, thinking of Sophie, he supposed that most of the tokens were probably motivated by love or for love. 'Love wishes,' he concluded.

The Wishing Tree was smaller than Neil had remembered, and it seemed to be ailing. A trick of time perhaps, or was it the tree itself battling against decay or old age, or even the onslaught of so much metal. 'Perhaps it's being poisoned by love offerings?' he wondered. 'Certainly, it must have clung determinedly to that hillside for generations,' he reflected, as he examined some of the older coins, a few dating back more than a century. One or two looked really ancient, with unfamiliar inscriptions and images on the little of them that remained, for most of these early offerings had been incorporated into the growing tree, absorbed by slow degrees into the living trunk. But although he examined the cash hoard with curiosity, his professional eye kept being drawn back to the health of the tree. It was definitely sick, and he suspected that its days were numbered: what future then for those hardy souls making the pilgrimage to Argyll to entreat the tree's magic properties? Something made him mumble an apology to the hawthorn as he took out his penknife. He selected a healthier branch and took two small cuttings. It was a long shot – they would probably dehydrate on the way back home – but at least he would try to keep them alive.

Looking back on that gentle summer evening, Neil remembered staying beside the Wishing Tree for several hours, his thoughts wandering free down the pathways of his mind. Some memories were recent, like those of his father and Sophie: others were more distant, like those of his mother. With some difficulty he recalled his first outing to the Wishing Tree many years before. His father had been unusually quiet and withdrawn at the time and to Neil the expedition was more of an adventure than anything else. Although he had been told that his mother Eleanor had cancer, he was too young to understand what that meant and the information hadn't really registered with him: he was more interested in the tree itself and its fascinating collection of coins. At the time he had picked up an old half sovereign to examine it further, but his father had sternly told him to put it back to avoid "the wrath of the tree." Neil's next visit he recalled more vividly: the wind; his father struggling to remain composed, trying to read a poem that his mother had written shortly before she died; then Jim choking with emotion and leaving Neil to finish the last verse in his clear, high, sing-song voice. Then the scattering of Eleanor's ashes and an unusually strong gust of wind carrying her remains out towards the sea and the islands that she loved so much. Later in his reverie Neil pondered the enigma of the tree itself and how it was that such a nondescript hawthorn should have become the object of so much attention. He marvelled that in this day and age, souvenir hunters and currency collectors had not stripped it bare. He imagined that some of these coins must be pretty valuable by now, thinking how rare it was to find something more precious than the offerings themselves: the respect of each visitor for the symbolic tokens of previous tree pilgrims. That respect was worth much more than mere cash. He couldn't imagine a phenomenon like this further south surviving the odds against people's greed and selfishness and it made him proud to be a Highlander. Then he wondered about fear as a motivation: 'Maybe folk left the coins alone out of fear of becoming cursed? Maybe it was simple anxiety that kept the offerings where they were, rather than respect for others?' Neil's matter-of-fact side kicked in then, and he suspected that whatever the reason, it was probably due more to the tree's remoteness than anything else: the sheer difficulty of reaching it. In a far-fetched moment he even wondered whether he should even make his own offering to the health of the tree itself – wishing for its return to vitality and a longer life. He imagined that Sophie would have said how daft that was - the tree couldn't grant a wish for itself - and as he thought of Sophie, he longed to make his wish for her and the safe delivery of their baby and the desire for them all to be together forever. But then the words that Ann had spoken earlier that day resurfaced in his mind, "Neil - promise me ye'll pray for Jim."

When he was a small boy, his mother had given him an old seventeenth century coin from Massachusetts that she had received in a pile of loose change. It was damaged - someone had drilled a small hole through it - but Neil was fascinated by the silver tree design on one side, partly worn away with the handling and rubbing of countless transactions. As a child he had always treasured it and kept it safe. When Eleanor died, Jim gave his son some keepsakes of hers, including a silver necklace. Neil decided to put coin and chain together and wear them around his neck. Somehow it had become a habit and during the years since her death, the necklace had rarely been removed. Now he instinctively unbuttoned his shirt and took out coin and chain. Neil was not a deeply spiritual person and neither was he anything but an occasional worshipper in any conventional sense of the word. Although as a child he had dutifully trotted off to Sunday school every week, after his mother had died, Jim stopped going to church except at Christmas and Easter time and that was OK by Neil too. Praying was therefore not something that came readily to him. But as he offered up his familiar Massachusetts coin, attaching it by its chain around the trunk of the Wishing Tree and closing his eyes that evening, he felt his mind clearing itself, unburdening its cares and worries and becoming at one with the moment. As if in a trance Neil found himself articulating his fervent wish that Jim would somehow recover from his accident.

When he recounted this experience to Sophie some time afterwards Neil couldn't remember whether he had actually spoken the words himself or whether they had simply been in his head. Before arriving at the Tree, he had anticipated making some kind of intercession to God, or even imploring the spirit of the Wishing Tree itself but what he actually found himself doing that soft summer evening was having an unexpected conversation with his mother. At the time it seemed perfectly normal and natural and it was only in retrospect that he realised what a bizarre experience it had been: mystical, in truth. It was as if Eleanor's ashes had returned from the sea, manifested in the shape of a shimmering angel that illuminated the Tree, and the first words that she spoke to him were "Don't worry." That much he was able to remember. But although he was unable to recall the exact phrases that she had used at the time, he did remember her words as having been immensely reassuring and consoling. She stayed with him for a while ('was it a minute or an hour?' he wondered later) and then she vanished. But just before she disappeared from his side, his mother sang to Neil the lullaby with which she used to sing him to sleep every night as a child. What remained with him long after his pilgrimage to the Argyll Wishing Tree were the adapted words of an extra verse:

Ally bally, Ally bally bee
Sitting by the Wishin' Tree
Bringin' oot your wee bawbee
To make a wish for Daddy.

And then she laughed - a long, silvery, pealing, joyous, reassuring laugh that always lifted Neil's spirits as a child and made him feel wanted and loved and cherished - and the laughter reminded him of Sophie. When he awoke as if from a dream, his first feeling was a certainty that there is much more to life than we will ever know: much more to life than life itself and that in the end - despite everything

- all would be well. His second feeling was of inexpressible love: for his mother, his father, for Ann but mostly for Sophie.

Sophie! My God! He had promised to call her back not long after their disjointed call all those hours ago and now the summer evening was well advanced. The sun's giant orb was gradually sinking into the dazzling sea and a golden glow illuminated the western sky, signalling the promise of fine weather tomorrow. He should be making his way back before it got dark. Dampening his handkerchief from a nearby pool, Neil wrapped it around the two hawthorn cuttings, placed them carefully in his haversack and started to head back down the moorland track.

He took out his mobile phone and pressed the speed dial for Sophie.

"Hi darling. It's been an eventful day," he said. "Have you got lots of time, because there's so much to talk about…"

Chapter 18

News travels fast in Argyll and when Neil got back to Cedar Cottage it was to a sympathetic reception from Duncan and comfort food prepared by Lorna. Ann was there too and although reluctant to join in any conversation at first, still traumatised by the morning's events and feeling in no mood to be sociable, she became increasingly glad of the company and conversation. Inevitably all the talk was of Jim's accident, which lent a reflective and melancholic mood to the evening, but as time went on, the conversation about Jim, life, the universe and everything began to have a cathartic effect on all of them. Neil didn't mention his Wishing Tree experience, and the others didn't ask. He knew that although Ann would understand, Duncan and Lorna might have seen it as a convenient excuse for some mild ribbing in the interests of lifting his spirits and Neil was in no mood for that. Whether it was his long phone call to Sophie earlier, the shared conversation of friends at dinnertime, or the reassuring vision of his mother, Neil slept a deep and dreamless sleep that night, despite the maelstrom of the day's events.

The following day the hospital phoned to confirm that the tests had shown 'positive', or in other words they were going to have to operate on Jim later that day. Already prepared for this unwelcome update, Neil alerted Ann to the news and made arrangements to leave for Edinburgh, putting his business into Craig's semi-capable hands and putting Robbie into Duncan's feckless hands. Also prepared for the worst, Ann had managed to negotiate two days leave of absence from Miss Lacelaw and agreed to Neil's offer of a lift down to Edinburgh. By late morning all the preparations had been made and Ann and Neil were on the road, heading south. En route Neil phoned Sophie again. "The hospital called. They're going to operate on Jim in about an hour. Looks like Ann and I will be down in Auld Reekie for a couple of days."

"Have you got somewhere to stay?" she asked.

"No. I guess we'll find a B&B somewhere."

"Don't book anything yet, I've got an idea," she replied.

Half an hour later she phoned him back. "Good news! We're all staying at Dee's."

She went on to explain that as she was in exam revision mode it didn't matter where she stayed and that it might as well be in Edinburgh as St Andrews. She added that whilst Dorothy had been sanguine about the news of her pregnancy, her mother had thrown a complete hissy fit and had gone into a major rage about her 'wasting her life and that if her father were still alive he would be extremely upset and disappointed'. But at least it had the effect of cementing her acceptance, albeit with extreme reservations, of Sophie's engagement to Neil - "this backwoodsman of yours" as Jane had labelled him. Her benevolence did not extend to giving them houseroom in Edinburgh however, since she apparently had guests already, although Neil sensed that this was probably an excuse for her not having to put herself out. By contrast, when Sophie had explained to Dorothy why she, Neil and Neil's godmother were going to be in town, her grandmother had insisted in putting all three of them up. Neil also sensed some mother-grandmother agenda at play in which the unsuspecting Sophie might be a pawn, but then quickly dismissed his conspiracy theory: Dorothy was after all a genuinely kind lady and Sophie was the apple of her grandmother's eye.

"So you see it's all fixed," Sophie said to Neil in a matter of fact way.

"Is there a double bed then, Moneypenny?" he asked in a Sean Connery accent.

"Don't push it double O seven," she retorted in an M tone of voice.

Neil was both relieved at not having to find a place to stay and apprehensive at the outcome of his father's operation. He looked forward to seeing the redoubtable Dorothy again. But on the other hand, Ann was less comfortable about the prospect of staying in a complete stranger's house even although she had listened to Neil talking fondly about Sophie's grandmother on several occasions. "Don't worry Ann, you'll get on with her just fine. She doesn't suffer fools but what you see is what you get. She won't beat about the bush. She'll be dead straight with you." He spent the next few minutes retelling the story of how he had first encountered Sophie's grandmother on the day of that rugby match all those months ago. As they approached Loch Fyne Neil pulled in at the restaurant on an impulse and despite Anne's protestations, he insisted on treating her to lunch.

"We've got several hours before they'll let us see Jim at the hospital anyway and it's the least I can do for you after all the great meals you've cooked for me," he said, but when it came to ordering, neither of them was particularly hungry. It was difficult to find one's appetite when the reality was that 150 miles away Jim was going under the knife. As they waited for their modest serving of oysters, they deliberately steered clear of the subject of hospitals for at least five minutes until Neil updated Ann on the phone call he had received from the hospital that morning. Recounting the surgeon's careful and oh so politically correct terminology which suggested that Jim "might not retain the full range of mental faculties that he previously enjoyed before his accident," Neil translated this as "Prepare for your Dad to be a cabbage."

Despite it being too early for the main tourist season, the restaurant was surprisingly busy. The table next to Ann and Neil was occupied by a late middle-aged couple who had evidently run out of anything meaningful to say some time ago and who were only interested in eavesdropping on conversations about other, more exciting lives. Sensing that he was being overheard, Neil abruptly changed the subject and after a while their conversation drifted into the evergreen subject of Miss Lacelaw and whether or not she was going to sell the estate. "I overheard her on the phone saying that she's going back to the States for at least three months this summer," said Ann "I think she might be going to sell Ardcairn and go back home for good."

After toying with their food, they resumed their gossip about Miss Lacelaw's latest local gaffes and even managed a forced chuckle or two on the journey south. This was just what they both needed to keep their minds off the reality of Jim's life-threatening surgery and the potential result of him "not retaining the full range of mental faculties that he previously enjoyed before his accident".

After Argyll's rural rhythm Neil usually found the lively pace of Edinburgh stimulating, but today he was having a stressful time wrestling with roadworks, diversions and temporary traffic lights. It seemed as if the whole city's road network was being dug up all at the same time. Once-familiar routes were now one-way streets going the wrong way, but eventually, after several wrong turns, Neil's instincts guided them both to the Royal Edinburgh Infirmary.

"The operation took around two hours," the surgeon explained, ushering Ann and Neil into a small anteroom. They sat down, listening intently. "It was of course fairly major surgery but there were no, ah, complications. I'm pleased to say that he has regained consciousness since his operation but you'll probably find him um, groggy with the after-effects of anaesthetic and he may not be completely, ah, with-it." Choosing her words carefully, surgeon McNaught hesitated, searching for the right diplomatic idiom. She went on to emphasise the fact that Jim's "accident was, ah, quite severe" and that they should prepare for Mr McLeod not being "um, fully compus mentis" for a while (or even for the rest of his life) thought Neil. They should also not be surprised if "he, um, didn't fully recognise" them for example. By now Ann and Neil were fully expecting the worst as they shuffled anxiously into the spotless but spartan recovery room. Jim was propped up on several pillows, staring out of the window and looking pale, distant and withdrawn.

"Two visitors for you Mr McLeod," said the Doctor briskly. Jim turned round slowly with a blank expression on his face. He examined them curiously for a few seconds. Neil was the first to break the silence.

"Dad," he said simply.

Jim's face wreathed itself in smiles.

"Why did ye no tell me you were comin'?" he said at last. "I would have worn my best pyjamas instead of this thing – it's no ma style," he added jokingly.

"Dad, you've had us all so worried. How are you doing?"

"Och, no bad son. Is that Ann?" he said turning towards her. "D'ye like my new heidpiece?" he asked, touching a fresh bandage liberally wrapped around his cranium, hiding the scars of the operation. I'm the original Frankenstein now," he joked. "What took ye both so long anyway? I'm needin' a lift home the now."

Ann gave a noise somewhere between relief and disapproval. "You're staying right here Jim McLeod. We've all been worried sick about you."

His father made a half-hearted attempt to protest, talking about catching up with all the things he needed to do at home, but Ann interrupted him abruptly, "You're a piece of work Jim. You know you could be dead from your accident. The doctor said you'd be in here for a week at least and here's where you'll stay."

Neil feared that his father might be a 'difficult' patient, but this was much worse (and much better) than he had expected. He reinforced Ann's message, "Dad, there's no way I'm taking you home 'til the doctors have done all their tests and said that it's OK."

They stayed talking for a while during which time Neil anxiously searched for any signs of impairment to "the full range of mental faculties that he previously enjoyed before his accident" but apart from a slight and hopefully temporary diminution in his father's eyesight, none were evident. With increasing relief Neil and Ann dared to allow themselves the unanticipated and miraculous hope that here was still the old Jim they had known before yesterday's catastrophe. But they were wrong about him not changing. During the next few months he demonstrated that - if anything - he was much more energetic, more 'full of beans' as he might have put it himself, than before his accident. It was as if - jolted into the realisation that life was so precious and short - he had somehow taken on a new lease of it. Whether or not the bang on the head was instrumental wasn't clear but each time Ann and Neil visited Jim during those next three days, rather than the broken old man they kept expecting, they found him increasingly and astonishingly full of joie de vivre.

Neil had intended to wait until his father was fully recovered before surprising him with the news about his impending fatherhood but once he told Jim where he and Ann were staying, the subject of Sophie inevitably cropped up. Talking at length about his fiancée, somewhere in his enthusiasm the news about her pregnancy just slipped out. Jim immediately became animated. "That's wonderful son, she's a lovely lass" and then, after a short pause, "I'm going to be a Grandad!" Then something happened that Ann and Neil least expected. Jim subsided into quiet tearfulness, gently at first and then more fervently. Ann - who had been standing beside his bed all this time - knelt down and took his hands in hers, gently rubbing them, making soothing noises and looking intently at him, her face full of concern. By contrast Neil turned away, confused and unsure of what to do, embarrassed at seeing his father crying.

He walked over to the high hospital window and looked down at the world outside. An ambulance was drawing up at A&E, its blue lights flashing. Neil had always known that his father was more reserved than outgoing, the product of a stricter upbringing in a world where girls dressed nicely and were helpful and boys rough and tumbled, a world in which big boys certainly didn't cry. Over time, he had come to understand that his father's extrovert banter was really a façade, in truth shielding a very private persona. Afterwards, when he cast his mind back to the start of his father's new lease of life in that austere hospital room, Neil would try and rationalise Jim's emotional outpouring. He supposed that it was linked to a realisation by his father that whereas he might easily be dead by now, instead he faced perhaps a decade or more in which his life could be lived to the full. Since the death of his wife Eleanor, Jim's approach to living had had a lacklustre edge to it, a kind of resigned fatalism. It was not exactly pessimistic but in no sense could it be described as optimistic either. Now there was the promise of a new generation of McLeods and a life to live that he had come so close to losing. Whether Jim's tears were tears of loss for the life he had not lived large or whether they were tears of joy for the new chance he had now been given, Neil could only guess, but as the crying continued it seemed as if time itself stood still within that small white hospital room.

Outside, the world still turned and ambulances came and went. Neil observed one stopping and the paramedics wheeling out an old man on a trolley. From a distance Neil couldn't tell whether he was alive or dead. In philosophical mood now, he started musing about his own life and wondered whether, at the end, he would look back with satisfaction and say that he had made a difference, or whether he would look away with resignation and say, "If only". A mother with a boisterous son in tow was heading away from the hospital towards the car park. Released from the confines of visiting hours, the boy was clearly letting off steam, running across the road and capering about enthusiastically. Through the double-glazed window Neil could just hear the mother's raised voice scolding her child. Then he watched her get out her mobile phone, flick back her hair and put the phone to her ear, and in that action there was something that reminded him forcibly of Sophie. His attention was now glued to the mini drama being played out in the car park below, and Neil continued to watch to see how it would unfold. The mother finished her brief call and rounded up her boisterous stray and in doing so her body language told a different story from the previous scolding. Neil watched her pick up the child lovingly, give him a cuddle and secure him into the car seat. Then she turned around and in that instant Neil gave a start, instantly transported back to the Wishing Tree. Even from that distance the woman appeared uncannily like his own angel mother. Neil gripped the radiator with both hands and his heart skipped a beat, forgetting for a moment about his invalid father and longing again for the mother he had hardly known, concentrating his whole attention on her doppelganger in the carpark below. As the woman looked around the hospital grounds it seemed as if some impulse had taken hold of her persona. Instead of walking round to the driver's door she paused, raised her head slowly and looked towards the window from where Neil stared down, transfixed. He yearned to reach out to her and somehow touch her but all he could do was watch helplessly. The woman looked in his direction for several seconds and to Neil it seemed at first as if she was seeing right through him. Then her gaze focussed directly upon him, and the Universe stood still. Seconds later she smiled, got into the car then drove slowly away. And now - despite himself - it was Neil's turn to find himself crying tears of yearning and nostalgia for a dead mother's lost love. His emotion found its release in an outpouring of tears. Behind him Ann could be heard sobbing loudly. Eventually Neil turned back to regard his father and

Ann. Jim's sobbing had subsided and Ann's eyes were red. 'What a trio' Neil thought.

"Look at us all greetin'," he said, wiping his eyes with the back of his sleeve, "You'd have thought that both parents had died or something."

Jim looked at him strangely. After a pause he said, "They say that you dinna dream under anaesthetic but, well, I had this strange dream about your mother Eleanor…" he began, and then his voice trailed off.

"I know Dad. It's OK. Everything's going to be OK."

By now the candles had guttered down to stubs and the fire in the grate had nearly burnt itself out. Only a pile of embers remained, casting a subtle glow across the floor of the library at Arcairn house. Nothing moved in the still of the night. The only discernable sound was the gentle ticking of the grandfather clock in the corner of the room. David and Eleanor were spellbound, hanging onto Ann's every word.

Ann paused for a few moments. Her thoughts dwelt on Jim and how close he had been to dying all those years ago. A tear slid gently down each cheek, although it was too dark in the room for David and Eleanor to notice. Even now Ann still felt Jim's absence acutely. And yet her tears were of gratitude as well as sorrow: gratitude for the new lease of life that Jim had enjoyed after the operation and gratitude for those precious years that she and Jim had enjoyed together.

It was Ann who eventually broke the spell. She sighed, got up slowly, walked over to the log basket and bent down to place some more fuel on the fire. As she straightened up, the flames began to take hold and the shadows retreated for an instant. Eleanor looked up at Ann meaningfully, "So that's how I got my name. Mum never really explained it to me."

"Your mother picked a name for you that would be dear to him - to Neil I mean - and so you were given the name of his mother, the mother he never really knew properly. Of course, before you were born we were all convinced that you were going to be a boy, although Sophie herself was never as quite as sure. When you turned out to be a girl, and after Neil..." Ann hesitated. "But now I'm getting ahead of myself. That's for later." She paused. "Maybe tomorrow," she added with a start, suddenly conscious of the late hour now that the firelight had re-illuminated the library clock face.

"No, no, you can't stop now," Eleanor pleaded. "Go on Ann. Please!" she implored. "What's happened to Nei- to my father?"

"Hang on a minute!" David's tone brought them back to reality. "Darling, have you seen the time?" His voice had an edge of concern to it. "Do we have a key to the front door of the hotel? They'll all have gone to bed by now."

Eleanor looked at her watch. "Gosh, I had no idea."

Ann smiled. "I can make a bed up for you here if you'd prefer to spend the night in your new home?" she offered.

Once again Eleanor and David exchanged a glance, both sharing a telepathic moment. "Thank you very much," they replied in chorus, laughing at their seemingly choreographed reply.

After several minutes of lighting fresh candles, replenishing the log basket and pouring more drinks, the three of them settled down again into the comfortable Chesterfield leather furniture. Ann brushed some imaginary crumbs from her skirt and collected her thoughts, casting her mind back all those years ago. For a while she watched the fire in silence as fresh flames licked around the logs in the grate. David and Eleanor waited patiently for her to start but Ann remained silent, reliving old memories. After a minute Eleanor gently prompted, "What happened to Jim, Ann? You were saying about the hospital. And what about my Mum and Neil?"

"Well, at the time there was a lot of talk about them getting married and of course your mother was pregnant with you, but I don't think that she and Neil were particularly interested in a church wedding. They just wanted some kind of out of doors blessing. But Dorothy and Jane - Sophie's mother - well, they both wanted a conventional wedding. With Sophie expecting you, I think that they were keen to make everything legal and above board, as you might say, what with your mother being Jane's only child. Dorothy helped out course. She may have been thinking about her link to the future I suppose. She told me in Edinburgh about the Montgomery wealth and that her great grandchild would eventually inherit. I suppose that's how you were able to afford Ardcairn?"

"We're both very lucky, we realise that." replied Eleanor. "David and I pooled all our resources - and we borrowed - to buy Ardcairn. After Mum died, we came up to the area on a visit and just happened by chance to see that the Estate was for sale."

"We fell in love with it on a road trip around Scotland." David smiled warmly at his wife. "But that's another story. And I'm lucky that with my software company I can be based anywhere where there's broadband. Even India," he chuckled.

"Well these things are sometimes meant to be," continued Ann, "but it's a miracle that Ardcairn was on the market at all. Miss Lacelaw owned the estate for twenty-five years and although she threatened to sell it from time to time, somehow she never did. I think this place had a stronger hold on her than even she realised. But saying that, she never really settled here properly. As the years went by, she spent more and more time in America. Eventually she stopped coming back altogether. Since then, it's really been just me and the old house, like my mother before me when Colonel Rutherford was alive. Of course, she was the head housekeeper and there were other housemaids to help her. I remember her telling me one time that..."

Eleanor realised that Ann was going off on a tangent and gently interrupted, "Sorry Ann, but you were about to tell us about Jim. And about my Mum and Neil? Did they get married?"

"Ah yes, well. When we got back to Dorothy's house after seeing Jim at the hospital, she was so pleased to see us. She made a great fuss over Sophie and Neil. Of course we were all emotionally drained by then, and... "

Ω❧❈❨

Chapter 19

Later that day Neil and Dorothy left the hospital and made their way across town to Ravelston Avenue. Dorothy was delighted to see Neil again after his first visit all those months ago when he had brought Sophie's ring with him. Sensing that he and Ann were both overwrought after their emotional visit to the hospital, Dorothy tried her best to put them at their ease and make them feel at home. And 'home' was the feeling that did greet Neil as he walked through the front door of The Grange that evening. Less intimidated by its genteel grandeur than before, he revelled in the familiar smell of leather and lilies in the drawing room and the now-familiar pictures adorning its walls. But although he was as pleased to see Dorothy as she was to see him, Neil was more excited at the prospect of seeing Sophie again and as Dorothy showed them around the house he kept glancing surreptitiously at his watch. He would have to wait though: a text arrived from Sophie saying that her train was going to be late. Unlike Neil, Ann was rather less relaxed in Dorothy's presence. Although well used to the opulent environment of a large house, it was as an employee rather than a guest, and she fidgeted a little uncomfortably whilst Dorothy fussed over them both.

When Sophie finally did appear, she looked bright eyed and blooming, relieved to hear about Jim's successful operation. Conscious of Dorothy and Ann's presence, there was a certain restraint to the embrace that she gave Neil, but the two older women could sense the young lovers' mutual affection clearly enough. Tactfully they withdrew, leaving the couple to 'unpack and catch up' whilst they took tea in the garden. And - just as

Neil had predicted - Ann soon warmed to Dorothy, her previous worries proving groundless as she sat in the garden gazebo alongside her host, sipping Earl Grey tea in the early spring sunshine. As they got to know one another better their conversation became less stilted, Ann telling Dorothy about her childhood in Argyll and the vagaries of the various owners of Ardcairn, Dorothy recalling stories of Sophie as a child: her tomboy scrapes, her diabetes and her passion for painting. That led the conversation on to Sir Charles and the talk became more serious but no less cheerful. By her second cup of tea Ann knew that she was going to enjoy her brief stay with Dorothy and was already starting to harbour mixed feelings about having to leave the following evening, but she appreciated Jim's need to recuperate properly before returning to Argyll.

Their conversation was interrupted by the arrival of Neil and Sophie looking rather flushed, arm in arm, each clasping a mug of tea with their free hand. Sophie appeared radiant although her hair was a little tousled, whilst Neil's face registered equal measures of happiness and sheepishness. Tactfully avoiding the question of what had taken them so long to unpack, Dorothy waved them over and plied them with questions about St Andrews and Sophie's studies and about Neil's forestry business. At one point in his explanation he made an innocent remark about his plans to branch out into arboriculture, failing to see the pun and becoming self-conscious at the general mirth and teasing that ensued. Neil took his business very seriously. Once the joke had been pointed out, and many other gratuitous quips thrown in by Sophie about 'getting to the root of things' and the like, with his feathers thoroughly ruffled, it took him a little while to regain his sense of humour.

Dorothy eventually rescued him, stating, "Neil, I have one or two trees in the garden that I'd like you to look at. They're getting quite big now and I think it's time they had some – what's the expression? Oh yes, surgery." Neil agreed to examine them but at the word surgery thoughts of his father flooded into his head again and the conversation once more drifted towards to Jim, his accident and the extraordinary signs of early recovery. "It seems quite miraculous that he should be so compos mentis after his operation," commented Dorothy innocently. Ann and Neil exchanged a meaningful glance but neither said anything, beyond agreeing with Dorothy that, "It had indeed been a miracle."

"Now, speaking of miracles, let's look at this young granddaughter of mine," declared Dorothy, making Sophie sit down beside her as if she were still a young girl. "It only seems like yesterday that you were climbing these trees," she added, gesturing to the garden. "I still can't believe that you're going to be a mother soon." Then her tone became more moralising, "I hope you two are going to show some sense of propriety and get married? When *are* you intending to tie the knot anyway?" she added, as Sophie and Neil shifted a little uncomfortably in their chairs.

"We're going to do something about it once my exams are out of the way Dee," said Sophie, clearly dissembling.

"Now I know that marriage is out of fashion these days, but I will help you organise an Edinburgh wedding if you wish. I know the vicar of the Church of the Good Shepherd very well and of course it's just around the corner. You could have the reception here if you wanted? That could be my wedding present to you. Naturally you will receive something rather more substantial when I shuffle off this mortal coil, Sophie."

Sophie admonished her. "Don't be so morbid Dee. Anyway, Neil's going to keep me in the manner to which I'm accustomed. Aren't you?" she teased. Then she added, "But thank you all the same" and sat on the floor beside her grandmother.

For a while the conversation revolved around the logistics of an Edinburgh wedding. Although Sophie and Neil harboured thoughts of getting married at 'their' Ardcairn tree they realised that for many members of Sophie's family that scenario would be impractical. It was a tempting proposition though, knowing that the coast would be clear with Miss Lacelaw being in the States that autumn. However, in the end they decided that the best thing would be to have a summer wedding in Edinburgh and an autumn ceremony of blessing in Argyll and before they had time to change their minds Dorothy telephoned the vicar and fixed up an appointment for the following afternoon. After that she took them on a detailed tour of her surprisingly large garden, amazing Neil with the extent of her botanical knowledge. Neil listened carefully to what she had to say, learning a great deal about trees that he didn't know. He was secretly pleased when he was able to enlighten her once or twice with a few tree facts of his own.

Later that evening he telephoned the hospital and spoke to the same Doctor McNaught who had previously shown such restraint and diplomacy in her choice of words. This time she was noticeably less inhibited, informing Neil that Jim was doing "extremely well" and that if he continued to recover so quickly, he could be allowed to recuperate at home in "oh, four or five days". When Neil spoke to his father on his bedside phone, Jim insisted that he would be fine that evening without receiving visitors and was sleepy in any case and would look forward to seeing him and Ann tomorrow. So instead of battling with the

Edinburgh traffic again, Neil helped Sophie gather herbs from the garden whilst Dorothy and Ann prepared dinner together.

During a convivial evening the four of them enjoyed the last of some vintage champagne from a once substantial collection that Sir Charles had laid down years ago. In deference to Dorothy, Neil had shown a polite reluctance to open a bottle, but Dorothy insisted, saying that she "hardly ever entertained these days". She made a dual toast, "to Jim's successful recovery and my impending great grandmother-hood," adding that "it would be a kindness to finish it", the 'it' of course being the champagne. Then she proposed a toast to "absent friends" remarking - rather pointedly - that it was a "pity that my daughter-in-law was too busy this evening". Taking her pregnancy and diabetes seriously, Sophie only took the odd sip from Neil's glass. After Dorothy had embarrassed Sophie with stories about her childhood and Ann had reciprocated in Neil's case, the talk eventually turned to Sophie and Neil and their future plans together, and the baby which would doubtless change their lives completely.

Before they all went to bed Dorothy initiated Neil and Sophie into the 'ring trick'. Creating an atmosphere of intrigue and mystery she made Neil pluck out one of Sophie's hairs and tie an end around her signet ring. "Usually it's a wedding ring," Dorothy explained pointedly, "but I suppose Sophie's wayward signet ring will do." All four watched closely as Neil was made to dangle the ring from its slender hair cord over Sophie's abdomen. No-one was more surprised than he when the ring twitched violently and started to move about in vigorous circles. Dorothy and Ann – who had seen this phenomenon before – compared notes on the direction of swing and both agreed that the child would be a boy, much to Neil and Sophie's scepticism.

But this mini drama was brought to an abrupt halt by the sound of the telephone ringing. All repartee ceased abruptly as thoughts of Jim and hospital and emergency complications sprang to mind, but to their somewhat mixed relief, the caller turned out to be Jane. "Let me speak to Sophie please Dorothy," she said, not offering any apology as to the lateness of the hour. "Now, Sophie" she went on sarcastically, "when you do manage to find a break in your hectic revision schedule tomorrow, I want you to bring the father of your child over to meet me."

"He's got a name mum."

"You've named your baby already?" The voice at the other end of the phone sounded incredulous.

"Yes… well no actually, but we think it's going to be a boy."

"You *think*?"

"Well, you see we did this kind of ring thing and what you do is, you…" Her explanation was cut short.

"What about your father's name: Thomas," interrupted her mother abruptly.

"Yes Mum but we really don't…."

"Now *he* would know what the best thing would be for you if he were still on this earth. You know I really fail to see how you're going to be able to have a baby and continue your studies and anyway, what about your diabetes?"

Sophie rolled her eyes at Neil. Her mother was onto her favourite hobbyhorse – nagging.

It was much later, after Ann and Neil had helped Dorothy to wash up and put away the dinner plates and Ann and Dorothy had slipped off to bed, that Sophie eventually came off the phone and said to Neil. "Meeting with Mum tomorrow. After we've visited your dad. I told her about the Edinburgh wedding thing. No pressure, but she's starting to draw up a guest list already."

Neil sighed, "Oh God! Why don't we just let her and Dorothy get on with it. We can concentrate on organising an Ardcairn service."

"Mmm. You know that Dorothy's put you in the spare room next to mine, at the back of the house?"

"Sho, Moneypenny, your plache or mine?" said his Sean Connery bedroom voice suggestively.

"Forget it Bond, the bed squeaks like a mouse on speed."

* * *

But at some stage in the middle of the night it was discovered that the solid oak floor of the rear bedrooms at number five Ravelston Avenue was not only sturdy, but gratifyingly silent.

Chapter 20

After that year's dry spring, late June on Scotland's west coast was reverting to type. Constant soft drizzle and early summer warmth had combined to create a Highland hothouse and now the vegetation was exploding into what Dorothy would have described as "a riot of green". Everywhere, trees, shrubs and bushes were bursting forth in another season's growth spurt for which Argyll is renowned. With winter dormancy now a distant memory, Ardcairn's arboreal giants were thrusting upwards and outwards again, driven by the longer days and the warmer temperatures. Tourists driving along Argyll's roads would point animatedly to the rhododendrons that lined the Atlantic oakwoods and commercial spruce forests, admiring their colourful display of purple flowers. Neil's view was rather more prosaic. Observing that these bushy weeds increased their forest foothold with every year that passed, he saw - not a pretty purple addition to Argyll's flora - but an alien invader, smothering the forest floor and turning commercial plantations into uneconomic liabilities. But as well as cursing the well-meaning landowners who had originally introduced this Asian weed, Neil was aware that cutting unwanted 'rhody' growth provided a useful addition to his core forestry business. And it also conferred the advantage of being never-ending work, "like painting the Forth Rail Bridge" he had once remarked to Duncan. For no sooner had the thick stems been cut or flailed than they sprang up again, gathering strength for their next ecological onslaught.

Since their Edinburgh interlude Sophie and Neil had spent far less time together than they would have wished, and that fact was getting them both down. Neil returned home to Taynuilt late one night having enjoyed a precious weekend with Sophie at St Andrews, vicariously living the life of a university student. To mark the occasion Sophie had thrown a small engagement party. She invited her close friends but with her pregnancy and the exams looming, the occasion had, of necessity, been muted. Neil was pleased to see Annabelle again and some other familiar faces as well, but he was all too aware of the brevity of time. Sunday evening came around much, much too quickly. So it was not surprising that, driving through the Argyll wetness the following morning and lamenting the inexorable growth of 'rhodies' he was feeling rather sorry for himself. Work was a good antidote to such feelings however, so whilst Sophie was throwing herself into exam revision nearly two hundred miles away, Neil was driving to a business meeting at Oban, with Robbie accompanying him as usual. Also beside him - for a change - was Jim. Though only recently discharged from Edinburgh Infirmary and still wearing an impressive head bandage, he was surprisingly full of vitality. Today he was joining Neil on his latest venture - to complete the acquisition of a small arboricultural business in Oban, a business that spent a lot of its time cutting and spraying *Rhododendron ponticum* and undertaking tree surgery for the 'good and the great' in the Lorn area. The boss of 'Oban Tree Amigos' had always preferred the hands-on side of work to the admin side and generously (or foolishly) under-charged customers that he knew well (which happened to be most of them). Finding the financial side of his operation much tougher than he had imagined, he had approached Neil with a view to becoming a subsidiary of 'McLeod Forestry', thereby maintaining some autonomy and continuing to do the practical stuff, but within the comfort and safety net of a larger outfit.

The wipers steadily flip-flopped Argyll's persistent raindrops off the windscreen. Neil was thinking about his father's collapse and the probability that in some measure, Jim's accident may have been due to his intense dedication and long hours spent in the workshop helping his son grow his business. A while ago Neil had decided that the best way to avoid a repeat of the accident - and also to let Jim save face - was to move the McLeod Forestry machinery and tool shop up to the barn at Lonan Farm and employ a full-time mechanic there. Neil could make the necessary arrangements before he moved into the Farm himself. That would shift the centre of gravity away from Cedar Cottage and remove the excuse for Jim to spend so much time fixing and servicing the Company's machines.

"But you ken all those hospital tests showed nothing wrong wi' me," emphasised Jim for the second time that morning, as the car approached Oban.

"I know Dad. I just think you were overdoing it. You *are* supposed to be retired after all," reproached Neil.

"I'm no a one for sitting around on my bahookie and vegetatin'," retorted Jim. "I need to keep busy. Anyway, *you* canna talk. Look at ye creeping back from St Andrews like a hiedless horse at God only knows what time last night, and then up wi' the sparrows this mornin'."

Neil couldn't disagree with that, but he wouldn't be deflected from his decision. "It's not that your work isn't really helpful to the business Dad," he said, "but I don't want you being under so much pressure. The business can afford a mechanic. And anyway, when I move out to Lonan Farm the big machines will need serviced there. You know Craig's brother stays close. He's well qualified and seems keen and I reckon he's up to it. I'm going to offer the job to him on a trial basis. And you can always come over from time to time and help out."

Although his father tried to deflect him, Neil would not be moved. But as they passed the entrance to Ardcairn, he did eventually capitulate, "OK, what if you continued to look after the chainsaws? That's no small task."

Although he continued to go through the motions of protesting, deep down Jim knew that Neil was probably right. He had been reflecting on his son's business success for some time now, for since its modest beginnings the enterprise had come a long way, thanks to Neil's natural flair and aptitude. Jim admired his success and - if he was honest to himself - he was also a little envious. Neil enjoyed a lifestyle that the young men of Jim's own generation could only ever dream of. Part of Jim's motivation for helping Neil out was the vicarious buzz of the enterprise culture that he himself had never enjoyed. He had helped his son to get started but now - if he was honest to himself - his work was done: the business had grown to the point where it had become both self-sufficient and able to expand without him. In any case he had his own reasons for wanting to ease off his workload and by the time they reached Oban, Jim agreed with Neil's proposal to wind down his input, albeit putting up some show of resistance. As they drew up to a large garden on the northern edge of town, they spotted the white van with 'Oban Tree Amigos' emblazoned on the side and four men lopping the branches of a sycamore tree. Jim's sense of humour returned and he said in an Irish accent, "So if it's tree amigos, why are there four of them?"

Neil laughed as he got out of the Landrover. "Maybe they couldn't count. That's why their figures are in such a mess."

The boss of Oban Tree Amigos was out of sight up the largest of the sycamore trees. From somewhere in its canopy, he shouted down that he would "no be long" and at that moment the owner of the house emerged from the front door carrying four mugs of coffee. Even without the purple cope Neil recognised the Bishop at once.

"Good morning. I'm sure I recognise you?" The Bishop put it as a rhetorical question, setting down the tray of mugs and glancing at the McLeod Forestry sign on the side of the Landrover. A look of recognition crossed his face and he half smiled. "Ah yes, I remember now, Neil, isn't it? This year's Hogmanay entertainment. Certainly gave us all something to remember. Quite livened up the evening," he beamed.

Neil looked sheepish, not quite knowing quite how to treat this comment. "Thank you, sir, reverend: sorry, I'm not sure what to call you."

"Well, if you're being terribly formal it's your Grace, but you can call me Bill," he said with a kindly twinkle in his eye.

Neil grinned and reminded the Bishop of the occasion of his own first Oban Ball several years ago and how pleased he had been to have been helped by the Bishop's dance set through some of the more obscure reels.

"Now, Neil, please tell me that you're still with that young lady you left with after that, ah, kerfuffle," he said diplomatically.

"Yes your Grace, Bill. In fact if it's alright with you, I'd like to ask you something…" Their conversation was drowned by the sound of a chainsaw firing up somewhere in the branches overhead and the Bishop gestured to Neil to move around the side of the house in order to communicate better.

An hour later, the various legal transfer forms having been signed, Jim and Neil shook hands with the four tree amigos and left them to complete their chipping and tidying up operations. Uncharacteristically Jim suggested that he and Neil should celebrate by having lunch out in Oban. Invariably used to eating a simple lunchtime piece prepared the night before, they both felt rather decadent at this idea, but it seemed an appropriate way to celebrate Jim's steady recovery and the incorporation of 'Tree Amigos' into 'McLeod Forestry'. Having found a suitable restaurant and been shown a table in a quiet corner, Neil remembered his inadvertent pun at Dorothy's and started the conversation by joking that he would have to change the name of the company now that they had an 'arboricultural branch'. "How does 'McLeod Trees' sound to you, Dad?" he asked Jim.

But his father wasn't giving him his undivided attention: he was wrestling with a rather more important matter of his own. Uncharacteristically serious for a moment he put down his menu and turned to Neil. "Son, there's something I've been wanting to tell ye," he began.

Neil looked up from his own menu and regarded his father attentively.

"It's like this…" continued Jim. Neil waited for him to form the right words.

"You see, ever since your mother Eleanor died, well, it's no been the best of time for me. Ann and I… well you ken we've been close this past wee while and since the accident we were both thinkin' that, well life is short and all…"

"Dad, are you telling me what I think you're telling me?" said Neil, his face starting to break out into a grin.

"Aye son. Ann and me…we've decided tae tie the knot. Looks like it'll be two McLeod weddings this summer."

"That's fantastic news!" exclaimed Neil "This calls for a toast," and he summoned the waiter over.

"Ye ken I'm no supposed to be drinking the now, wi me in ma current state."

But Neil would not be deterred and ordered a half bottle of champagne. They waited while the waiter went through the motions of pouring two glasses.

"Here's to you two and a long and happy life together," toasted Neil.

"And here's to Ann – and absent friends," rejoined his father.

"And the future of McLeod Forestry," added Neil.

They raised their glasses and drank. Life was good and there was everything to look forward to.

Chapter 21

With the stress of her last exam behind her, Sophie was like a caged bird released. Neil had just collected her from Taynuilt station and they were driving the short distance to Lonan Farm for the start of their summer together. Robbie was clearly excited at seeing his master's friend again. He knew that she was always good to him, sometimes spoiling him with the odd snack when master wasn't looking and often giving him walkies when Neil was busy at work. Robbie was starting to become familiar with the sights and sounds and smells of Lonan Farm. For the last few days Neil had been moving his stuff in and piling supplies of decorating equipment into one of the downstairs rooms. He had also installed a new double bed upstairs but when Robbie had tried to claim it as mutual territory Neil had pushed him off, giving him the consolation prize of a new dog bed downstairs.

"I can't wait to get stuck in to making Lonan ours," Sophie said. It's going to be a fantastic summer. And the wedding in August. Oh Neil," she enthused, one hand on his thigh and the other on Robbie's head. "I'm so happy." His tail wagging furiously, Robbie tried to ingratiate his way into the front seat but despite Sophie's pleading, Neil wasn't having any. As Neil stopped for Sophie to open the farm gate the collie looked at her hopefully. "Don't worry Robbie, we'll take you for walkies soon," she said and at those words the collie pricked up his ears and wagged his tail even harder.

"First things first," announced Neil as he drew into the farmyard. Before Sophie could make a move he opened the passenger door, grabbed her, bundled her up and swept her over the threshold. "Be it ever so humble…" he began, but Sophie's kiss interrupted any further conversation.

Much later, after Robbie had given up all hope of exercise, the two lovers surprised him by whisking him off on a tour of the farm boundary. Grabbing a spade and a bag, Neil suggested to Sophie that they make an inspection of the farmland that had accompanied the sale of the house. They started by beating the bounds to where the enclosed inby fields gave way to rougher moorland. As they walked, Neil outlined his plans for improving the land. He explained how he was going to apply for a grant from the Forestry Commission in order to plant some more shelterbelts to protect the farm from easterly winds and regenerate the native birch and oak remnants that straggled alongside the small hill burns. They climbed over the stock fence to join a rough track that threaded up the hill above the farmhouse. Neil expounded on the theory that it had once been an old drove road, used in the past by local farmers and cattle traders to take their beasts on the long journey southwards to the markets of the Central Belt and long before that, that the track had been an ancient route into west Argyll. Some of the older local folk still referred to it as the 'Road to the Isles'. Nowadays it wasn't much used by hikers and climbers since it didn't form a designated trail or a Munro mountain access track, but the occasional walker could be seen exploring the area.

Sophie and Neil climbed up past the farm boundary towards the top of the hill. From there they admired the striking views that swept down towards Loch Etive, the Lorn Peninsula and the sea. Somewhere below them, nestled within a fold in the landscape, lay Ardcairn Estate and 'their' tree now hidden from view. The two lovers discussed for a while how they might contrive a service of blessing there at Ardcairn after the Edinburgh wedding.

"Now, speaking of blessings," said Neil changing the subject, "there's a wee planting ceremony we should do." He explained to Sophie about taking the Wishing Tree cuttings and how - contrary to his expectations - they had rooted successfully and so he had transferred them into larger pots. "This is an ideal site," he explained pointing to a sheltered spot not far from a burn. I'll come up later in the Landrover and put a wee fence around it." And so it was that summer evening that a living scion of the dying Wishing Tree was lovingly planted on a different Argyll hillside by Neil and Sophie and, later that same day, enclosed by a stockproof fence to give protection from the mouths of hungry sheep and deer.

A couple of days later the two lovers were sitting in the newly decorated kitchen of Lonan Farm, Neil drinking coffee, Sophie sipping hot water, and both of them looking at a calendar and discussing the coming months. "So it's going to be a busy year then, what with our wedding in Edinburgh next month, and then your Dad and Ann's wedding later this year, and maybe our service of blessing in September, if you can persuade the Bishop of Argyll to do the honours, that is."

"Well he seems up for it. And let's not forget the baby under construction either."

Sophie patted her bump, just discernible now. "Yeah, Thomas or whatever we're going to call him – or her," she added quickly. "Mid-December. Which reminds me, I'm supposed to make an appointment for an ultrasound scan at the hospital. Any evening next week OK?"

"Sure," replied Neil absent-mindedly, putting his hands alongside Sophie's and gradually slipping them down her bulge.

"Oi, keep your hands to yourself!" exclaimed Sophie.

"You know I can't help it," he replied, "Seeing you pregnant makes me so horny."

"You wait 'til my breasts get bigger" she replied. "You won't be able to keep your hands off me then."

"I can't keep my hands off you now," he retorted as he started fumbling with her bra strap. Robbie, knowing that this was the prelude to being completely ignored for at least half an hour, sighed heavily, lowered his head onto his front paws and assumed the epitome of doggie martyrdom. With only Neil around, he had been conditioned to expect a morning constitutional but today was starting to look like a dead loss on the walkies front…

Chapter 22

"Do you want the good news or the bad news?"

The following week Neil could be seen pacing up and down the Craignure ferry terminal on Mull, his mobile phone glued to his ear. His restless toing and froing was in stark contrast to the relaxed demeanour of other folk waiting in the afternoon sunshine for the Oban ferry, for at this time of the year most of the passengers were either holidaymakers admiring the view or locals reading their newspapers. Those few tourists who did notice Neil mistook his impatient pacing as a state of excitement, but in truth he was anxious, apprehensive and mostly annoyed that the usually punctual ferry was running so late.

"Give me the bad news," said Sophie.

"OK, the bad news is that I may be late," he announced. "They're sending a replacement ferry and it should be here in," - he checked his watch - "about half an hour." He listened to his fiancée's response and then continued "Look Soph, you go on. I'll catch you up at the hospital just as soon as Calmac get me out of here."

* * *

On this occasion his fretting wasn't connected with work. In truth, Neil had spent a very enjoyable day on Mull in the company of an enthusiastic London merchant banker, inspecting the latter's portfolio of commercial woodlands. That morning he had collected his client from a chartered flight at the small airstrip on the island's east coast. From there they had spent an enjoyable, informative and unusually sunny day driving around the island, inspecting one plantation after another. Neil's enthusiasm - not to mention his extensive knowledge of forestry - had rubbed off on the urbane Londoner whose day away from his city desk had been equally enjoyable but much more educational. The banker had shown an inexhaustible interest in his forestry investment and had exploited the opportunity to pick Neil's brains. They had spent much of the day discussing soil types and drainage, species choice and silvicultural systems, growth rates and yield classes, and the general state of the timber market. Neil's client knew that impressive growth rates were achievable on Mull but had not realised that Sitka spruce could reach commercial maturity in only thirty-five years. As they criss-crossed the island Neil explained about the use of selected provenances of Sitka, the species' love of the Gulf Stream climate, the fertile brown earth soils common on the island and the resulting rapid growth rates. He had then gone on to explain about the potential perils of windthrow, insects, deer damage and fire. So passionate had Neil been about forestry, and so intently had his client listened, that both of them lost track of time. After finishing their inspection of the plantations it was mid afternoon and lunchtime had somehow passed them by. So they sat beside the landing strip in the summer sunshine eating sandwiches and drinking real coffee - a thoughtful gesture arranged by Sophie that morning - and waited for the chartered Cessna to return. Whether it was the sunny weather or simply the warmth of Neil's empathy, in the end his city client had agreed much more advantageous terms and conditions terms than Neil could have dared to hope for.

After waving his client off, Neil began to appreciate with rising excitement that McLeod Forestry was now in possession of a long-term contract to carry out a significant programme of forest management on Mull. He was pleased not only with the agreed terms of the contract but also by the fact that the business now had enough work ahead of it to support a further expansion. This agreement would give him leverage to extend his bank loan in order to expand the growing fleet of forestry machines.

Neil's network of contacts extended to several potential sub-contractors on the island, some of them fellow ex High School pupils who had become bored sitting around waiting for life to happen to them and had started to dabble in the world of forestry. He knew that they weren't always the most motivated bunch in the world but at least they were 'machine savvy' and, importantly, they were tied to the island by working wives. Outside the tourist season, finding work on Mull was often difficult and they would be glad of some steady seasonal employment. Sure, they would need some skills training but there were grants available and experience would come with time. Neil smiled. He could lease some new machines and bring the older ones over to the island. 'That would please Craig,' he thought. Craig was always going on at Neil to update his machinery. Neil knew that operating off the mainland would carry its own set of problems and additional costs, but the sawlog market was on the up and he calculated that even under the worst-case scenario he should be able to make a sizeable surplus given the scale of the programme ahead of him.

Having waved the Cessna off and arrived at the ferry terminal in good time, all in all Neil should have been happy, but he wasn't. Although excited at the Mull contract, he was also frustrated: the Oban ferry was very late, Sophie was due a scan at the hospital that evening and it was now touch and go as to whether he would get back in time to join her for her appointment.

* * *

"And what's the good news?" asked Sophie.

She listened while Neil gave an explanation of his day with the rich client and how McLeod Forestry was now "poised to expand its offshore operations." Resisting the temptation to tease him about his plans for global expansion, she made encouraging noises whilst Neil spelt out what the expansion could mean for the business. Sophie knew how important this contract was to Neil but she also knew how much he'd been looking forward to seeing the scan of the baby. So when he started railing against the vagaries of Calmac she tried to calm him down. "Not to worry darling. I'll head over to the hospital soon and expect you when I see you. Alright. Love you," and she folded up her mobile phone and put it in her bag. Neil or no Neil she would have to keep her engagement: it was not easy rescheduling hospital appointments at this time of the year with so many tourists swelling the usual admission statistics and waiting times. When Neil had dropped her off in Oban that morning on his way to catch the Mull ferry Sophie had looked forward to the prospect of a day's shopping for supplies: food, furniture, wallpaper and plenty of paint. Since settling in at Lonan Farm she had been enjoying the creative process of putting her mark on the farmhouse, gradually transforming what had once been a run-down and neglected interior into a comfortable and presentable home. By now the builders had done most of the heavy work, knocking down some walls, adding a couple of upstairs windows and constructing a small building at the rear of the farmhouse to house a woodchip boiler that Neil had recently ordered. The skill now lay in choosing just the right combination of colours, fabrics and finishes to make Lonan farmhouse more than the sum of its parts and Sophie was confident about that and about it making their house a home.

Her appointment for an ultrasound scan at Oban hospital had been scheduled for early evening and planned around the Calmac timetable, but the MV 'Lord of the Isles' ferry breakdown had thrown those plans into disarray. After putting her phone back in her bag Sophie glanced at her watch: without Neil to collect her it was probably time she should be going. She could walk from town to the hospital and with luck he would arrive in time to catch the scan, collect the supplies and take her home.

Some minutes later, as she looked up at the now familiar hospital entrance Sophie thought back to the last time she had been in there: the saintly taxi driver Malcolm, the objectionable Morag and the reassuring doctor Liston. She still treasured the painting of Loch Etive that she had almost completed on that fateful day in which Neil had entered her life. Occasionally she would take it out of its hiding place in her folio of work and examine it. Even she had to admit to herself that despite some raindrop streaks it still remained one of her most accomplished watercolours. She sometimes contemplated finishing it - it wouldn't take her long - but for some reason that she couldn't quite put her finger on, she never did.

There was only one concern nagging at Sophie that day - the dread of bumping into Morag Govan at Oban General. It wasn't that she worried about any residual feelings that Neil might still have for Morag. She knew him well enough to know that as far as he was concerned Morag was genuinely in the past. It was just that she was a part of his history and therefore an unwelcome complication. Sophie would rather keep things simple and not deal with her at all. So it was with some trepidation that she entered the waiting room shortly after the hospital receptionist had informed her that, "a nurse will be along to see you soon Miss Montgomery."

As she took a seat, Sophie briefly wondered whether she should have registered herself under the name of McLeod, which was, after all, a common local name. The name Montgomery might attract the unwanted attention of a certain nurse and she could do without that. But seconds later her worst fears materialised. Idly flipping through the pages of a magazine, Sophie was waiting to be summoned when an all-too-familiar voice broke the silence with a harsh "Ms Montgomery?" and there before her was the unmistakable figure of nurse Govan scrutinising her latest patient censoriously. "Ah yes," she announced. "I wondered when we might be seeing you here." Sophie remained silent, biting her lip whilst Morag made a show of flipping through her case notes. "So, you're here for an ultrasound scan. I won't ask who's the father," she snapped contemptuously.

"Look, if this is difficult for you perhaps there's someone else who can see me?" responded Sophie.

Morag pointedly ignored her question. "How much water have you drunk. Fluid intake?"

"Uh, about a pint," Sophie replied, gathering all her things together in a hurry and following the disappearing figure of nurse Govan down a corridor. This hospital was clearly Morag's domain and there was no doubting as to who was in control of the situation here.

"You'll need to drink more. The scanner won't work properly otherwise."

"But…"

"No 'buts'. You'll have to drink this," ordered Morag, dismissing Sophie's protests. She stopped at a water fountain, filled a plastic cup brim full and thrust it towards Sophie. "I'll be back in ten minutes. Wait here," she said over her shoulder gesturing to a nearby consulting room.

Sophie groaned inwardly. She was already bursting for a pee and the idea of drinking more was barely thinkable but what else could she do? 'Was Morag telling the truth?' she wondered. She drank the cupful and then, in a supreme effort of mind over matter, started to pace up and down the room trying not to think about going to the ladies.

It seemed like an age to Sophie before nurse Govan returned. Morag had actually been in the canteen drinking a cup of tea herself and enjoying the masochistic knowledge that Ms Montbloodygomery's bladder was doubtless in distress by now. 'Well she deserves it' thought Morag, 'It's time to make that little bitch suffer for a change.' Returning to find Sophie agitatedly pacing the small consulting room, Morag barked dismissively "Lie down please!"

"Look, I know this isn't…" began Sophie.

"Lie down please!" repeated Morag, practically thrusting Sophie onto the examination trolley and reaching for the tube of gel used to make a connection between uterus and scanning probe. She always warned first time mothers-to-be about this gelatinous substance. If you weren't used to it, was cold – very cold. Not having been warned, Sophie wasn't expecting it and gave a gasp when Morag squirted a liberal supply onto her bare midriff. She almost pissed herself: it took all her concentration not to.

"Not expecting that?" taunted Morag, "well I dare say there'll be more pain when your time comes."

Once again Sophie bit her lip. She had had just about enough. But just as she was going to remonstrate with Morag and insist that she be seen by another nurse, the screen changed from a uniformly grey fuzz, suddenly clearing to reveal the recognisable form of a tiny embryo. Sophie gasped. All thoughts of aching bladder and frozen abdomen now forgotten, she gazed at the precious image of a growing baby there on the monitor: her baby, Neil's baby, their baby.

Morag, offensively loquacious up until that moment, also fell suddenly silent. It was as if the TV screen had become a physical link to the unborn child. Here was an image expressing the result of love between a man and a woman, between Sophie and Neil, between Sophie and *her* - Morag's - Neil. Morag's hand started to shake as she gazed at the monitor in denial. Her hand faltered. She could have - she *should* have - been the mother of Neil's child. This should have been *her* baby. The blood drained from her face. Two things then happened simultaneously. Morag fainted, dropping the scanner onto the floor, and Sophie peed herself. The urine flowed in a torrent off the bed towards the prone figure of Nurse Campbell below.

At that moment the door opened and in walked Doctor Liston. He quickly rushed over to the collapsed figure of Morag and picked her up, sitting her on a chair and putting her head below her knees. Morag said faintly "I dinna feel too well Doctor Liston. I have to… get some fresh air."

He looked at the mess on the floor. "Not to worry," he said reassuringly, "these things happen," but whether this was directed to Morag or Sophie wasn't clear. "I can take over now," he added, but Morag was stumbling her way out of the door already, helped by the arrival of another nurse. Torn between helping the Nurse Govan and helping the patient, in the end, Doctor Liston turned towards the patient lying before him in a considerable state of dampness and embarrassment. "Not to worry," he reassured her. These things happen all the time. Now, it's Montgomery, isn't it?" he said, glancing at her case notes, "Ah yes, Sophie Montgomery. I've got a feeling we've met before, is that right?"

Sophie looked up at his comforting face and said, "Well yes – and no. I was in here briefly a while ago. I had a diabetic… incident."

"Of course, I remember you now," he smiled, "the scarlet pimpernel."

"The what?"

"You know: they search her here, they search her there, they search her everywhere. Turned out you were on a train halfway to Edinburgh," he laughed, whilst Sophie's features became, if anything, even more uncomfortable. "Congratulations on your forthcoming baby by the way. Don't worry, we'll get you cleaned up in a jiffy. Do you want to know if it's going to be a boy or a girl?"

"But I thought… the scanner…" Sophie tried to hide her embarrassment.

"No need to worry," he reassured her, realising the reason behind her awkwardness. This is a brand-new machine; the latest generation of scanners. Gives you clear images without the mother's bladder needing to be too full."

"Oh, I see," replied Sophie slowly. She paused. "Yes please Doctor Liston," she said, "I would like to know."

"Oh, just call me Philip," he replied. "We like to keep things informal here and no doubt we'll be seeing you again to check up on the baby's progress?" he asked, manipulating the scanner and examining the screen intently. "Now, about… the… gender…"

Only a few metres away but in reality a lifetime removed, Morag sat on the closed lid of the staff toilet, sobbing uncontrollably.

Chapter 23

"Oh God!". Neil groaned, woken by a faint scratching at the bedroom door. "Go away!" Outside, a wagging tail could be heard brushing enthusiastically against the carpet of the upstairs landing.

* * *

Like the rest of that summer's events, the Edinburgh wedding came and went in a flash. One minute Neil and Sophie had walked up the aisle of the Church of the Good Shepherd as Mr McLeod and Miss Montgomery and the next they were a married couple, surrounded by a sea of guests. Brushing aside Neil's suggestion that he buy her a new wedding ring, all Sophie wanted to adorn her finger was her beloved signet ring. To her it symbolised a link with the past as a connection with her Grandfather Charles, a link to Neil and the present, and a link to the future - the Tree of Life motif. Neil had eventually given in to her wish but insisted that as he would not be buying her a ring, he would pay for it to be reduced to the correct size. He sealed their marriage by slipping the ring on to Sophie's wedding finger for the third time since they had met. This time it finally felt snug, secure and permanent.

With the service over, they emerged into the bright sunlight outside the church. Several curious passers-by stopped and stared at the couple as they held hands, kissed and went through the ritual of posing for the cameras. For Neil these moments passed in a surreal flurry of new faces and a blur of names and introductions. Southern Scots accents, most of them belonging to Montgomery accountants, lawyers and doctors, contrasted with the softer Highland lilt of assorted McLeods. Sophie's relatives were generous of spirit towards Neil if not generous in largesse, showering the couple with much confetti but not much in the way of wedding presents. Neil supposed that their personal canniness with the bawbees may have explained the array of expensive cars lining the roads around The Grange that day.

Most of the older male Montgomery guests came up to Neil at some time or another during the reception to proffer their congratulations, clap him on the back and tell him that he was "a very lucky young man". Neil responded graciously, giving the sincerity of those well wishers the benefit of the doubt. But the womenfolk were sometimes rather catty and with Sophie's mother Jane he was aware of a certain lingering tension and coolness that tended to surface at times of stress - like the marriage of her daughter for example. But, as only to be expected, Jane's reserve was in stark contrast to Dorothy's warmth and generosity. True to her word she had funded the lavish reception herself, pulling out all the stops and making the place worthy of royalty, providing a marquee and huge sprays of lilies and ordering catering fit for a King. Looking almost as pleased as the newly-marrieds themselves, she showed off Neil to everyone, almost as if he were her own grandson, which, in a sense, he now was.

However, amongst Sophie's friends were a few young men of Neil's age who were less than happy at having lost the prospect of marrying into Montgomery wealth. Envious of Neil as the chosen one who would forever enjoy the pleasure of Sophie's beautiful body (not to mention her forthcoming inheritance) they united in their resentment, retreating into a seditious cluster, generally lurking about and casting aspersions about 'woodcutter', 'lumberjack' and 'Sophie marrying beneath her'. If Neil did occasionally overhear these barbed remarks, he took it all on the chin. His was the prize and he loved Sophie and that was all that mattered to him. Remembering the very first words that Dorothy had said to him - "Are you another of those exasperating boys who are always pestering her?" Neil grinned at the nay-sayers like a Cheshire cat, which annoyed them even more. Neither Henry nor Morag were invited of course, and much to Sophie and Neil's relief, neither turned up to the service.

There were far fewer guests on Neil's side: some old school friends, a sprinkling of distant cousins over from Canada and New Zealand, and even an Edinburgh-based business client or two. Duncan and Lorna were present of course and Craig and his mechanic brother and even two of the Tree Amigos who, after receiving puzzled looks from well-dressed wedding guests, gave up trying to explain the joke. Although a few McLeod Forestry employees had made the effort to attend, they looked rather uncomfortable at first and generally kept themselves to themselves. However, they perked up a bit when they saw the marquee in Dorothy's garden with its well-stocked complimentary bar. Shunning the vintage champagne, they proceeded to acquaint themselves thoroughly with the comprehensive selection of beers on offer.

The one black spot tarnishing the day's brilliance was the absence of Jim and Ann. The morning before they were due to travel south Jim had had a mild relapse and the local doctor decided that it was in his best interests not to go. Although Jim tried to insist that Ann be there to represent him, in the end she stayed north too, to "make sure he didn't get up tae mischief". Both Jim and Neil knew that as godmother to Neil and now recent friend of Dorothy, Ann's decision would have been a tough one for her to make.

Talking it over with his father the night before he was due to head south, Neil had said, "Dad I'm gutted about your not being able to come. It'll not be the same without you. But Sophie and I have had an idea. We know it's important to have a church wedding in Edinburgh and everything but what we'd really like is some sort of service up here. Not another wedding of course but a service of blessing and we really want to have it at Ardcairn."

"You cannae abuse the trust of Ms Lacelaw, son," he replied, "It wad no be right to use the house and no fair to Ann either."

"I know Dad. I've learned my lesson. But we thought that we might have a service of blessing outside, in the arboretum. The Bishop's up for doing that - I spoke to him in Oban that day we were there, remember - and we can invite Taynuilt friends and Craig and the lads and have a wee reception somewhere local. Miss Lacelaw's away until Christmas; she told Ann herself."

Jim thought it over for a while. "Well now how's this for an idea son," he suggested. "Why not make it a double celebration? Me and Ann getting' married in Oban in the morning, and in the afternoon you and Sophie can get blessed like two monkeys in a tree and then we can all have a ceilidh at Lonan in the evening." And shortly before Neil left for the Edinburgh wedding, he and his father had earmarked a couple of provisional autumn dates for a double celebration.

In the marquee at The Grange during the quiet lull before the guests arrived, Dorothy engaged Neil in a conspiratorial conversation in which she reminded him of the Montgomery motto and made him promise to always take care of Sophie. "And maybe I'll come up to Argyll from time to time to make sure that you do," she teased with a twinkle in her eye.

"I'll guard her bien," he replied, "and you know that you're always welcome in our home Dee." Then spotting Sophie approaching he said in a louder tone, "My wife and I would love it if you came to stay."

"Are you coming up to see us?" asked Sophie, "Oh do come Dee, it would be great to show you around Argyll!" she said excitedly, but all she got out of Dorothy was a vague "We'll see dear. You never know," just as the vanguard of guests arrived.

At the formal line up Neil dissolved any awkwardness lingering after the wedding service by repeated references to "My wife and I…"

"Aye and the wean an' all!" came Duncan's voice from the floor, much to the amusement of everyone else. From that moment on the mood of the reception lifted perceptibly. All differences, resentments and judgements were cast aside as the serious business of enjoying themselves began to occupy the guests.

"This doesn't mean I'm up for changing my name you know," murmured Sophie in Neil's ear during a brief lull in the proceedings, "after all I mean to make the Montgomery oeuvre an art collector's dream, donchaknow dahling."

"Well my own collection's unique," he replied, "you're the only oil painting I'll ever want."

"I should think so too," butted in Lorna who was next in the queue, "I'll be cuttin off your todger with yer chainsaw if ye're plannin' on sticking it elsewhere, Neil McLeod."

"Aye, well make sure it's the biggest saw you can find, Lorna Fraser," he retorted and gave her a smacking kiss.

"You're getting' horny and cheesy at the same time O husband of mine," said Sophie in a sing-song tone of voice, "that's a very bad sign".

"Well you know what we can do about that," he murmured suggestively in her ear.

"Absolutely no chance bub, we've got a reception to finish first," she replied giving him a mock look of sternness and his arm a punch.

"Ow! Well you can always sign your masterpieces SM. That'll keep us both happy."

Years later, when she found herself able to paint again, Sophie always signed off her work with a characteristic intertwining of her initials. For her, that act of closure was always the most emotional moment of a painting, for whenever she combined an S and an M into the corner of the canvas, she would be reminded of her grandfather's interlocking CM monogram in his paintings, and Neil's words that day.

Occasionally the conspicuous absence of Jim and Ann interrupted Neil's enjoyment and after proposing a toast to the health of 'my lovely wife' Neil made a point of making the next toasts to 'absent friends' and 'Jim and Ann'. Then Duncan responded in a show of braggadocio, toasting the health of 'the wee bairn to be' - just in case there might possibly be any wedding guests who didn't by then know that Sophie was expecting - and much to everyone's mirth he managed to imply that somehow he was the one responsible for its conception. Looking back at the reception, Neil savoured many special moments: Duncan's hilarious best man speech; Sophie delivering her own wedding speech using a sketch of Neil and Robbie as a visual prop; the female vicar doing a surprisingly good imitation of a rap artist; and the McLeod Forestry staff starting a conga and showing some straight-laced Edinburgh maidens what Argyllers wore under their kilts. The rest of the day passed in a blur of champagne and laughter and dancing. Throughout it all, Neil was on his best behaviour, being as charming as only he knew how, and by the end of the day he had gained almost universal approval from the older Montgomery invitees. Late that evening, after the band played the Last Waltz, the guests drifted away one by one or crashed out in a state of inebriation. The last two standing were Sophie and Neil.

He nibbled her ear and murmured in an over-refined Edinburgh accent, "There's something on my 'to do' list right now Mrs McLeod."

"I can guess what it is."

"Do you know what Ravelston coalmen carry their coal in?" he continued.

"No – but I've a feeling you're about to tell me."

"Seeax."

* * *

The scratching at the bedroom door became more insistent. Half awake now, Sophie turned over and said sleepily. "Poor dog. Go on, let him in. He hasn't seen us properly for days."

Feeling sleep-deprived Neil grunted. "Is this what babies do, wake you up in the middle of the night?" he asked. What time is it anyway?"

* * *

It had been Sophie's idea to honeymoon on the Scottish islands. Although Neil was far keener to travel somewhere exotic - "and *warm*" he stressed - in the end they agreed to defer their proper honeymoon until after the baby was born. It would be expedient to give the Oban Ball a miss this year - for obvious reasons - and anyway the baby's arrival would put paid to that suggestion. So Neil added a sidecar to his Triumph and they spent a few short but sweet days on the bike, honeymooning on three wheels, island-hopping around the west coast and returning late after a long ride from Lochaline ferry. True to the long range forecast the high-pressure system had held, and the days had been blissfully warm, perfect for biking, with stunning views and quiet roads. Partly on account of Jim's liking for whisky, they visited a couple of distilleries. As a thank you present to Jim and Ann for looking after Robbie during their road trip, Neil had presented them with a selection of Islay malts and their collective Black Bottle blend. Anticipating the couple's homecoming, Jim had returned Robbie to Lonan Farm and now, the morning after the honeymooners' return, Robbie was clearly delighted to have them back. Having arrived home late, tired and aching, Neil and Sophie had paid only the briefest of attention to Robbie the night before, and now - the morning after - he considered it high time that his attention deficit was rectified. Hearing muffled sounds coming from his master's bedroom Robbie's tail wagged ten to the dozen on the landing carpet. How was he to know that the sounds of affection coming from the other side of the door were nothing to do with a homecoming welcome?

* * *

Sophie looked at her watch. "Six thirty" she said sleepily. "Go on, let him in. He won't give up now."

Neil groaned again, rolled out of bed and opened the door.

One happy Border collie streaked like greased lightning into the room, jumped onto the bed and started licking Neil's face.

"Oh God!"

Chapter 24

With the Scottish honeymoon still fresh in their minds, Neil and Sophie's lives started to take on a new routine. Whilst Neil continued to throw his energies into McLeod Forestry, Sophie signed up for a distance-learning course. Her mornings were spent studying towards her History of Art degree, in the afternoons she painted the house, and when the light was good enough, she painted canvasses instead. Recently one of the outbuildings had been converted into a studio with a sizeable window looking northwards towards Loch Etive and the mountains beyond. If she stood by the studio's large pane of glass Sophie could just make out the tallest of the Ardcairn trees in the distance. Inspired by this distant view, the changing light and its effects on the landscape, she worked diligently on a series of studies depicting the Ardcairn Douglas fir, each image evolving one by one from a lifelike painting of the tree itself into an impressionistic representation of a giant green druid.

"Hmm," said Neil one evening, creeping into the studio and looking over Sophie's shoulder as she laboured on the last of the scenes in the fading light, "It's good, but what is it?"

She jumped. "You startled me. How long have you been standing there?"

"Not so long as you'd notice," he said enigmatically. Then in an American accent, "Looks like some crazy drug-fuelled hippy trip to me," as he put down a bottle of lemonade and started to pour two glasses.

"More like hypoglycemic-fuelled," responded Sophie. "Remember when we first met and I was out of it? My diabetic coma? I couldn't see straight or anything. Well that's what the tree looked like to me."

"What, a jolly green giant?" joked Neil. Handing her a glass of lemonade he said, "Are you going to sell it to Miss Lacelaw then?"

"No way José. I was thinking of maybe setting up an exhibition here sometime."

Neil's mind immediately focussed on the possibilities. "An exhibition, eh? That's great. We could send out invites to everyone we can think of and maybe advertise it in the local paper. It's bound to be popular."

"Hmm." Sophie didn't share the same conviction of her artistic abilities that Neil did. "Trouble is, I can't think of a name," she said.

"What's wrong with The Jolly Green Giant?"

"Not the picture numb nuts: the gallery."

Neil glanced out of the huge window at the tops of the Ardcairn trees turning golden green in the evening sunset.

"Why not call it the arboretum gallery?"

Sophie's wine glass paused mid way to her mouth. "The Arboretum Gallery!" she cried. Neil, that's brilliant!" and she put down her glass, stood up and gave him a hug. "And everyone who comes here can make a donation and we'll give the money to a woodland charity."

"Not on your Nelly," he remonstrated, his mind racing ahead once again. "We'll use the donations ourselves to plant lots of different trees in the inby fields. In future people can come for a walk in the woods here as well as buy paintings."

"Brilliant again!" continued Sophie, excited by his idea. "And maybe they can dedicate a tree to someone special and then they'll come back each year to see it grow and visit the gallery as well!"

"Good thinking Batwoman. Well, here's to the Arboretum Gallery then, Mrs M!" announced Neil pouring another lemonade for himself.

"Yeah, Mrs McLeod to you, but Ms Montgomery to my buyers, don't forget."

"Mrs, schmisses," he quipped dismissively, and clinked his glass to hers in a toast to its future success: "The Arboretum Gallery!"

* * *

Two weeks later the morning of the McLeod nuptials dawned bright and clear. Keen to convey an atmosphere of informality, but at the same time anxious to ensure that nothing would be left to chance, Neil and Jim had put a lot of time and effort into planning the day. With the service of blessing dependent upon the low-key but unapproved use of Ardcairn estate, apart from the weather the one remaining worry nagging at Neil during the days leading up to the ceremony was the potential bombshell arrival of Miss Lacelaw. Along with Morag and Henry, she was one of the few people definitely not on the guest list. If she did turn up unannounced it would ruin everything, particularly given that most invited guests knew nothing about the Ardcairn subterfuge and those that did would not be expecting her sudden arrival. Whilst the invitations stated 'Rose Cottage' they remained silent on the particular matter of the policy woodland part of the programme. In fact, including Duncan, Ann and the Bishop, only a handful of people knew that the plan for the actual service was to walk from Rose Cottage to the Douglas fir grove. The day before the McLeod double celebration Neil had checked and rechecked with Duncan and Ann that Miss Lacelaw wasn't going to give them any nasty surprises by turning up again unannounced. After managing to phone her in New York on some contrived pretext or other Ann was able to reassure Neil that yes, she had spoken to Miss Lacelaw herself and that no, there would be no spontaneous unwelcome interruptions. Duncan confirmed that he had received telephone instructions from his 'paymaster' recently and also got her to confirm that she wasn't coming back to Ardcairn for several weeks. "But I cannae vouch for the Powder-puff Pooch," he warned Neil, "It may be a white wedding after all."

"Service of blessing," Neil corrected his best friend, amused and reassured at the same time.

Wanting to do his best for Neil, Duncan had taken his factoring role seriously for a change and in the days preceding the service he had made a special effort to ensure that the grounds of Ardcairn were in tip top condition. He had fettled the lawns and hedges, roped off parking places for all the guests, cleared an entirely new pathway into the conifer grove and strimmed the grass underneath. Walking round the garden with Duncan the day before, Neil had been hugely impressed with his efforts. "You've put a lot of graft into it Duncan. It's looking better than I've ever seen it," he said complimenting his best friend and clapping him on the back, "I owe you mate."

"Ach, you can always gi's a job if Miss Lacelaw kicks us into touch. For starters she'll no be happy wi' ma new pathway," joked Duncan, but only half seriously.

"There's a job for you right now in McLeod Forestry if you graft like this."

"Aye, but can ye afford me?" winked Duncan mischievously.

For his part Neil had contracted a local joiner to clear out and fix up Lonan farm's large wooden barn and put up some temporary seating. Sophie had added her own artistic touches to the dance floor with streamers, coloured lights and bunting, lending the whole place an air of festive gaiety. For guests invited to the service of blessing, Ann had prepared a tour de force cold buffet lunch at Rose Cottage, with a generous array of local and exotic dishes. Now fully recovered from his recent relapse, Jim had dealt with a myriad of last-minute details and had generously insisted on paying for both the ceilidh band and the evening caterers at Lonan Farm. In return, Neil's surprise present to Jim and Ann was the hire of a sleek white Rolls Royce to take them from the Oban registry office back to Ardcairn.

Ann and Jim were keen to have a 'quietish' service and so it turned out to be, with only a dozen or so well-wishers turning up at the registry office. With Ann wearing a lilac outfit and matching hat and with Jim dressed in his best McLeod kilt and jacket, they appeared both smart and formal. Although to a casual onlooker they might have seemed outwardly diffident about the occasion, to the small circle of invited friends their joy and delight could be in no doubt. Old friends who had seen Jim becoming more introverted after the death of his first wife Eleanor, remarked at his recent blossoming and the re-emergence of his old persona after all these years. For Ann's part, although she appeared her usual unassuming self for most of the time, the twinkle in her eye had taken on a more intense gleam than ever before and those who knew her well rejoiced in her new-found happiness.

Their wedding service was over in a matter of minutes. From a flurry of confetti outside the Oban registry office, the Rolls Royce whisked them off to Ardcairn and Rose Cottage where what had started as a small cluster of guests was swelling into a lively throng. When Neil and Sophie headed up the Ardcairn drive a few minutes ahead of the Rolls they heard the unmistakable sounds of bagpipes in the distance long before they saw Duncan wrestling with them. Dressed in his slightly crumpled Fraser kilt he was belting out 'Marie's Wedding' to the alternate delight or anguish of arriving guests. Also waiting to receive them was the Bishop of Argyll looking resplendent in purple attire, complete with staff and mitre. When the Rolls appeared and Jim and Ann alighted to much cheering from those guests that knew them, the Bishop looked confused. "Shouldn't it be you and Sophie arriving in the wedding car?" he asked, turning to Neil. Having been left in the dark about the complications of a double celebration, his mistake was understandable, and no one enjoyed the moment more than him when the complication was explained. "A double celebration? Well, well. You Taynuilt McLeods certainly know how to live life to the full," he remarked kindly and made his way over to join the knot of guests congratulating Jim and Ann.

Hovering self-consciously in the background was a cluster of local villagers whom Sophie didn't recognise, as well as a few familiar faces that she did, including Dr Philip Liston and Gordon and Stephen Grey from the Oban Ball. A sprinkling of former Oban High School friends were also there, including John, up from Edinburgh. Many of Neil's local forestry contacts were present, including the whole McLeod Forestry workforce - looking much more at ease here than they had done in Edinburgh. Arriving by taxi from Taynuilt station were several of Sophie's St Andrews friends, including Annabelle. Welcoming each new arrival, Neil kept looking at his watch and playing for time, delaying the moment when the entourage would set off towards the arboretum. One important guest was still missing.

"Shouldn't we be making our way?" asked Sophie.

"In a minute," he replied. "I just want to check that everyone's here."

"Looks like everyone's here to me. Who could possibl-... Dee!" she yelled at the top of her voice, as the taxi drew up again and Dorothy's familiar features could be seen beaming through the passenger window. Grinning, Neil looked at Sophie closely and then at her grandmother, registering yet again how strikingly similar and good looking they were in so many ways.

"Hello Dee," he said conspiratorially, after Sophie had rushed over to give her a hug, "Welcome. Thanks for coming."

"I wouldn't have missed it for the world," she replied. "Besides, I want to see this famous place where you two first met."

Sophie admonished her grandmother. "You said you couldn't come."

"Ah yes, well. Neil and I wanted to surprise you," she added, a mischievous smile on her face, "I can be quite good at keeping secrets you know."

"And my husband also it seems," replied Sophie giving him a knowing look. "I hope you haven't got any more secrets I should know about."

"None you *should* know about," he agreed provocatively, whereupon she pretended to give him a kick, much to Dorothy's amusement. "Come on, we can get started now."

When the entourage finally reached the Douglas fir it seemed to Sophie and Neil that 'their' tree and trysting place that had once been so secret and secluded had now lost its intimacy. The rhododendrons had been cleared back by Duncan and the tree trunk was clearly visible. But to everyone else beholding the giant fir for the first time, their overwhelming feeling was not of seclusion, but of grandeur and stature: here was a veritable giant amongst Scotland's mightiest conifers. The wedding party slowly took their places around the rim of the surrounding hollow and whilst Sophie and Neil took their places on either side of the trees' mighty trunk, the Bishop officiated in the middle. Although the service was an informal affair with occasional moments of humour, it was no less solemn for being light-hearted. By now it was early afternoon and as the couple repeated their wedding vows the sun kept promising to break out from behind a single cloud, but in the end it remained obstinately hidden.

"And now I would like to invite Mr and Mrs McLeod senior to come forward and join Mr and Mrs McLeod junior," the Bishop added spontaneously, much to Neil's pleasure and Jim's evident embarrassment.

"This wasnae in the order of service," muttered Jim darkly as he and Ann shuffled forward self-consciously. The circle of guests parted to let them through, revealing Neil and Sophie grinning at them like a pair of hyenas beside the huge trunk of the Douglas fir. As both couples came together the Bishop continued, "In closing I would like to be the first to congratulate both Neil and Sophie and Jim and Ann and wish all four of you a long, happy and prosperous married life. I will now finish with the words of a Gaelic Blessing." Several of the more devout guests bowed their heads and closed their eyes, whilst the remainder observed the proceedings, savouring the closing moments of this memorable outdoor service.

"Deep peace of the running wave to you. Deep peace of the flowing air to you," began the Bishop. At that instant the sun began to make a slow reappearance from its hiding place behind the cloud, gradually bathing the group in its afternoon warmth.

"Deep peace of the quiet earth to you. Deep peace of the shining stars to you." With the trunk of the old fir now fully illuminated, a few of the more observant guests smiled as they now noticed a carved heart with an N and an S on either side of it.

"Deep peace of the gentle night to you; moon and stars pour their beaming light on you." A soft breeze stirred the upper canopy and then wafted down to the lower branches of the mighty tree as if sighing back its own blessing.

"Deep peace of Christ, the light of the world, to you; and may the blessing of our Lord Jesus Christ, father, son and holy spirit be with you all, evermore."

"Amen." The word rippled around the circle of assembled guests and then a spontaneous surge of applause rang through the glade as Neil and Sophie kissed each other and Ann and Jim stood awkwardly holding hands. The group remained under the tree as the guests' cameras clicked repeatedly. They all basked in the sunshine, savouring the moment, and then the Bishop started to engage Sophie, Ann and Jim in small talk. John made his way over towards Neil and - noticing the carving on the rough bark of the fir - he turned to his friend. "Congratulations mate, you may be needing another initial for the wean when it comes along. Maybe two if it's twins."

"Aye, and if a certain somebody catches you defacin' her prize trees again ye may be needin' an R, an I and a P for your own memorial," added Duncan, joining his ex High School friends.

"Don't worry Lacelaw lacky, I've peed on my own memorial often enough," punned Neil.

"It's a wonder the tree's still alive then," retorted Duncan.

"What's still alive?" asked Sophie, returning to the group.

"My tombstone," said Neil gesturing to the tree and patting its bark fondly as if it were an old friend.

A sudden gust of wind swayed the canopy and swept roughly the lower branches as the cloud obscured the sun again. Ann tugged at Jim's arm motioning him away. Sophie shivered. "Enough morbid chitchat guys," she said, "come on, we're keeping everyone waiting," and she dragged Neil, John and Duncan off towards Rose Cottage.

In a surprise of her own making, Lorna had spent several hours during the days before the service collecting and drying silver birch leaves. She knew that people loved to throw confetti at weddings but if Miss Lacelaw were to discover hundreds of paper hearts and horseshoes on the ground, she would immediately demand someone's head on a plate. As caretaker of the estate grounds, Duncan would be held responsible and that might cost him his job. And if he did lose his job, she would be the only breadwinner in their relationship. So she handed out baskets of leaves to the wedding guests to dispense and as the two McLeod couples stepped forward onto the newly-strimmed path they found themselves in a blizzard of natural confetti. When they reached the Ardcairn driveway some minutes later their clothes and hair were still strewn with birch leaves. There, in the afternoon sunlight, the stunning panorama of Loch Etive and the distant hills greeted their gaze, adding a theatrical backdrop to the man-made beauty of Ardcairn's grounds. Sophie paused momentarily to savour the view and found herself drawn as though by an invisible thread towards the semi-circular garden bench close to the house. She meandered slowly up to it and leaned lightly on its oak frame, shading her eyes from the sun. Gazing out over the panorama spread out before her she felt a raw sensation that started as a tingle down her spine and ended up as a lump in her throat and at that moment her growing baby made its first kicking movements within her womb. Whether it was this stirring of life inside her, the evocative scent of Ardcairn, the view of the hills, the distant sound of Duncan's pipes or a combination of all of these things, even Sophie couldn't tell, but for some reason she found herself overwhelmed by emotion. Tears of bliss started to roll gently down her cheeks, splashing onto the oak seat below.

Abruptly aware of her absence from his side and seeing her in the distance on her own, Neil made his excuses to the animated group of undergraduates who were debating the existence of God and strolled the short distance up the rise to join her. He put his arms around her waist and felt her body shaking as she sobbed quietly.

"What's wrong Soph?"

"Nothing... I'm just... so happy."

"I do love you, you know," he said, and after a while her shuddering subsided. She took his hands in hers but this time she directed them lower, down over her abdomen to where tiny feet were kicking inside. Mother, father and baby remained locked together, oblivious of the rest of the world, while - for a few brief moments - time stood still.

Their peaceful moments of togetherness were dramatically shattered by the roar of an engine sounding from somewhere behind them. They both jumped in shock, turning round to see what on earth was making all the noise. Emerging from its hiding place behind the house and roaring up the drive at high speed like a large red mechanical monster sped a McLeod Forestry forwarder with none other than Craig at its controls, grinning like a lunatic. He had fitted loudspeakers to the outside of the machine and in a Mad Max moment he now turned on a cassette tape. This was his surprise present to his boss and he was not going to allow Neil to forget it. He shot up the drive and headed straight towards the couple. Everyone else gasped and stepped back out of his way, fearing some dreadful accident. But as Craig pressed the play button the speakers started to blare out raucous music that many guests recognised as Billy Idol's 'White Wedding'. And as the forwarder drew alongside the guests, they could see that the machine bolsters had been decorated with giant ribbons and in its grab it held aloft a huge log, skilfully carved by the McLeod cutters into the shape of a champagne bottle. As the giant machine thundered past the guests lining the driveway, they could see attached to its trailer a battered old sofa fitted with seatbelts, whereupon their shock swiftly turned to amusement. Craig drew the machine to a sudden halt beside Neil and Sophie and amidst much cheering they were made to climb up onto the sofa and then paraded down the drive with Idol wailing "In the midnight hour she cries 'more, more, more!'" through the speakers at full volume.

The same unconventional transport was later used to chauffeur the couple up to Lonan Farm after the lunch reception at Rose Cottage. Now it was Neil's turn to get his own back at the tourist traffic as he and Sophie waved back at the accumulating convoy of vehicles stuck behind them on the Taynuilt road. Not that the road users seemed to mind all that much. Almost all the cars that honked at them before overtaking were doing it to encourage rather than protest. Somehow, someone managed to take a photo of them both smiling and waving and amongst many others in Oban the next day, Morag opened the local newspaper to read the caption 'Sofa so good for newlyweds' with a large photograph of Neil and Sophie. Their picture even made it to the nationals and during the next few days Neil received one or two congratulatory calls from long lost High

School contemporaries who had moved to England and seen his face beaming out from the pages of the Times.

The forwarder proved its worth in more ways than one that day. Halfway through the evening ceilidh at the Lonan barn, a local power cut plunged the farm into sudden and total blackness. As it was well away from the glare of any street or other light, there was nothing to relieve the total darkness and the dancers were abruptly forced to stop their reeling. Taking advantage of the situation, some of the more amorous couples could now express their mutual feelings rather more physically. Several men found themselves in receipt of lingering kisses and exploratory tongues from ardent dance partners, whilst a handful of girls found themselves subject to wandering hand trouble from their male admirers. Unplugged but undaunted, the resourceful dance band started to play 'Will ye go, lassie go' during the unlit minutes that followed and many of the guests joined in the chorus.

Neil thought fast. He knew that he had an emergency gas lantern in the house but on its own that would not be nearly enough to keep the ceilidh going. But Craig was already a step ahead of his boss and had managed to grope his way through the darkness to locate his trusty forwarder. Now he started it up and drew it alongside the barn. Before he turned off its engine, he switched on its impressive array of boom lights that were designed to enable the machine to work in the forest at night. The bank of bulbs instantly bathed the barn in an intense pool of light, hastily forcing some surprised couples to moderate their intimacy. Minutes later, with the help of Neil and the addition of two other giant forestry machines, the barn was surrounded by an even brighter illumination than before. Now, apart from a few absent couples (who would have sneaked off to find a private spot in any case) everyone joined the only well-lit space at Lonan Farm that evening and the ceilidh band promptly resumed their programme of reels in the barn with renewed vigour. Much later, everyone was having such a good time that nobody actually noticed when the power and the farmhouse lights did come on again.

Chapter 25

A few weeks later, finding himself with some free time in Oban, Neil decided to nip into one of his favourite haunts to buy a new pair of motorbike gauntlets. After propping up his Triumph outside 'Oban Bikes' he headed inside, placed his helmet on the counter and went over to inspect the range of new and second-hand bikes crowding the showroom. For a change he shunned the solid tourers and cruisers and homed in on the Japanese racers instead. He spent several minutes admiring the sleek design lines of the latest 'plastic rockets' as Duncan called them and was just crouching down to examine the workings of a striking red Kawasaki when a voice came from somewhere behind him. It was Steve, manager of 'Oban Bikes', who knew Neil reasonably well from his regular visits to the shop.

"Is there anything I can help you with there?"

As Neil straightened himself, Steve recognised his face. "Ah, if it isn't Neil McLeod? Congratulations by the way, I saw your picture in the paper."

"Hi Steve, oh yeah, *that* picture. Rumour has it that I'm fitting sofas into all my machines now - for health and safety reasons."

Steve laughed and then started asking Neil about business and they spent the next few minutes discussing life, the universe and forestry. Then he asked, "Are you interested in the Kawasaki XT then? That one's almost new. Returned just yesterday by one of our customers. You'll know him in fact – Grieg Govan."

That was a minus point as far as Neil was concerned. Firstly, he could do without being reminded of Morag and secondly, although he didn't know Morag's brother Grieg all that well, he did know how he treated his bikes – roughly. And yet, the price tag was alluring. "What's wrong with it?" he asked.

"Nothing's wrong with it. We had to take it back after the customer – ah…" he lowered his voice, "defaulted on his instalments," he explained.

Neil pulled a face but Steve continued, "It's only got 2000 miles on the clock. Hardly run in, in fact. I've checked her over and tested her myself. She's sweet."

Neil had always wanted something speedy ever since he had acquired his first machine at the age of sixteen. It was a small battered old trail bike which he had learned to ride off road, ripping across the countryside, chewing up tracks, falling off frequently and generally being a nuisance to the neighbourhood. A visit one day by the Taynuilt bobby and a stern talking to by his father afterwards had persuaded him to see the error of his ways. Leaving his brief but colourful tearaway phase behind, Neil got his motorbike licence and stuck to the tarmac after that. There was more than enough fun to be had burning up the quieter roads of Argyll. He had bought his trusty old Triumph from someone in the village soon after passing his driving test and although he was still sentimentally attached to it, it did have a habit of breaking down fairly regularly and he simply didn't have time to fix it anymore. Although he derived a lot of pleasure from biking the Argyll roads (as did Robbie on occasions) he had been thinking about getting something newer and faster for some time. The modern Jap bikes that zipped up from Glasgow for day outings always left his slower Triumph in their wake and he grudgingly admired their superior roadholding and acceleration. Controlling these bikes at speed required total concentration and Neil admired the skill of their riders. Most were considerate and professional, but Neil had also seen his fair share of daft behaviour by reckless riders, which reflected badly on all bikers and gave them a bad name. Every year there were accidents on the local roads - some fatal - but Neil was a responsible rider on the whole, who never touched alcohol when biking, who knew the road system like the back of his hand and who - most importantly - knew his limitations. He also knew that when Sophie's baby arrived, he would have less time to enjoy two wheels. This was going to be his last chance to indulge himself for a long while. He was sorely tempted by the price of the Kawasaki but concluded that it was just a bit on the high side. There was also the matter of Sophie's reaction. Although she had occasionally taken the Triumph down a few of the remoter roads with Neil behind her, her growing abdomen had put paid to pillion trips for a while and Neil knew that the appeal of two wheels might wear off once the baby arrived.

"It's tempting..." Neil paused.

Steve thought for a moment and went on, "Tell you what. Seeing as it's you, I'll knock ten percent off the asking and let you test-drive it for a week. After that you can look me in the eye and tell me that you don't want it."

Neil laughed. He recognised a good salesman when he saw one and Steve knew him well enough to know that his technique was very likely to succeed.

"I'll have your Triumph brought round to your house later today if you tell me where, and you can take the XT away right now," Steve added.

Neil hesitated. "It's over Taynuilt way," he said, thinking that that might put Steve off.

"Not a problem."

Neil hesitated again, "I would have to sort out some insurance." He was beginning to run out of excuses for not taking up the offer.

"Oban Bikes have a franchise arrangement. It's basically a corporate discount scheme. Or you can use my phone and call a broker?" suggested Steve.

Neil hesitated for a third time – and was lost.

"Thanks, Steve" he said, grinning broadly.

*　　*　　*

Sophie put down her OU study pack and looked out of the bay window. An unfamiliar sounding bike was roaring up the drive, scattering loose stones as it went. As the rider stood up on the footrests and waved his left arm in a salute, she recognised Neil's form. She put down her essay and went outside to meet him. "I thought you were just off to buy some gloves, not a new bike?" she said reproachfully as he pulled the Kawasaki back onto its stand.

Neil took off his helmet and said somewhat sheepishly "Yes, well, strictly speaking it's not new and it's not mine… er, yet."

"Well? What's the story, morning glory? Where's your Triumph?"

"The bike shop's bringing it over later today," Neil replied.

Sophie frowned as she looked at the speedometer dial. "A hundred and sixty miles an hour. Bloody hell! It's more Kamakazi than Kawasaki. It looks pretty lethal to me."

"Pretty is right," Neil replied. "But it's not lethal, it's safe as houses. Honest."

"Yeah, right. And so useful for the three of us."

Sophie's sarcasm wasn't lost on Neil. "I know Soph but I've always wanted one of these and it was a bargain. And anyway," he added, "I've got it on approval. I might not buy it."

"Aye right. As if. I know you Neil McLeod," she replied disapprovingly.

Changing the subject he asked, "Anyway, how's the world's worker? And how about some coffee?"

"I've nearly finished my essay on Klimt. You know, I reckon if I worked hard, I could even finish my degree in two years. Lonan is so great for studying: much better than Uni." Sophie's scepticism about the motorbike changed to enthusiasm about the farm. "It's so peaceful here. Or at least it was until you arrived."

"And what about when the baby arrives?"

"Och I'll still be able to work. We'll make a routine. And Lorna's offered to help. I reckon she's getting broody herself."

They went through into the kitchen. "You know, this woodfuel system's the best thing ever," said Neil taking off his jacket and jersey. "This place seemed so… unloved when I first saw it, cold even, and now look at it." He patted her large bump, affectionately and Sophie grinned. "Warm and cosy and a proper home with you two here." They sat by the kitchen table talking about his bike, her growing bump and their plans for the future. "We must invite Dee up now that Lonan's habitable," suggested Neil.

"Funnily enough she was on the phone this morning and I said the same thing. We discussed some dates but I didn't want to agree anything without you."

"Sooner the better. We've only got a few weeks until the big day. Or we could wait until baby arrives and invite her then. The spare room's perfect, thanks to you. Tell you what, why don't we both see her in Edinburgh next weekend, after the match?"

"I've been thinking about that," she replied. "I'm really not too keen on going just now. I mean I can't really see I'm going to enjoy Murrayfield with a bulge like this and my insulin's been going up and down like a yo-yo recently."

"But I got you a ticket," he protested, "you must come."

"Why not invite Dee instead? You know she loves her rugby."

Neil paused to ponder this suggestion. Why not indeed? "Well, if you think she'd enjoy it, I mean. Let's phone her. But later.

Lunch first. And then how about a walk up the hill with Robbie to see how our tree's doing?" From where he had been lying quietly the collie pricked up his ears at the 'W' word and wagged his tail briefly. After lunch, with Robbie joyfully cavorting about their heels, Neil and Sophie made their way slowly up the hill behind Lonan towards the old drove road and the place where they had lovingly planted the Wishing Tree cuttings several months ago. When they reached the sheltered hollow, they noticed with a good deal of satisfaction that the small hawthorns had put forth new and vigorous growth. "A good omen," suggested Neil. "Maybe our boy will come here and make wishes," he said after bending down to remove some of the vegetation surrounding the young plant.

"What makes you think it's a boy?"

"The wedding ring trick remember? I haven't forgotten even if you have," Neil teased.

"Ah yes, said Sophie in a knowing tone of voice, "well we'll see, won't we."

"What's that supposed to mean?"

"We'll see!" repeated Sophie. She was being deliberately mysterious and despite Neil's cross-examination she wouldn't be drawn further on the subject.

* * *

The day before the rugby International, Sophie was in her studio finishing her composition of Neil and Robbie on the Triumph and half listening to the radio. She was tired today

– the baby's frequent kicking had distracted her from her painting. She paused as the Scottish news came on. For some days the rail unions had been threatening strike action and she was anxious to know if Neil's planned trip to Edinburgh would be affected. Sure enough, the news was bad. "Talks to avert a one-day rail strike by members of the Transport and General Workers Union failed to reach a solution yesterday. At ten a.m. today the Union issued a statement to confirm that they are calling a twenty-four-hour stoppage which will affect the entire rail network tomorrow. Only a limited service will operate in the central region and all trains to and from the Highlands have been cancelled."

When Sophie told him the news later that day Neil groaned. "Dammit! I'll have to drive down to Edinburgh now." But even as he swore, a thought entered his head, and he sensed an opportunity to turn defeat into victory. "What's the forecast for the weekend?" he asked.

"Why?"

"Well maybe I'll take the Kawasaki."

"Babe, don't do that – it's a hell of a drive down and back. Take the bus – or the Landrover."

"That'll take forever. Anyway, you're not coming, remember? So I can take two wheels no problemo. And parking at Murrayfield will be a doddle."

But Sophie was sceptical, and as the evening shadows lengthened, she wrestled with conflicted feelings. She knew that Neil loved his rugby and that after this match, there might not be a chance for him to go to an International for a long while: he had said so himself only recently. Also, with the baby due in only a matter of weeks, this might be his last chance to enjoy a long ride on his new toy for a while. But still a doubt nagged at the back of her mind. And yet, who was she to talk him out of going?

The TV was on in the room but neither of them was paying any attention to the news. Sophie was still distracted, thinking about Neil's trip south.

"Why don't you stay with Dee after the match and come back on Monday?" she suggested, "I can phone her tomorrow to see if that's alright."

In the background the weatherman's voice was saying, "Earlier on today, apparently, a woman rung the BBC and said she heard that there was a hurricane on the way..."

At the word hurricane they both pricked up their ears and turned to the TV.

"...well, if you're watching, don't worry, there isn't! But having said that, actually the weather will become very windy but most of the strong winds incidentally will be down over Spain and across France."

"There you are Soph," said Neil, going to the next-door room and switching the TV off, "No worries chicken curries. Let's go to bed."

Chapter 26

That Saturday an unlikely pair could be seen wending their way towards the rugby match at Murrayfield. The stadium was bedecked with colourful pennants that fluttered briskly from its crown of girders. One of the figures - a tall young man wearing a McLeod tartan scarf - was protectively shepherding the other - an old lady - through packed throngs of English and Scottish rugby supporters. At one point the old lady paused to buy a jaunty saltire hat from a street hawker. Its white cross and blue background bobbed steadily amidst a sea of fans: saltires, tartan tammies and Scottish lions flowing inexorably towards the match. As they approached the stadium Neil and Dorothy were inadvertently shoved by a group of inebriated Scots fans in kilts who wheeled about lifting cans of lager high above their heads and chanting rugby songs. At the time Neil was a little anxious but Dorothy made light of it. "This is just like the old days with Charles," she exclaimed excitedly, "I haven't enjoyed myself so much for ages. It's not the same as seeing it on telly."

"You just wait until the match starts," responded Neil, "Scotland are going to give England such a thrashing."

"I wouldn't be so sure," countered Dorothy, "It could be a close-run thing," and there and then, as they waited to go through the turnstile, she began expounding her reasons as to why the game would be a close call.

* * *

Seated in Lonan arboretum gallery, Sophie took a sip of hot water and gazed at the distant view through the large plate glass window. Below her in the distance, the tops of Ardcairn's tall trees were starting to sway in the stiffening afternoon breeze whilst flocks of seagulls wheeled high in a slate grey sky. She put down her cup and snapped open the two locks of her artists' painting case. Before she resumed work on the final painting in her Ardcairn tree series she stepped back from the easel and examined the other paintings propped against the wall. Starting at the first canvas with its representation of the giant Douglas fir, she observed with satisfaction how they gradually metamorphosed one into another, the final painting ending up as an impressionistic druid. The first paintings in the opus were complete but there was something still not quite right about the last one. It just didn't seem to complement the others in the way that she wanted it to. "Hmm," she said half audibly to herself. Neil's comment about it being a "jolly green giant" had been uncomfortably close to the mark and now she had to work out how to make the image more like a druid and less like Jack and the beanstalk. Frowning with concentration, she studied her composition intently, looking to see how she might improve it.

*   *   *

After battling through the crowds and the strengthening wind, Dorothy and Neil jostled their way past the turnstile and found their seats inside the stadium. Able to relax now, they started to revel in the pre-match buzz and the chanting of the capacity crowd, and they chattered animatedly about the forthcoming clash. As they waited for the two competing squads to emerge onto the pitch, Dorothy continued to expand her well-informed analysis of each teams' strengths and weaknesses and how they might affect the forthcoming match, whilst Neil listened to her thorough knowledge of the sport with undisguised admiration.

* * *

Finally working out how to make her creation more authentic, Sophie sat down and took another sip of water. She had just embarked upon the first strokes of paint when she felt a sharp kick in her abdomen. "Oi, junior!" she exclaimed, rubbing her belly, "I'm not a rugby ball you know." Reminded thus of the match, she leaned back to turn on the radio behind her and tuned into the sports channel. The distinctive Scots patois crackled over the speaker "…and with the two mighty teams poised to settle some old scores here at Murrayfield, the atmosphere this afternoon is electric. I can see the referee with the two captains now. He's taking a coin out of his pocket and he's asking the English captain to call…" Sophie turned the volume down a little, picked up her brush again and resumed her work.

* * *

The match had started well, with the home squad scoring the first try. Like all the other Scots fans, Dorothy cheered vigorously and yelled her approval. Most of the crowd went wild, already anticipating an easy victory, but soon afterwards England took advantage of some sloppy play by the opposition to first equalise and then, converting their try, move ahead. The Scots' cheers swiftly turned to a mixture of boos and whistles and the atmosphere became more antagonistic. At that moment Neil felt his phone vibrate once in his pocket. A text. He'd check it out at the break. Just before the half-time whistle went, Scotland seized an opportunity to break through the English defences and score a drop goal: 8-7 to the home team. The stadium erupted with cheering Scots fans.

* * *

The eaves of the arboretum gallery emitted sporadic moaning from gusts of wind that competed with the commentary on the radio. Sophie was only listening with half an ear to the rugby, so absorbed was she in the steady progress she was making. Having completed her work-around and adding a few finishing touches to the canvas she decided that she would go into the house and watch the rest of the match on TV. But just as she started to clean up her brushes, she felt a rush of fluid between her legs. "Shit! Great timing junior," she exclaimed and reached over for her mobile phone.

* * *

At half-time Neil battled his way down the steps to buy two coffees from a booth just outside the stand. He joined a queue of impatient supporters waiting to be served by the stall that seemed to have the shortest queue but although the line was short, the service was slow. It was only after a lengthy delay that Neil eventually found himself towards the front. A phone went off in the pocket of someone behind him and as it did so it reminded Neil that he had a text waiting to be read. Retrieving his own phone from his pocket he saw that the message had been sent from Sophie. 'It was probably wishing him love and the home team luck, he imagined. He clicked on the 'read' command just as the people in front of him collected their refreshments and were turning to go.

"Who's next please?" came the vendor's voice as Neil read the text.

There was a short pause. "Can I help you?" came the vendor's voice again, louder this time, but Neil - unaware of anything except the text - stood motionless, stunned, as he read and re-read Sophie's message. 'Waters just broke. Baby wont wait. Will taxi to Hsptl. Dont hurry back. Love u xxx.' In disbelief he read the message yet again. This wasn't supposed to happen for another three weeks. His mind raced, trying to take in the enormity of the situation. 'What the hell to do now?' he wondered. People in the queue behind him were clucking and tutting and telling him to get a move on but Neil was completely oblivious to their disapproving noises.

"Oi, son, ye'r keepin' others waitin." The vendor was losing patience. "Ye want somethin or not?"

Jerked rudely back to the present, Neil came to his senses. He looked at the man vacantly. "Er, no, thanks," he mumbled and stumbled his way blindly back up towards the terraces.

* * *

Having phoned for a taxi and notified the hospital of her impending arrival, Sophie rushed about the house throwing things into a holdall that she might need in hospital. She was conscious that with the baby coming along this early, her stay there might be an extended one. Frantically pulling open drawer after drawer she desperately hunted for the one nightie she possessed that wasn't overtly erotic. Discarding an array of silky, lacy, frilly and downright kinky garments, she eventually located something suitable hiding at the back of a wardrobe. 'Will it still fit me now?' she wondered, holding it up to inspect it and picking up her phone at the same time. Still no text back from Neil. 'Not to worry,' she thought, 'He probably won't have

registered the call with all the noise and mêlée of the match.'
Then she phoned Dorothy's home phone, but naturally there
was no reply from her grandmother either. 'Why would there be
if they're both at the match' she realised, and in case Neil didn't
get her text she left a message on her grandmother's
answerphone, "Hi Dee. The baby's decided not to wait and I'm
off to the hospital soon. Could you let Neil know when he gets
back. Give him my love – and lots of love to you too. Byeeeee!"
Dorothy didn't have a mobile phone so there wasn't much more
that Sophie could usefully do just now to inform the people she
loved the most. She would let her mother know from the
hospital and as for Neil's parents, well Ann would only worry
and Jim would want to take Sophie to Oban himself and he was
such a slow driver. She knew that a taxi would be much quicker
and less fuss. She put the phone down on her bedside table,
intending to pack it later and as she did so, momentarily
distracted, she glanced at the framed photograph lying there. In
it, Neil and Sophie were hand in hand at their service of
blessing, embracing each other underneath the spreading
branches of the Ardcairn fir. The afternoon sun highlighted
their features with a gentle glow and with their faces half turned
out towards the camera, half leaning in towards each other, it
was clear that here were two young people deeply in love. As
she gazed at the image, Sophie's face formed a half smile and
she drifted back in her mind's eye to all the times that she and
Neil had spent under the tree, talking, making love and just
enjoying their company. She remembered what Neil had said to
her in bed the day before: "When junior appears we should take
him there and make it our family tree."

Her reverie was rudely shattered by the sound of a horn
honking from outside. The taxi! It was early. She needed to
finish packing! On an impulse she shoved the photo into the

holdall before grabbing her hairbrush and cosmetics and stuffing them into her bag as well. Then she hurried downstairs.

* * *

Neil shoved his way back through the crowd as fast as he could. His mind was racing. Sophie had sent the text just over half an hour ago. She would probably be on her way to hospital by now: in fact she might even be there already. Barring any problems, his journey north should take about three hours. He wondered whether he would even make it back in time for the birth. But he would have to get Dorothy home first and that could take another forty-five minutes - at least. Rapidly pressing the speed dial keys for Sophie's number he waited in vain for her to answer. "Come on… Come ON!" he muttered to himself as he barged his way roughly through the crowd back to Dorothy, but there was no answer. Eventually regaining the terraces, he spotted the familiar jester hat before he spotted Dorothy herself and despite the stress of the situation he couldn't help smiling. Unaware of Neil approaching from behind, Dorothy abruptly stood up, simultaneously waved her arms forwards and upwards into the air, then sat down again, a frail individual human drop in a Mexican wave of supporters that swept around the stadium. Spotting Neil, she shouted breathlessly, "This is new since my day – I forget what they call it."

"A Mexican Wave," Neil shouted back just as another one rolled its way towards Dorothy.

Looking flushed, she panted, "A what?" then standing up and waving her arms above her head once again.

"A Mexican Wave!" chortled Neil loudly. Then as he drew nearer, he bent his face towards her ear, confiding in a quieter tone, "Dee, Sophie's waters have broken and she's on her way to hospital. She sent me a text."

For a moment Dorothy studied his face, fixing his eyes with her piercing gaze. "Then you must join her," she replied imperturbably.

Another collective wave rolled past; this time unassisted by Dorothy.

"But what about you? I have to take you home."

"I'm not a child you know," she rebuked Neil, "I can take care of myself and besides, I'm enjoying myself far too much here. You go. I'll be fine. You'll be much quicker without me."

Towering above her small figure, Neil gazed down fondly at his grandmother-in-law. To all outward appearances, here was a fragile old biddy dressed in a silly blue and white hat, making a fool of herself in public. But what Neil's eyes took in was an extraordinary, vivacious and energetic old lady, living life in the moment and enjoying it to the full, and his heart went out to her. The thought crossed his mind that if he were half as alive as Dorothy when he reached her age then there would indeed be much to look forward to. He hesitated for a moment. "Are you sure, Dee?"

"Never surer. Now off you go. Give the proud Mother all my love."

"I will..." he half turned to go, "...and, Dee?"

Dorothy's forceful gaze held his eyes for several seconds.

"I... well... thanks," he said simply, in those few faltering words, conveying his love for her far more profoundly than any eloquent goodbye speech.

"Oh come here," she pretended to scold him, holding out her hands, just as the surrounding crowd started cheering for the two re-emerging teams. Right then and there, on the terraces, amidst the deafening chanting of seventy thousand rugby supporters, Neil and Dorothy embraced each other in a fond farewell hug. Several of the fans nearby stopped chanting for a second as they witnessed this impromptu cameo, briefly diverted by the emotional connection between a tall young man and a frail old lady. Then the whistle went, the spell broke and Neil turned to go. Just before he left the terraces, he looked back over his shoulder one last time. The famous Murrayfield roar was in full force. Somewhere back there in the stadium an old lady was having the time of her life.

* * *

"Alright, alright" Sophie yelled as the horn sounded yet again, "I'm coming." Grabbing her hastily prepared bag, she struggled to shut the farmhouse door against the strengthening wind. Finally managing to slam it shut and lock it, she stumbled outside to where the Etive taxi was waiting, its engine running. As she drew close the driver's window wound down and a familiar voice shouted, "Well Sophie, how's it 'goin'?"

"Malcolm! It's you!"

"Nane other. When Control radioed aboot a fare frae Lonan tae hospital I thought I'd tak the job. Wee bit early, eh?"

"Well yes, you are a bit but that's OK."

The taxi driver laughed. "No! You I mean. I thought the baby wasnae due yet a while?"

"Thanks Malcolm, is nothing secret around here? Does everyone know everything?" she continued, manoeuvring herself awkwardly into the car.

"Aye, just aboot. This is Argyll, ye ken," he grinned, letting off the handbrake.

As the taxi scrunched down the gravelly farm track Sophie rummaged distractedly inside her holdall. She had a nagging feeling that she'd forgotten something, but she couldn't for the life of her remember what it was. 'At least I've got enough money in my wallet,' she noted with relief, remembering the last time that she had been taken to the hospital by Malcolm. That incident at Ardcairn seemed like a lifetime ago now.

Still grinning, her driver looked in his rear-view mirror.

"You forgotten something? Cash mebbe?"

Sophie looked up. "Very funny. You'll be pleased to know that I can pay you this time."

"Neil cheering for Scotland then?"

"Sorry?" Sophie was still preoccupied.

"He'll be at Murrayfield?"

"How... how did you...?" Sophie began.

"Malcolm laughed. Like you say, nohing's sacred around here. Dinna worry. We'll get ye tae the baby factory in nae time."

Sophie smiled gratefully at his beaming reflection. "Thanks Malcolm," she said warmly. She stopped rummaging in her bag and sat back, fiddling with her hair, still preoccupied.

On a table in the empty bedroom of Lonan farmhouse Sophie's mobile phone rang out, unheard and unanswered.

* * *

The second half of the England v Scotland clash was developing into a veritable nail-biter. Things had started badly for the home team. After their marginal half time lead Scotland had rested on their laurels, allowing England the chance to score and convert a try. Just before extra time the home side seized a lucky opportunity and tucked away a drop goal and with only a few minutes remaining, the score now stood at England 14, Scotland 11. Seconds later the English retaliated with their own drop goal, increasing their score to 17. Now the match was going into extra time and with only another minute or two to go until the final whistle Dorothy was still yelling like a banshee, shouting at the referee and exhorting the flagging Scots squad to dig deep and give it their all. Every time the ref looked at his watch the home crowd whipped themselves up into an anxious frenzy. It seemed as if it was all over for Scotland. And then - just as all hope had gone - their lucky break came. Scotland's outside centre player body-swerved, found a gap in the English defences, and stormed towards the far end of the pitch as if his very life depended upon it. Veering through the remaining English players with three pursuing white shirts on his back, he managed to tuck a try into the extreme corner of the playing field: England 17, Scotland 16. Now the urging and exhorting of the crowd increased to fever pitch. But shortly afterwards, as the fly half started to prepare for the kick of his life, like a fountain being quenched, the roaring subsided into a hubbub and then a murmur and then an expectant, heart-stopping hush. The crowd was on tenterhooks, acutely aware that the referee was only waiting for the kick to be taken before blowing his whistle to signal the end of the match. The whole outcome of this game - and the tournament - depended upon Scotland converting this try and snatching victory from the jaws of defeat. But getting the ball through the posts from this angle would take the player's entire skill and a lot of luck besides. Even inside the shelter of the stadium it was clear that the strengthening wind could have a profound effect upon the shot. As the fly-half fiddled with the ball, trying to set it at just the correct angle, the silence was interrupted by gusts of wind that smacked into the stadium. The hush of the crowd was interrupted by the shrieking of wind vibrating the roof girders. It sounded like a demonstration of angry poltergeists. Like all the Scots fans lining the stadium that day or watching the match on TV, Dorothy felt her nerves straining and every fibre in her body willing the fly-half to convert the try. She clutched anxiously at her throat as the small Borderer took five paces back from the ball and two paces to the side. The crowd fell completely silent as the number ten player rocked on the balls of his feet for a second and looked up at the distant white H post. Then he leaned forward, gathered momentum, ran up to the ball and with one scoop of his foot sent it heavenward...

* * *

Despite the noise of the wind whistling in the stadium girders behind him, when Neil reached his bike he could tell that the roar of the crowd had subsided. He frowned, trying to guess what was happening back there. He felt a momentary twinge of frustration at having to leave such an epic clash. But he also knew that for the next three hours he would need to devote all his concentration to the road and not to Sophie or the baby or the rugby. Before strapping on his helmet, he tried one last time to phone Sophie. Still no reply. By now Neil guessed that she must be in hospital where she would not be allowed to use her phone. And yet, strangely, it was not switched off. 'She must know that someone is trying to call her?' he thought as he stood up on the kick-starter and lashed out with his foot. After several determined kicks, the Kawasaki surrendered to his efforts. With his helmet now secured, Neil was only vaguely aware of the momentous closing seconds of the match being played out behind him. He opened up the throttle, gunned the sleek red Kawasaki along Corstorphine Road, slipped through the self-assured Edinburgh suburbs and out onto the motorway. Beyond Stirling stretched the distant hills, the road to the isles, and Sophie…

* * *

Everything was happening much too fast for Sophie. Even as she was being escorted down the hospital corridor ('thank God Ms Govan's nowhere to be seen' she thought) she realised that she had left her mobile phone back at Lonan. An hour later, her contractions became stronger and more frequent and she was moved from a room that she shared briefly with another expectant mother, into a private birthing room. The duty midwife seemed a bit peculiar to Sophie and although she was trying to be as reassuring as she could, all Sophie wanted was for Neil's familiar face to be by her side. Her pulse rate soared and she became increasingly apprehensive and fretful as her contractions grew steadily in strength. With the baby not due for nearly another month Sophie was mentally unprepared for this journey into the unknown, especially with her diabetes. It worried her that, being so premature, the baby might not survive, and it also worried her that Neil was so far away. Beads of perspiration started to form on her brow and her back ('Why do they have to keep hospitals like ovens?' she kept thinking) and she winced in pain as yet another contraction sent her body into spasm. By now the hospital staff had hooked her up to a monitor. Studying the screen anxiously, the midwife picked up the internal hospital phone and spoke quickly to the person at the other end.

In an authoritative manner which still couldn't mask overtones of nervousness, she said, "Doctor Graham, I think you'd better come here."

* * *

Skirting the shores of Loch Lomond and swearing at the moronic traffic, Neil zoomed past a queue of leisurely Sunday afternoon drivers and tucked the Kawasaki into an opening ahead. This seemed to be one of those ill-fated days when the whole world was determined to get in his way and slow him down. Being held back by others was the one thing that stressed Neil more than anything and this afternoon he was becoming more and more harassed. He knew the road well - where to overtake and where not to - but perversely all the straight sections were clogged with pulses of oncoming vehicles. And for some inexplicable reason the traffic was uncommonly heavy as well. To make things worse the wind was getting stronger. From time to time, sporadic gusts took unexpected sideswipes at him. Adding to his problems, an intermittent engine fault caused an occasional loss of power for a second or two. In itself this wasn't serious enough to justify stopping his journey, but it was certainly unnerving. Just after Arrochar he seized his chance to pass a slow car pulling a trailer and sneaked into a small gap whilst an oncoming car flashed its lights repeatedly at him. "Eff you too, sunshine," shouted Neil as he gunned the throttle and accelerated rapidly. Then as he rounded a tight bend he hit the brakes again, groaning at the same time. Up ahead of him were two supermarket trucks travelling in a convoy "Selfish B's!" he cursed. 'Why did they have to do that?' It was a case of one lorry being unfortunate but two being careless and he saw no reason why they should travel together like a herd, slowing everyone else down and effectively stopping anything from overtaking. But as the road veered away from the side of Loch Long, Neil knew that the lorries would be slowed down by the twisty ascent of Glen Croe and the steep ascent towards 'Rest and be Thankful'. In his mind he was already anticipating where and when to pass them. But what he could not know was that the car that had flashed its lights was not admonishing him but trying to warn him of a hazard ahead...

After less than a minute Neil seized his chance. Through a right hand bend he glimpsed a clear stretch of road and instantly opened up the throttle. But almost immediately the engine paused and began to lose power. "Bloody hell!" Neil swore, desperately twisting and untwisting the grip and waiting for the power to pick up again. He saw that the lorry drivers had selfishly left too tight a gap for him to pull in between them safely and he was now committed to overtaking both of them. But the foremost lorry started honking its horn as Neil managed to accelerate around it and now the corner was changing from a right hand bend to a blind left hand one and a strong gust of wind came out of nowhere pushing Neil back. He opened the throttle to maximum and the bike stuttered again and then - too late - he saw the sheep. There was a screeching of brakes, a sickening thud and Neil's world went black.

* * *

Doctor Graham rushed into the birthing room. What she saw was an expectant mother, her hair matted with sweat, her face red with exertion and her mouth contorted into a suppressed scream of agony. The bedclothes were damp with perspiration but of most concern to her was a dark smudge of blood that had seeped out from between the patient's legs and was spreading slowly across the white bed linen. The midwife looked up anxiously as she came in and a hastily whispered conversation ensued between the two of them. Then "Sophie!" the doctor addressed her in a suspiciously cheerful tone of voice. "I'm afraid that some complications have arisen and we're going to have to perform a caesarean section on you. We'll need to put you under anaesthetic. I'm sorry that there may be a risk to your baby but it's in your best interest. Is there a number we can telephone to contact your partner or your parents perhaps?"

Sophie's consciousness was starting to swim alarmingly but even in her distracted state she could see right through the doctor's artificially upbeat tone. Realising that things were now indeed serious, she managed to mumble Neil's mobile number. Then an anaesthetist entered the room as, feeling another spasm, Sophie uttered a half scream of pain. Shortly afterwards a mask came up to her face and she gulped in deep draughts of gas. The doctor's white lab coat seemed to transform itself into the wings of a bright angel and shortly afterwards Sophie lost consciousness.

In the stadium Dorothy clutched anxiously at her throat as the small fly half looked up towards the distant goalpost and raised himself up on his feet. As the tension level in the stadium rose to breaking point and the girders shrieked out their unearthly wailing, the constriction in Dorothy's chest grew tighter and she felt her heart hammering uncontrollably. The player leaned forward, gathered momentum and took the kick. To the assembled Scots, collectively willing that kick to succeed, the ball's ascent seemed to take forever. It rose slowly upwards, describing a graceful arc as straight as a die towards the lofty white H post. With the whole fate of the match depending upon the success of this kick, several thousand fans held their breath in unison, craning their necks and willing the ball not to fall short. As its trajectory finally peaked and gravity started to pull it inexorably back to earth Dorothy's heart continued to pound like a jackhammer and now she realised that something was gravely wrong. She doubled up with pain as the ball approached the posts but even as her seizure gripped her, part of her conscious mind was thinking that the ball would fall short of the crossbar.

Long afterwards, people talked about the Murrayfield miracle that occurred that day. Certainly, it appeared as if the magic of some invisible hand was at work, for just when the ball looked set to go wide, a strong gust of wind enfolded it at the critical moment, giving it just enough momentum to career headlong against the upright bar. Spinning frantically, it bounced upwards, fell onto the horizontal crossbar and then toppled forward onto the ground behind: England 17, Scotland 18. The referee's whistle blew, and a victory roar erupted from thousands of Scots supporters inside the stadium.

But the exultation of a few fans occupying a small corner of the terraces that afternoon was short-lived. The old lady in front of them, who had been so eccentrically and delightfully enthusiastic throughout the match, had just slumped forward and collapsed to the ground. To their consternation she seemed to have stopped breathing and her lips had turned blue.

Chapter 27

At his official Oban residence, the Bishop of Argyll and the Isles tapped the barometer in his study for the third time that day and tutted uneasily to himself. All afternoon the needle had been falling steadily and now it was set to 'severe storm'. Distracted by the intermittent rattle of the windowpanes, the Bishop gave up working on his sermon. He picked up his spectacles from the desk and went over to the window. Outside, a dramatic scene was unfolding. All the treetops were dancing and swaying, thrown about by the strengthening wind. A few small boats caught out by the freak weather conditions were frantically beating their way back towards the safe haven of Oban harbour. Beyond them, out in the Sound of Mull, strings of wild white horses stampeded crazily towards the mainland. And now the first fat drops of rain started to beat at the casement window. The Bishop tutted again, threw another log onto the fire and turned the radio on. "Attention all vessels. The Met Office has issued the following shipping forecast at seventeen hundred hours GMT today..."

Craig was listening to the radio from headphones in the cab of his new green McLeod Forestry forwarder: "... forecast at seventeen hundred hours GMT today. There are warnings of gales in the following areas: Bailey, Rockall..." Having worked hard all day extracting sawlogs from Fearnoch forest, Craig was only too aware of the wind's strengthening force. From time to time a small branch clattered down onto the roof of his cab as the forest canopy swayed alarmingly overhead. He uplifted the last load of logs and added them to a large stack at the edge of the forest road. Only too aware of the approaching storm's power, he parked the forwarder out of harm's way beyond the falling distance of the nearest tree, put his belongings into his car and headed for home.

In Cedar Cottage Ann was making a pot of tea in the kitchen whilst Jim was poring over the Oban Times. She brought the tray through to the living room and placed it on the table. "… following areas: Bailey, Rockall, Hebrides and Malin. Here is the general synopsis…" Jim reached over and switched the radio off. "It's going to be a wild evening," he said. I dare say there'll be some windthrow damage in the forests by the morn. This wasnae predicted yesterday. It's come frae nowhere."

Ann poured out the teas in silence. All day long something had been preoccupying her and this evening she was unusually silent and broody. Jim looked up from his paper and asked, "Are ye alright hen? Ye've been very quiet today."

"Och I'm okay… it'll be likely the wind. It's been getting on ma nerves."

"Well as long as it's no me that's been getting on your nerves," replied Jim candidly, but in truth he was feeling a little edgy himself.

Ann held out a steaming mug to him and continued, "I hope they'll be alright at Lonan. It's awfu' out in the open up there. There's no so much shelter on a night like this."

"Ach they'll be fine," Jim replied, although he too shared Ann's sense of unease. "Mind you, Neil's away to the match so it's just Sophie up there on her own. I'll mebbe give her a phone later." He paused. "I'll just finish this Sudoku. It's driving me crazy."

All day long, a menacing area of low pressure that had started life deep in the north Atlantic Ocean had gathered potency and was now approaching the British Isles with the velocity of an express train. As it continued its relentless advance towards Argyll it grew stronger and stronger, adding strength and moisture to its already dark brooding clouds. Before the storm could unleash its remorseless fury on the outer isles, the Met Office had finally woken up to the threat, revising its forecasts and issuing severe storm and flood warnings. Calmac cancelled all ferry sailings and by mid afternoon the emergency services were on full alert. That autumn afternoon the west coast held its collective breath. By evening the storm beast had well and truly escaped from its cage and was on the rampage across Argyll.

On Mull the Merchant Banker's forests were having a hard time of it. Several of the more exposed compartments of spruce trees were falling about like ninepins under the assault of each battering squall. Rank upon rank of conifers peeled away from their neighbours and fell to the ground, each line adding to the carnage of the last. On the mainland, native woodlands and conifer forests alike were reeling under the force of the hurricane's strength. All Argyll's trees were suffering, but the newly thinned conifer plantations which twisted, bent and bowed to the fury of each fresh onslaught, were particularly vulnerable. It was only a matter of time before the extreme force of the wind destroyed the rotten, the unsound and the shallow rooted. Although some of the more open grown spruce and fir were secured to the soil by deeper roots, they too bent alarmingly as the gale increased. In the end even these trees succumbed to its fury, many of the taller ones snapping clean in two. Though more sheltered than most other estates, Ardcairn was not immune from the wrath of the Atlantic storm beast. Whoever created the estate's arboretum had wisely selected the site for its deep rooting soils and topographic shelter, and in the past Ardcairn's specimen trees had survived many a severe Atlantic gale unscathed. But this was no ordinary gale. This was the Great Gale, the gale that would be remembered for a generation or more, a night passed down in the history books as the worst storm event for over a hundred years. By evening the arboretum was reeling under the tempest's full malice and although the Douglas firs had anchored storm-resistant roots deep down into the earth, these were being wrenched mercilessly, plucked and torn by the fearsome gale. The squeals of branch rubbing on branch were almost like the wailing of prisoners awaiting execution.

Jim was anxious. Despite trying two or three times he could get no answer from the Lonan land line – just the answerphone. And when he called Sophie's mobile it rang but there was no reply. And Neil's mobile was switched off. Jim had even tried Dorothy's home number but all he got there was the answerphone too. After a while he turned to Ann and said, "This doesnae feel right. I'm goin' tae see what's happening at Lonan – it's no like Sophie not tae answer."

"It's a really wild night Jim. You said yourself there'll be trees down all over. Why not try the phone once more," she replied, but in truth Ann's misgivings were also growing by the minute and an inner voice was insisting that all was not well. But Jim's mind was made up and he resolved to drive up and find out what was happening. Just as he started to put on his coat the cottage lights flickered, remained on briefly and then went off completely, casting the room into near-total darkness.

"Blast!" he exclaimed, "The lines must be down. Now where did I leave that torch?" Once his eyes had adjusted to the gloom, he cast about by the glow of the wood fire until he had found a box of matches and lit some candles. Minutes later, just as he was preparing to face the wild Argyll night again, he noticed the headlights of a car approaching.

With increasing foreboding Ann pulled the curtains aside and observed the unmistakable patterning of a police Landrover drawing up outside. An acute sense of déjà vu swept over her. She put her hand to her mouth and gasped anxiously.

"What is it Ann?"

"It's the polis," she said nervously, "they're…" But before she could finish there was a firm 'rat tat tat' at the door. Jim opened it to reveal not the local constable who he knew well, but two unfamiliar uniformed officers, one male and the other female.

"Mr McLeod?" asked the male officer, the gale howling about him. Behind Jim the candles flickered from the gust of wind that swirled into the cottage, extinguishing the flame of the nearest one.

"Yes?"

"May we come in?" said the female officer, "I'm afraid we have some bad news."

They crossed the threshold and waited until Jim had sat down. He was pale now and the candle he held in his hand shook a little. Ann already knew in her heart the dreadful message they were about to relate.

"It's about Neil, your son, is that correct?"

Jim nodded dumbly.

"He was involved in a road traffic accident earlier today. I'm very sorry to have to tell you that he did not survive."

* * *

Back in Edinburgh Sophie's mother Jane was trying to ignore the phone. She had just finished a stressful day dealing with a string of surly customers and to top it all she had got completely soaked on the way home, battered by the strong winds and drenched by sheets of rain. She had run a hot bath, and had just got out of her wet clothes, looking forward to immersing herself in its scented water and relaxing after the rigours of the day. But there was something insistent about that phone. Its shrill *"bring, bring"* simply refused to give up and go away. Cursing a little under her breath she padded downstairs in her dressing gown and picked up the receiver in the hall.

"Double two seven eight," she said automatically.

"Are you a relation of Dorothy Montgomery?" asked the official-sounding female voice at the other end.

"Yes. I'm her daughter. Who is this?"

"It's Doctor Alison Vickers from the Western General hospital."

Sophie's mother sat down heavily on the hall chair. "What's happened?"

"I'm very sorry to have to tell you that your mother died earlier today." The doctor paused for a while and then added, "We appreciate that this will be a considerable shock for you, but we would be very grateful if you could come to the hospital at some stage to make a formal identification."

* * *

Focussed on his demanding task, the surgeon at Oban Hospital that evening was only dimly aware of the savage storm beast rampaging outside. His patient was completely oblivious to the elemental forces unleashing their fury upon Argyll. Anaesthetised, unconscious and stretched out on the operating theatre, Sophie was insensible to the hospital lights that flickered, died, and then revived, as the storm brought down the power lines and the emergency hospital generators kicked in. It would be several hours before she would regain consciousness and discover how that fateful day of the great storm had changed her life forever. Even as the doctor performed the difficult Caesarean operation, some of the mighty Ardcairn conifers were being wrenched and twisted about like giant ninepins. Although they were restrained for a while by their sturdier neighbours, it wasn't long before the gale wrestled them bodily down to the ground. As the surgeon completed the abdominal incision on his patient, he observed the mother's weak vital signs. There was a high chance that this could be a stillborn infant. But as he lifted the baby clear from its mother's womb, the tiny thing gave a start and a splutter and then an unmistakable wail emanated from its minute female lungs. That evening, as the storm mauled Argyll, a tiny new miracle started her life's journey on earth.

Chapter 28

The next morning, as the watery sun cast its pale light over the war-torn landscape, Argyll and the Isles emerged from its tempestuous nightmare. Everywhere, roofs had been ripped apart and telegraph posts thrown down. Trees had been tossed about like spillikins and many roads were blocked. At Ardcairn several of the once proud specimen trees were now lying forlornly on their sides, felled or snapped in pieces. Only one of the tallest Douglas firs had survived the Great Storm. In a defiant gesture of resistance, this giant conifer stood, battered but proud, battle-scarred but upright, impassively surveying the carnage and corpses of its compatriots. With neighbouring trees gone and the pale sunlight shining clearly on its trunk, the markings that had been carved into its side were now clearly visible. Future visitors to Ardcairn's arboretum would either look puzzled or smile knowingly as they saw the letters N and S and - in between them - the shape of a heart that had been etched by Neil into the bark of the Douglas fir that he had once described to Sophie as "our family tree."

Chapter 29

Looking back on those days and years following the Great Storm, when Sophie put the pieces of the jigsaw together, she recognised that she had undergone a prolonged nervous breakdown. The immediate result of giving birth and hearing the news of Neil's and Dorothy's death was a mild psychosis and weeks of hospitalisation in which her baby was mainly looked after by others. Later, post-natal depression kicked in. And all this was made worse by her diabetic condition. The two people in the world most dear to her heart had been forcibly wrenched from her life and she hadn't even had the chance to say goodbye properly. And so it came as little surprise to anyone that Sophie retreated more and more into herself, having no interest other than caring for Eleanor. Her withdrawal from the world was - she later realised - a kind of self-defence mechanism that dulled the pain a little, but never managed to remove it completely. She only returned to Argyll once and in secret, to scatter Neil's ashes at the foot of 'their' family tree, a tree that would now never see their family, would never witness their children playing beneath its branches. Shunning Argyll and its painful memories, Sophie devoted all of her energies to being a mother. It was only much later, once she started to paint again, that she understood what she had experienced: a protracted semi-existence, where suffering and denial were never far below the surface.

Even inheriting her grandmother's house and what turned out to be her considerable financial assets, did nothing to restore Sophie's spirits. The Edinburgh lawyers didn't take long to conclude the terms of Dorothy's Will and pass on to Sophie what amounted to a small fortune. She herself would of course have given it all away in a heartbeat to have had Neil back by her side. But those same legal terms and conditions that benefitted Sophie, became the last straw in her already threadbare relationship with her mother. Jane had never made a secret of blaming Sophie for everything bad in her life, including Dorothy and Neil's death. Furious that Dorothy had cut her own daughter out of her will, Jane suddenly and dramatically disappeared from Scotland - and Sophie's life - for ever. The rumour mill speculated that she had emigrated to Spain in the company of a long-suffering retired civil servant and when Sophie heard this from a friend of a friend, she was, in all honesty, relieved.

Sophie's withdrawal from Jim and Ann was an altogether more gradual and unintended process. She always held them dear in her heart and had never meant to lose touch with them, but in truth they were a raw reminder of her lost life with Neil, and she knew that that reminder worked both ways. It somehow seemed easier, as the years went by, not to see them: the grief was never far away, and the gloomy silences became longer and more awkward. Having set up her new home in The Grange, Sophie could never bring herself to return to Lonan Farm. When it was put on the market it sold quickly to English holiday home seekers. Having no financial worries herself, Sophie insisted that the proceeds of the sale went to Jim and Anne, who - whilst uncomfortable about it - eventually gave in to Sophie's insistences. But the early and necessary communications over Neil and Dorothy's funeral arrangements gradually became more sporadic. Letters gave way to annual Christmas cards and then eventually petered out altogether. Even when Jim died suddenly from a brain aneurism that the doctors attributed to his earlier accident, Sophie was unable to attend the funeral, being abroad on an exhibition tour. For she had, after some years, discovered the therapeutic healing power that painting could bring. Eleanor was too young to understand why her mother was throwing her energies into painting and exhibiting her work, and she was too young to understand why a gentle Edinburgh gallery owner's visits to the Grange became more and more frequent, and then permanent. She only knew this man with the kindly eyes and concern for her mother, as 'Daddy'. She was also too young to know that Sophie's diabetes was getting progressively worse with every passing year. Some years later Eleanor went to university and ended up in a steady relationship with her boyfriend David who was studying digital technology. Sophie managed to remain well enough to see Eleanor graduate with honours, but not long afterwards - when Eleanor and David had embarked on a gap year to the Far East - they received the news of Sophie's fatal diabetes-induced stroke. And so it was, in her early twenties, that Eleanor Buchanan found herself the beneficiary of Dorothy's - and then Sophie's - considerable wealth. With David's start-up tech company taking off, and the option of them living anywhere with good digital connection, they decided that Edinburgh was no longer where they wanted to be. An extended road trip around Scotland made them both realise that Argyll was exactly where they wanted to spend their lives together. Ardcairn was the beacon that summoned them home...

Epilogue

The newest recruit to prestigious Estate Agents G K Saville, Harriet was excited about concluding her sale but she was also anxious to get back to Glasgow. Her boyfriend's flight was due in soon - he had spent a week away on business - and there was some urgent 'relationship catching-up' to do. "And if you just sign here... and here," she said, pointing to the documents spread out on the occasional table. "we'll have our lawyers send over copies of the missives to you next week." She glanced at her watch. "I am sure that you will both be very happy here. Ardcairn is a wonderful place."

At that moment Ann entered the room and set down the tray. After she had been introduced to David and Eleanor there was an embarrassing moment when she dropped some spoons on the floor and looked a little flustered. Harriet put it down to her advancing years and rescued the awkward moment by asking the new owners, "Are you intending to head back south this evening?"

David replied, "No we're staying nearby tonight. We're planning to walk around the grounds tomorrow. We've a charter flight from Oban in the afternoon."

Harriet was just about to say something when her mobile phone rang. "I'm very sorry but this is an important call," she apologised, "would you excuse me for a minute?" and with that she stepped out onto the upper landing where her boyfriend's phone call would not interfere with any conversation in the drawing room. But the others overheard the occasional comment coming from Harriet, "...me too. Something for me? I can't wait... Look, I should be finished here soon. I'll get back as soon as I can."

Shortly afterwards she re-entered the room, but her mind was now focussed upon how quickly she could get away. Sensing her fidgeting, David said tactfully, "I think that we're finished with business now. Let's not keep you any longer Harriet. Why don't you make tracks. We can arrange to lock up if you show us what's what."

"Well if there's nothing more I can do?"

"Thank you, it's been a pleasure." David and Eleanor followed Harriet downstairs to the front door and watched as she shut the door of her shiny black saloon car and waved goodbye. "Give our regards to your colleague," shouted David. Shortly afterwards the car sped down the driveway and disappeared out of sight.

Postscript

Early the next morning a stray beam of sunshine stole its way through a gap in the brocade curtains of Ardcairn's master bedroom and alighted on the sleeping face of Eleanor Buchanan. She stirred drowsily and for a few seconds wondered where she was. Then she stole over to the window and drew back the heavy drapes. Below her stretched a scene of benign neglect. The garden lawns were overgrown and the privet bushes appeared bedraggled and uncared for. On one of the terraces stood a pond, choked full of weeds. In its shallows the verdigris sculpture of a heron remained exactly as it had done for years, frozen, transfixed in its perpetual hunt for a fish. Beyond the lawns, several birch seedlings were flourishing in the gaps of collapsed masonry from a once-impressive walled garden. It was more than clear to Eleanor that - unlike that of the house - maintenance of the Ardcairn grounds had stopped several years ago. Despite that neglect though, she could still discern echoes of the estate's former glory days illuminated by the brightening sunlight.

Beyond the unkempt borders and overgrown bushes lay a more timeless vision. In the inlet below the house, the retreating tide had exposed dark rocks festooned with glossy seaweed. Close to the shore, a knot of eider ducks bobbed and crooned to themselves amongst the wavelets, whilst further out, two wild white swans slid gracefully over the ripples. Below the line of crags fringing the horizon, shafts of sunlight played over late-season heather, dying bracken and the emerging tints of autumnal birch woods. Lost in the moment, Eleanor gazed and gazed at the view.

"What's the Lady of Ardcairn thinking about?" David's sleepy voice drifted up from the four-poster bed behind Eleanor.

She turned round and faced her husband, who could see that she had been quietly weeping. "I'm still trying to process Ann's bombshell from last night. You know – it's a lot to take in, discovering who your real father is but never knowing him. And I know this sounds awful but – well you know what I mean, our crazy decision to buy Ardcairn and not knowing it was such a part of Mum's past. You know she never once mentioned it. I guess she was so devastated when Neil - when my father - died, that she just moved to Edinburgh to forget it all and put it behind her and after all, Edinburgh's been my whole upbringing. And the Dad I've only ever known will still always be my Dad. And I know this sounds mercenary" she added, "but when Mum passed away this year and I inherited... well..." Her voice trailed off.

"So much to take in," David echoed. "I was thinking about last night too." He swivelled out of bed and joined his wife beside the window. "You know, after we'd gone to bed. After all those revelations. If my job wasn't so flexible about where I'm based, and if Ardcairn hadn't come up for sale just when we were looking around Argyll... well, we wouldn't be here, would we?" He paused. By the way, shouldn't I have been wearing protection?" he asked, putting his arm around her and gazing into her intense blue eyes.

"Um, I was thinking that too," Eleanor replied, looking a little sheepish.

"Oh well, que sera, sera," said David. "There's never really a right time, is there?"

Eleanor laughed. A musical tinkling laugh.

David turned his attention to survey the grounds through the window. Looking down, he frowned, "Hmm, there's a lot that needs to be done out there."

"I know but think of the fun we'll have restoring the garden its former glory! It's going to be great! Oh David, I'm so happy to be here. It's just so amazing!"

David agreed with his wife that there was nowhere else he would rather be, and no one else he would rather be with at that moment. Then he remembered all the help that Ann had given and changed the subject. "On a more immediate note I wonder what we should do about Ann?"

"What do you mean?"

"Well, isn't she a bit too old to continue doing the housekeeping?"

"Oh, I see what you mean. Perhaps it does seem a bit unfair."

Their discussion was brought to a sudden halt by the sound of gentle knocking at the bedroom door. It was Ann bringing them a cup of tea. David and Eleanor couldn't help exchanging a look and laughing, for in her inimitable way

Ann had answered their question herself. Yes she was old, but she was certainly not too old to be a very useful asset indeed. "I thought you might like a cup of tea," they heard her call through the door. "I'll leave it outside. Breakfast is ready downstairs when you want it." Setting the tray down outside the bedroom door she padded back down the corridor, adding suggestively over her shoulder, "It's a lovely day outside."

Later that morning, after exploring the gardens and shoreline, David and Eleanor found themselves drawn towards the arboretum. Approaching what little remained of the once-great collection of trees, they made their way to the foot of the giant Douglas fir. There, still clearly visible in its bark after so many years, were the weathered carved markings that Ann had talked about the night before. They lingered for a while under its shade, thinking about all that she had said: how Neil had first met and rescued Sophie there, how they had exchanged marriage vows underneath its spreading canopy and how Sophie had scattered Neil's ashes in a final act of closure many years ago. For a while the couple sat in silence listening to the soft fluting of a Robin coming from somewhere above their heads.

Before they returned to Edinburgh there was one final act of pilgrimage that Eleanor was determined to make. Before taking the road to the airport, David headed up the minor road towards Lonan Farm, parking the car at the foot of the track that wound up the hillside. He and Eleanor could see that the farmhouse had recently been extended and gentrified as a holiday home and that there was now no sign of a nearby barn or outbuildings. Sophie's vision of an arboretum had clearly come to naught, for below the farmhouse the fields were still open grassland, not young trees. But it was not the farm that they had come to see that clear autumn afternoon.

From the moorland above Lonan a gentle autumn breeze ruffled the heather, carrying with it the soft bleating of sheep and occasional mewing of a buzzard. In silence David and Eleanor climbed up the old drove road behind the cultivated fields and the surviving remnants of birch and oak woodland. "The Old Road to the Isles" Ann had called it and to David and Eleanor it seemed to possess an ancient, timeless quality. Unexpectedly soon they reached a break in the slope that revealed a small stock-fenced enclosure protecting a young hawthorn tree. There was no mistaking it. This was their goal, the one remaining living scion of Argyll's wishing tree, a cutting that Neil and Sophie had lovingly replanted over twenty years ago. But an unexpected sight met their gaze. Instead of just a young thorn tree that David and Eleanor had expected to see, they were surprised by the presence of a small collection of coins that had been pressed here and there into its bark.

Eleanor found herself strangely moved. At Ardcairn's arboretum she had expected to see the initials and heart carved by her parents. But here, off the beaten track, were unexpected signs and wonders. Somehow the legend of Argyll's Wishing Tree had managed to translocate itself to a new locus for a new generation of visitors and pilgrims. No guidebook or signpost had directed their footsteps. It must simply have been a case of word of mouth starting a new arboreal legend, literally growing a new place of homage. Eleanor felt in her pocket and unconsciously pulled out a one-pound coin. She examined it closely. Somehow it seemed fitting that the offering she was making to this wishing tree should be a coin bearing the image of another tree, an oak. Round the rim she read the inscription "Decus et Tutamen" and her classics education kicked in ('surprising how often it helped,' she thought). "An Ornament and a Safeguard," she said out loud. 'Now that is appropriate' she thought, 'A coin for ornament, the tree for safeguarding.'

High on that Argyll hillside, amidst the bleating of sheep and the soft, gentle breeze, Eleanor Buchanan placed the coin lovingly in a fork of a branch and made a silent wish.

David smiled. He knew instinctively what she was wishing for without having to ask. He watched her closely, waiting until she opened her eyes again. Eleanor's eyelids flickered and then registered his gaze. She regarded him with her intense blue eyes so characteristic of her mother Sophie and her great grandmother Dorothy before her.

And then she laughed - a long, silvery, pealing, joyous, reassuring laugh.

David took her hand in his. "Come on darling," he said. "Time to go."